LILY RENÉE,
Escape Artist

From Holocaust Survivor to Comic Book Pioneer

TRINA ROBBINS

Illustrated by
ANNE TIMMONS and MO OH

GRAPHIC UNIVERSE™ · MINNEAPOLIS · NEW YORK

Story by
Trina Robbins

Pencils by
Anne Timmons

Inks by
mo oh

Lettering by
Felix Ruiz and Cayetano Garza Jr.

Coloring by
Studio C10

Graphic Universe™
A division of Lerner Publishing Group, Inc.
241 First Avenue North
Minneapolis, MN 55401 U.S.A.

Website address: www.lernerbooks.com

Photographs on pp. 4, 79, 94, and 95 are courtesy of Lily Renée Phillips. The comic book art photographed on pp. 92 and 93 are from the collection of the author.

Main body text set in CC Dave Gibbons Lower.
Typeface provided by Comicraft/Active Images.

Library of Congress Cataloging-in-Publication Data

Robbins, Trina.
   Lily Renée, escape artist : from Holocaust survivor to comic book pioneer / by Trina Robbins ; illustrated by Anne Timmons and mo oh.
      p.   cm.
   ISBN: 978–0–7613–6010–0 (lib. bdg. : alk. paper)
   1. Renée, Lily — Biography — Juvenile literature. 2. Jewish children in the Holocaust — Germany — Biography — Juvenile literature. 3. Holocaust, Jewish (1939–1945) — Germany — Biography — Juvenile literature. 4. Germany — Ethnic relations — Juvenile literature. I. Timmons, Anne. II. Oh, Margaret. III. Title.
DS134.42.R46 R63   2011
940.53'18092—dc22
   [B]   2011001084

Manufactured in the United States of America
1 – DP – 7/15/11

CHAPTER ONE: *Vienna, 1938*

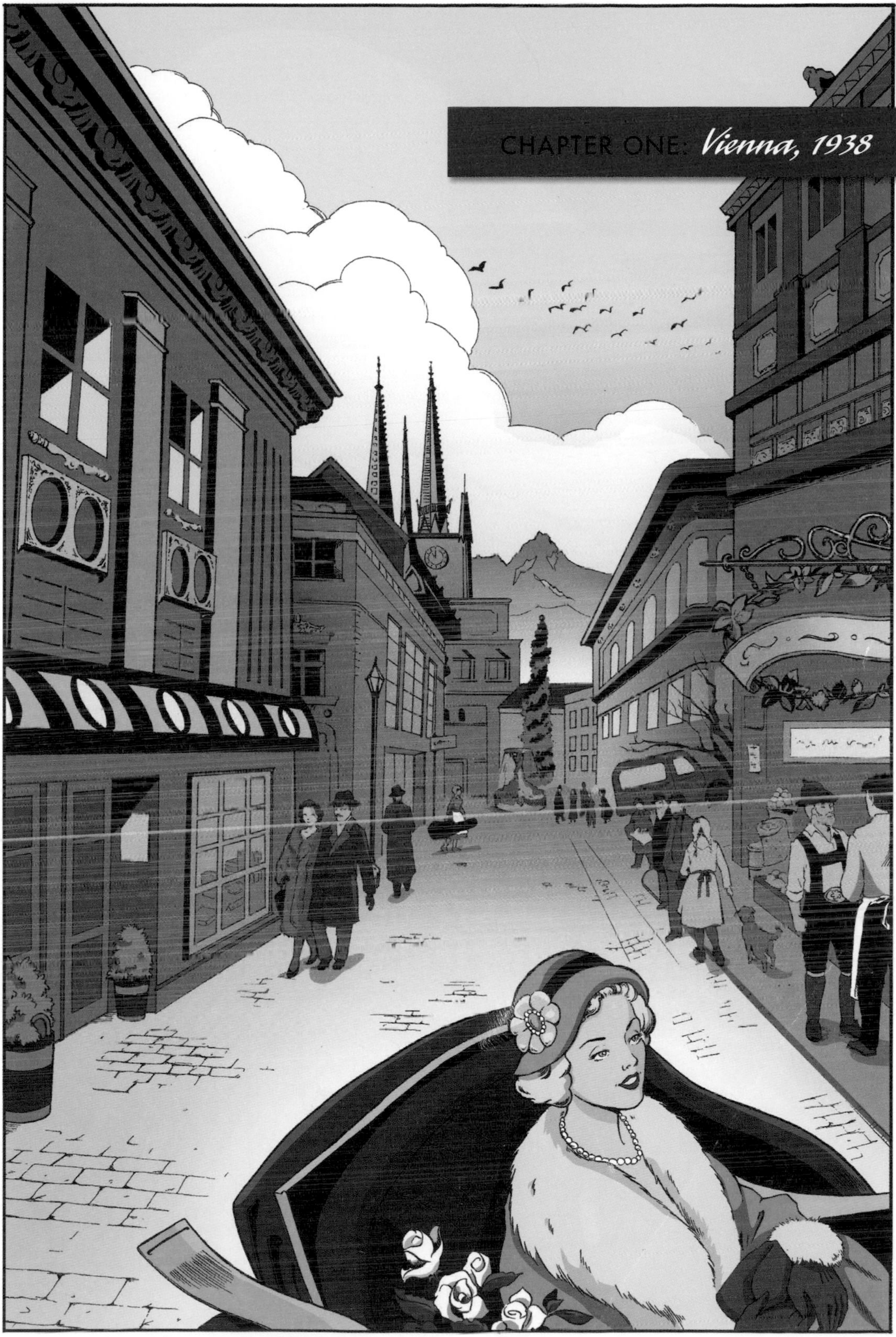

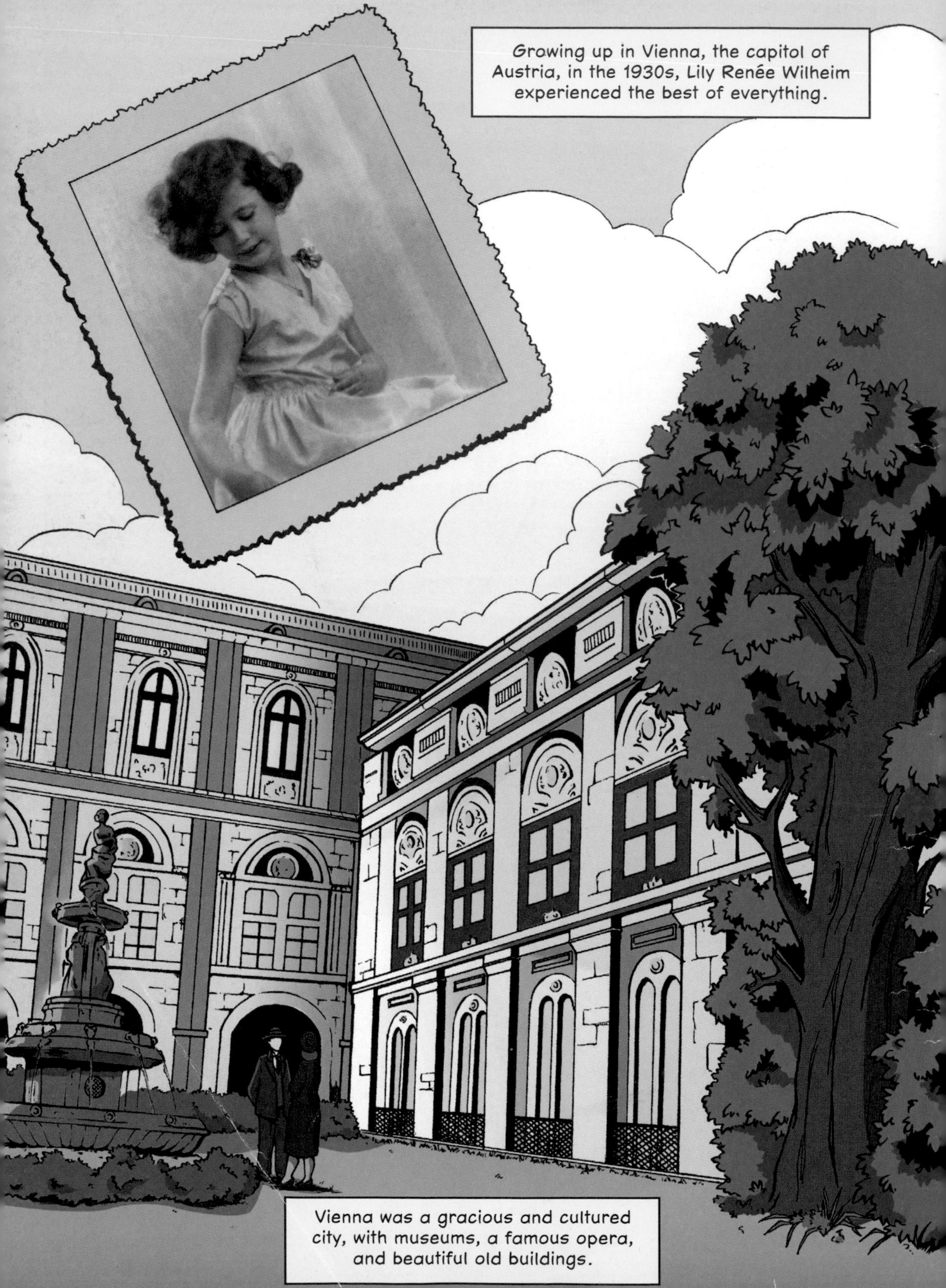
Growing up in Vienna, the capitol of Austria, in the 1930s, Lily Renée Wilheim experienced the best of everything.
Vienna was a gracious and cultured city, with museums, a famous opera, and beautiful old buildings.

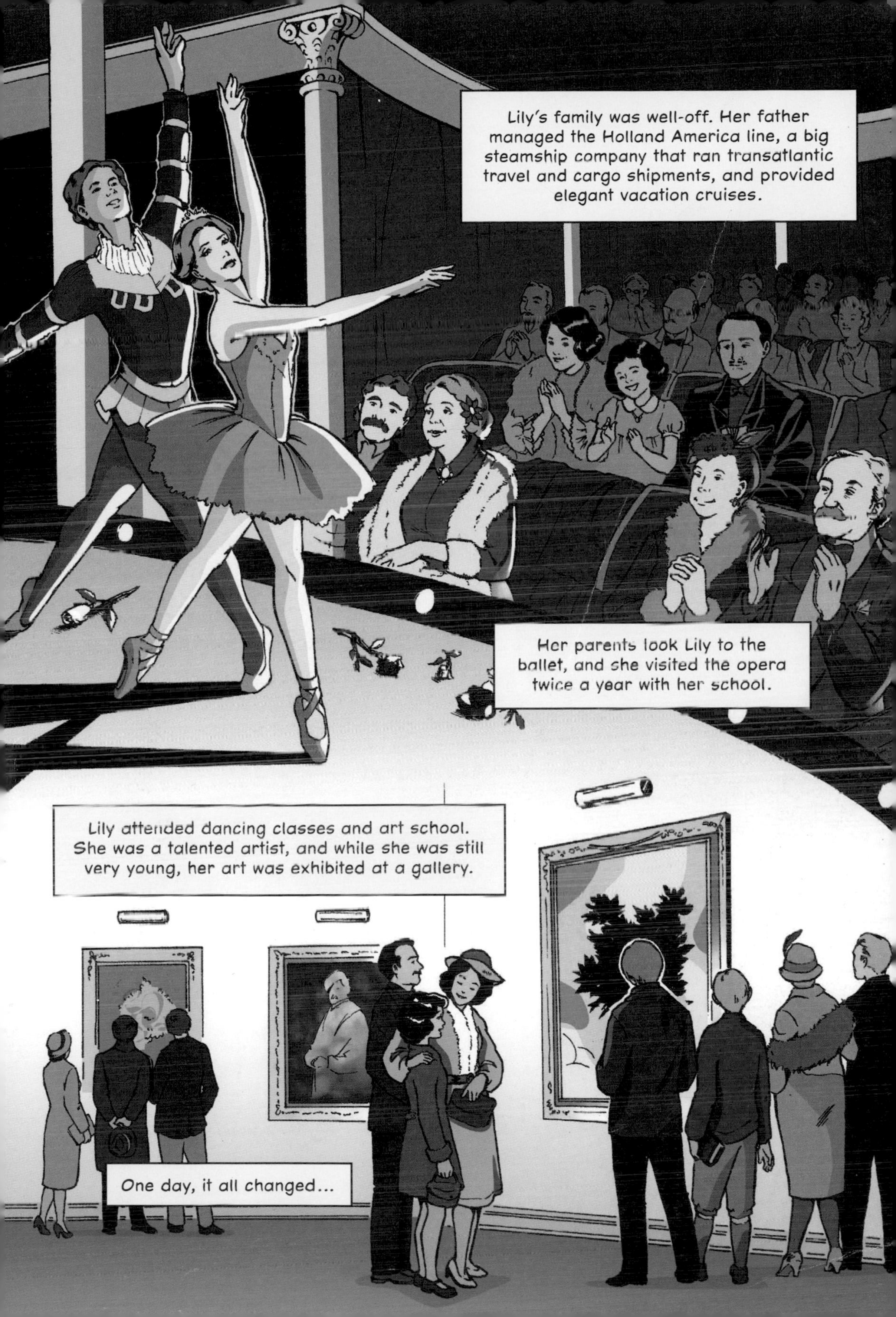

Lily's family was well-off. Her father managed the Holland America line, a big steamship company that ran transatlantic travel and cargo shipments, and provided elegant vacation cruises.
Her parents look Lily to the ballet, and she visited the opera twice a year with her school.
Lily attended dancing classes and art school. She was a talented artist, and while she was still very young, her art was exhibited at a gallery.
One day, it all changed...

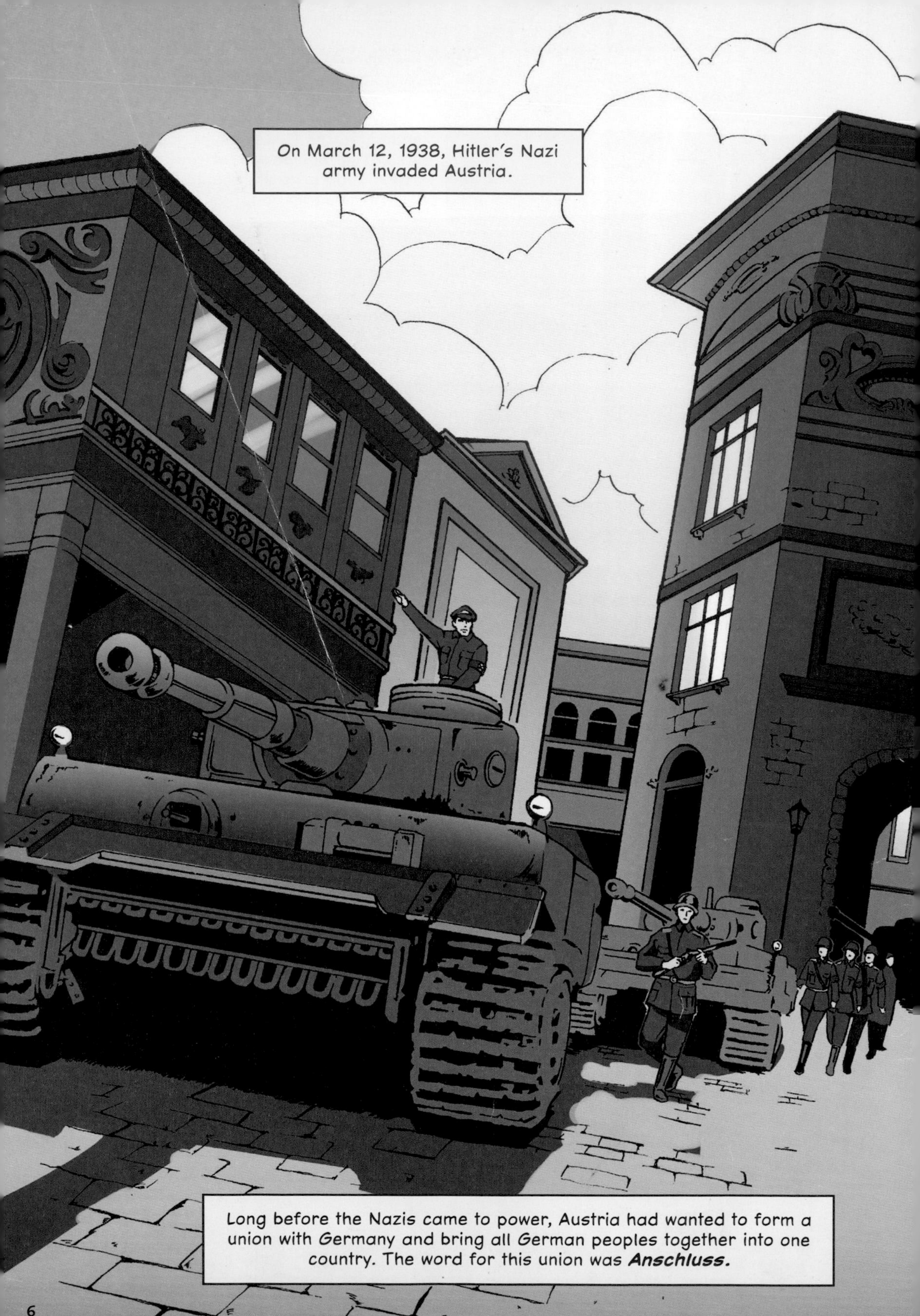
On March 12, 1938, Hitler's Nazi army invaded Austria.
Long before the Nazis came to power, Austria had wanted to form a union with Germany and bring all German peoples together into one country. The word for this union was ***Anschluss.***

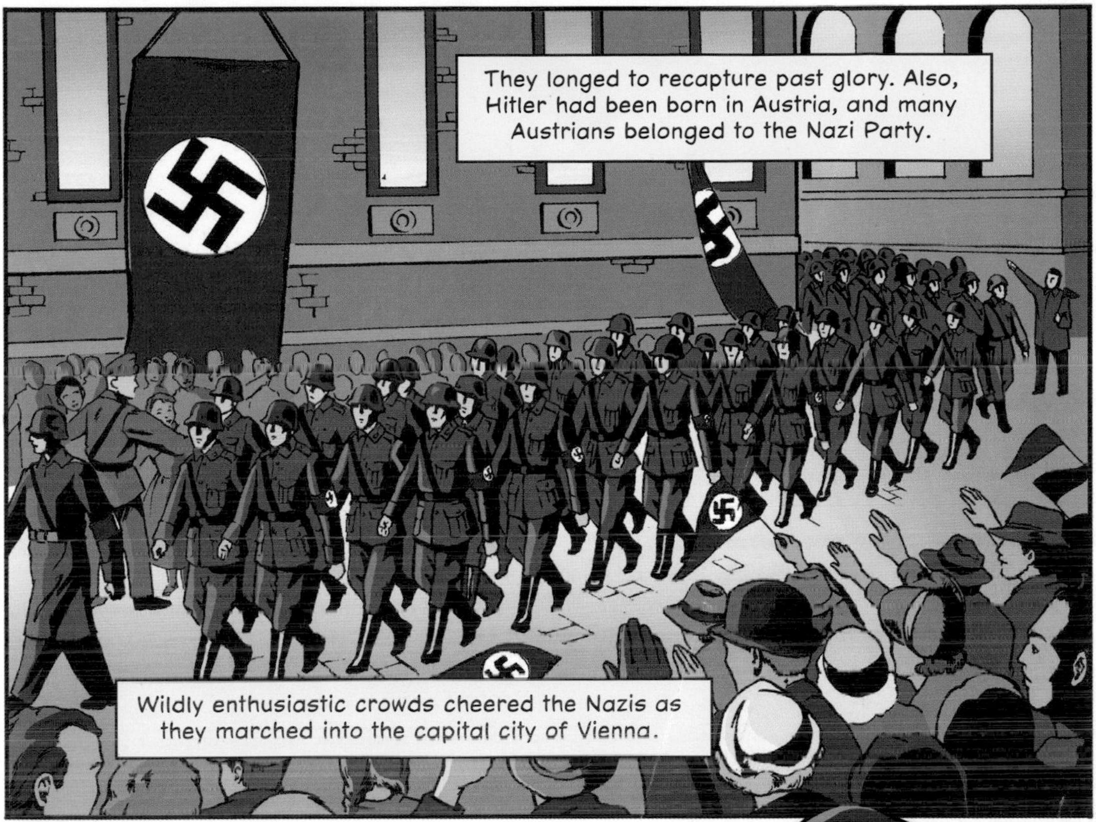
They longed to recapture past glory. Also, Hitler had been born in Austria, and many Austrians belonged to the Nazi Party.
Wildly enthusiastic crowds cheered the Nazis as they marched into the capital city of Vienna.

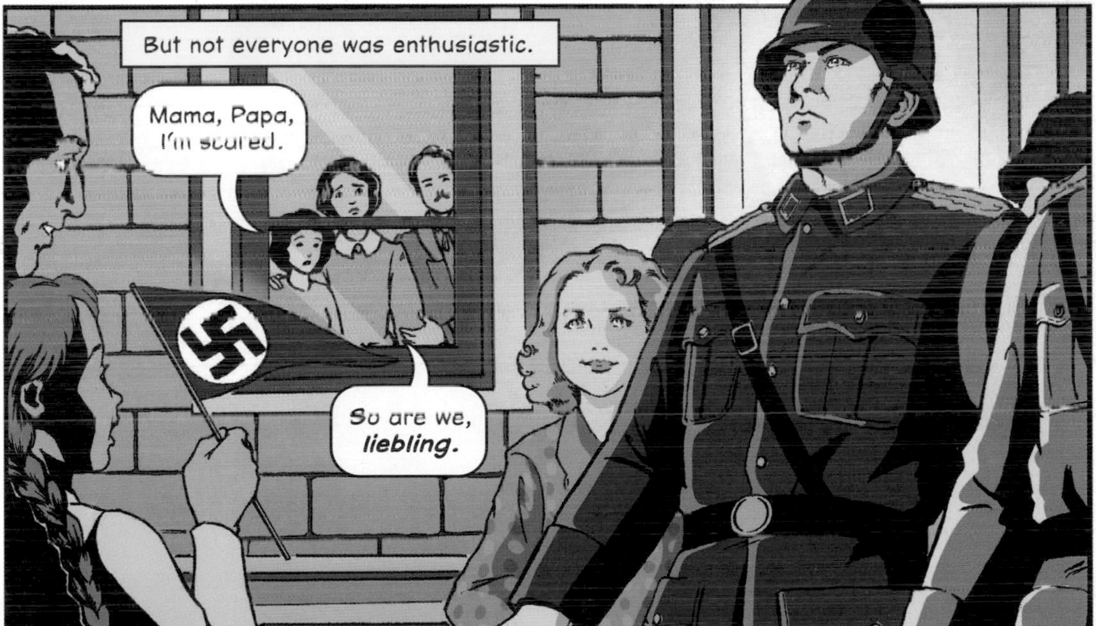
But not everyone was enthusiastic.
Mama, Papa, I'm scared.
So are we, *liebling.*
Lily and her parents were Jewish. They knew how fiercely the Nazis hated the Jews.

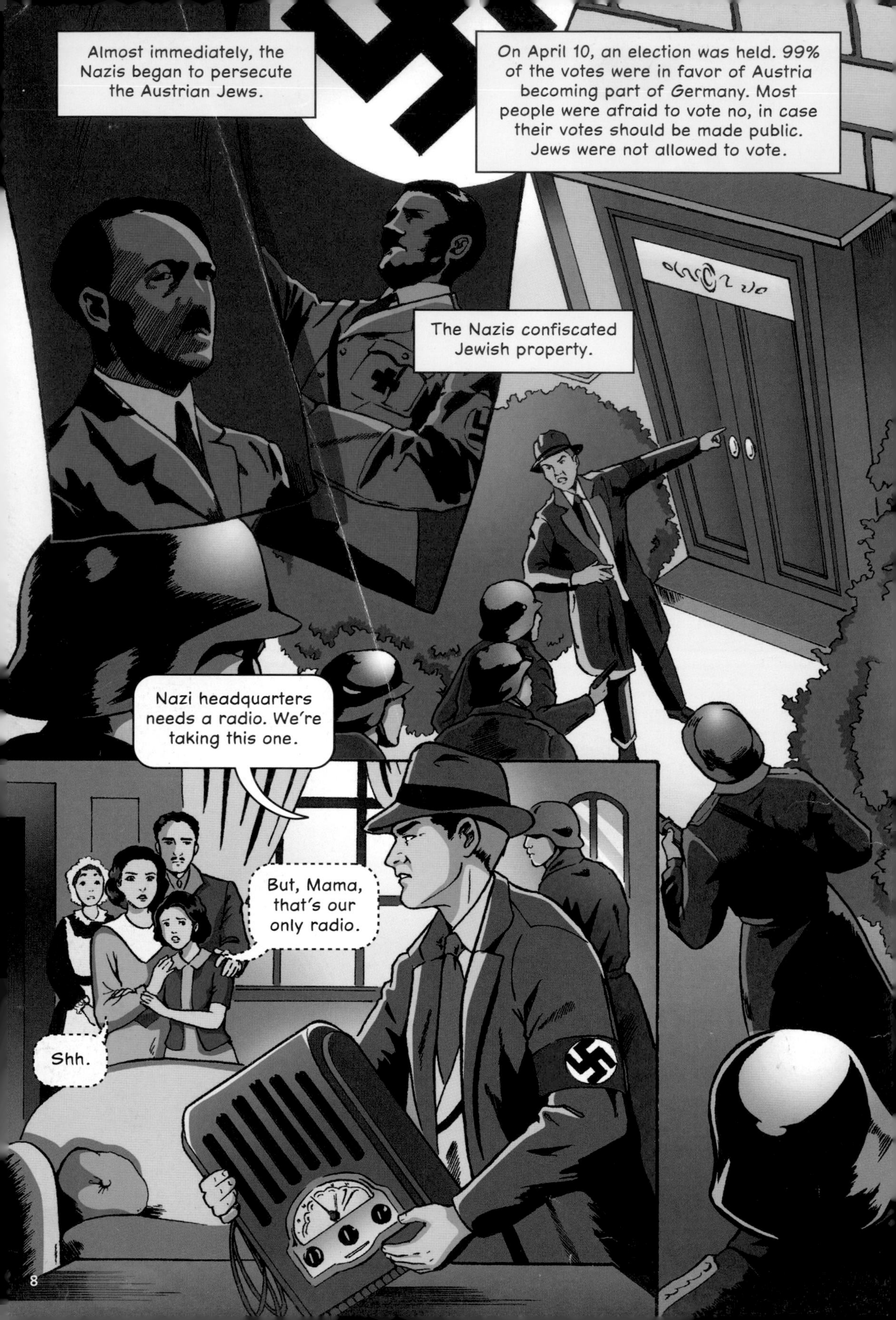
Almost immediately, the Nazis began to persecute the Austrian Jews.
On April 10, an election was held. 99% of the votes were in favor of Austria becoming part of Germany. Most people were afraid to vote no, in case their votes should be made public. Jews were not allowed to vote.
The Nazis confiscated Jewish property.
Nazi headquarters needs a radio. We're taking this one.
But, Mama, that's our only radio.
Shh.

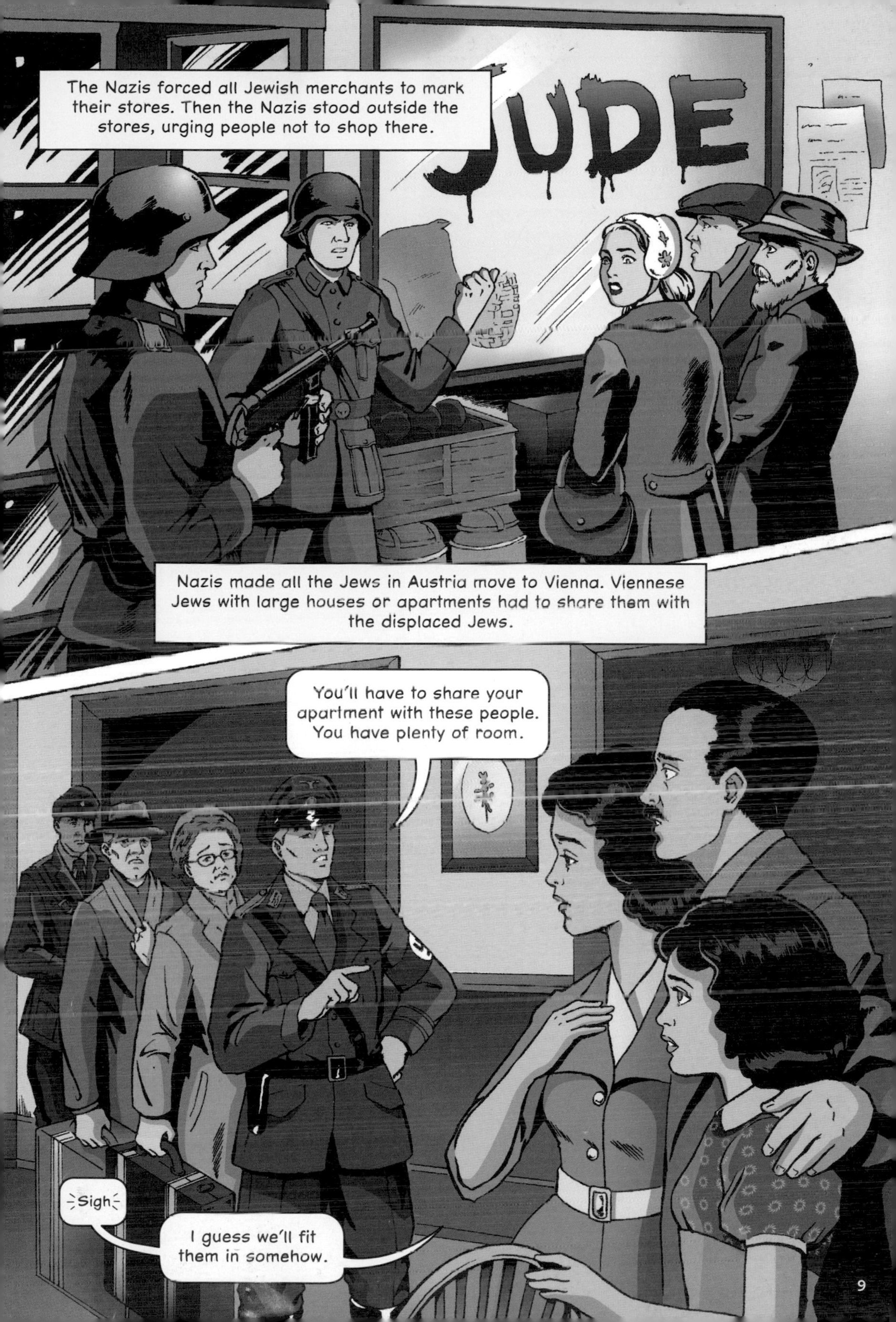
The Nazis forced all Jewish merchants to mark their stores. Then the Nazis stood outside the stores, urging people not to shop there.
JUDE
Nazis made all the Jews in Austria move to Vienna. Viennese Jews with large houses or apartments had to share them with the displaced Jews.
You'll have to share your apartment with these people. You have plenty of room.
Sigh
I guess we'll fit them in somehow.

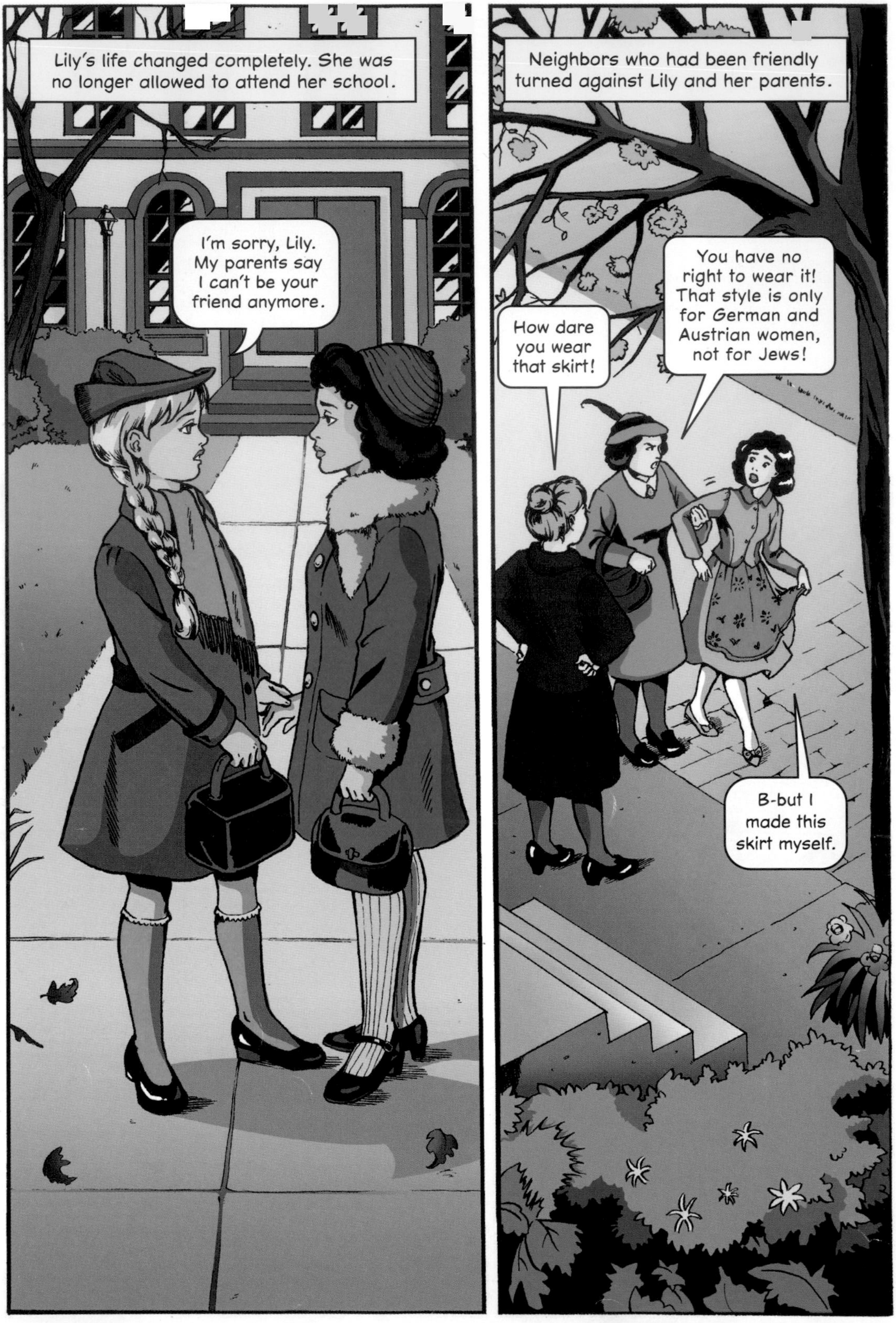
Lily's life changed completely. She was no longer allowed to attend her school.
I'm sorry, Lily. My parents say I can't be your friend anymore.
Neighbors who had been friendly turned against Lily and her parents.
How dare you wear that skirt!
You have no right to wear it! That style is only for German and Austrian women, not for Jews!
B-but I made this skirt myself.

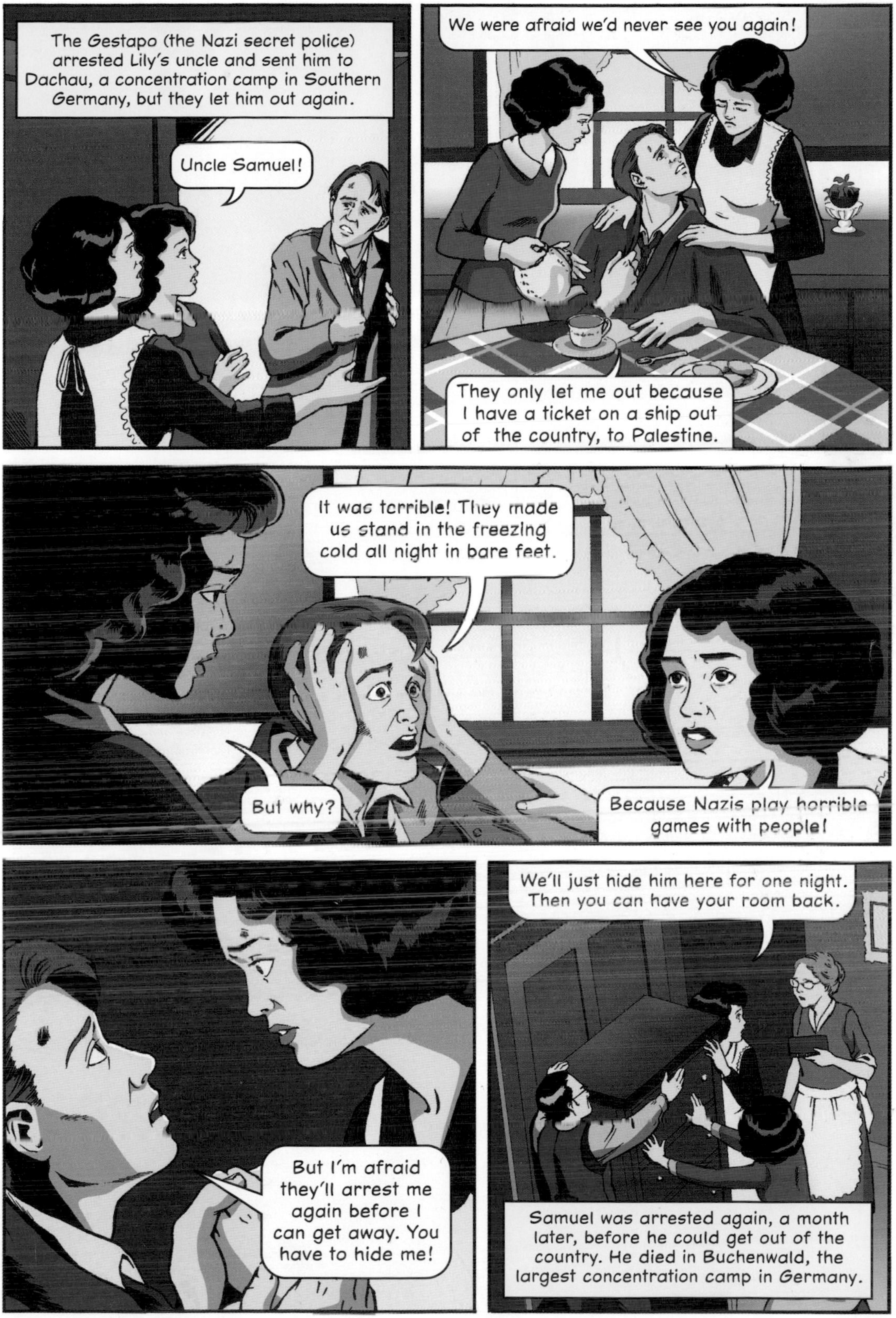
The Gestapo (the Nazi secret police) arrested Lily's uncle and sent him to Dachau, a concentration camp in Southern Germany, but they let him out again.
Uncle Samuel!
We were afraid we'd never see you again!
They only let me out because I have a ticket on a ship out of the country, to Palestine.
It was terrible! They made us stand in the freezing cold all night in bare feet.
But why?
Because Nazis play horrible games with people!
But I'm afraid they'll arrest me again before I can get away. You have to hide me!
We'll just hide him here for one night. Then you can have your room back.
Samuel was arrested again, a month later, before he could get out of the country. He died in Buchenwald, the largest concentration camp in Germany.

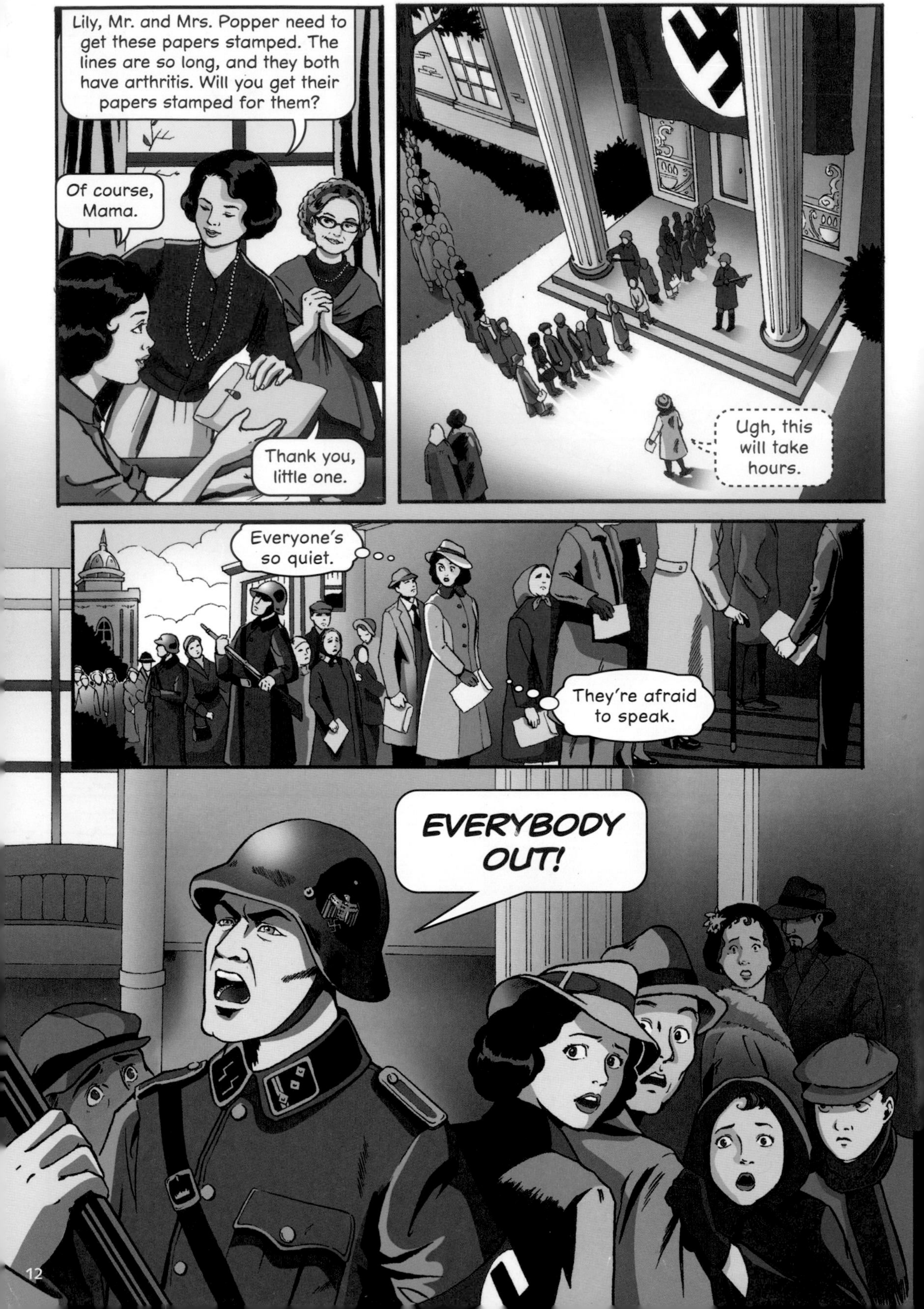
Lily, Mr. and Mrs. Popper need to get these papers stamped. The lines are so long, and they both have arthritis. Will you get their papers stamped for them?
Of course, Mama.
Thank you, little one.
Ugh, this will take hours.
Everyone's so quiet.
They're afraid to speak.
EVERYBODY OUT!

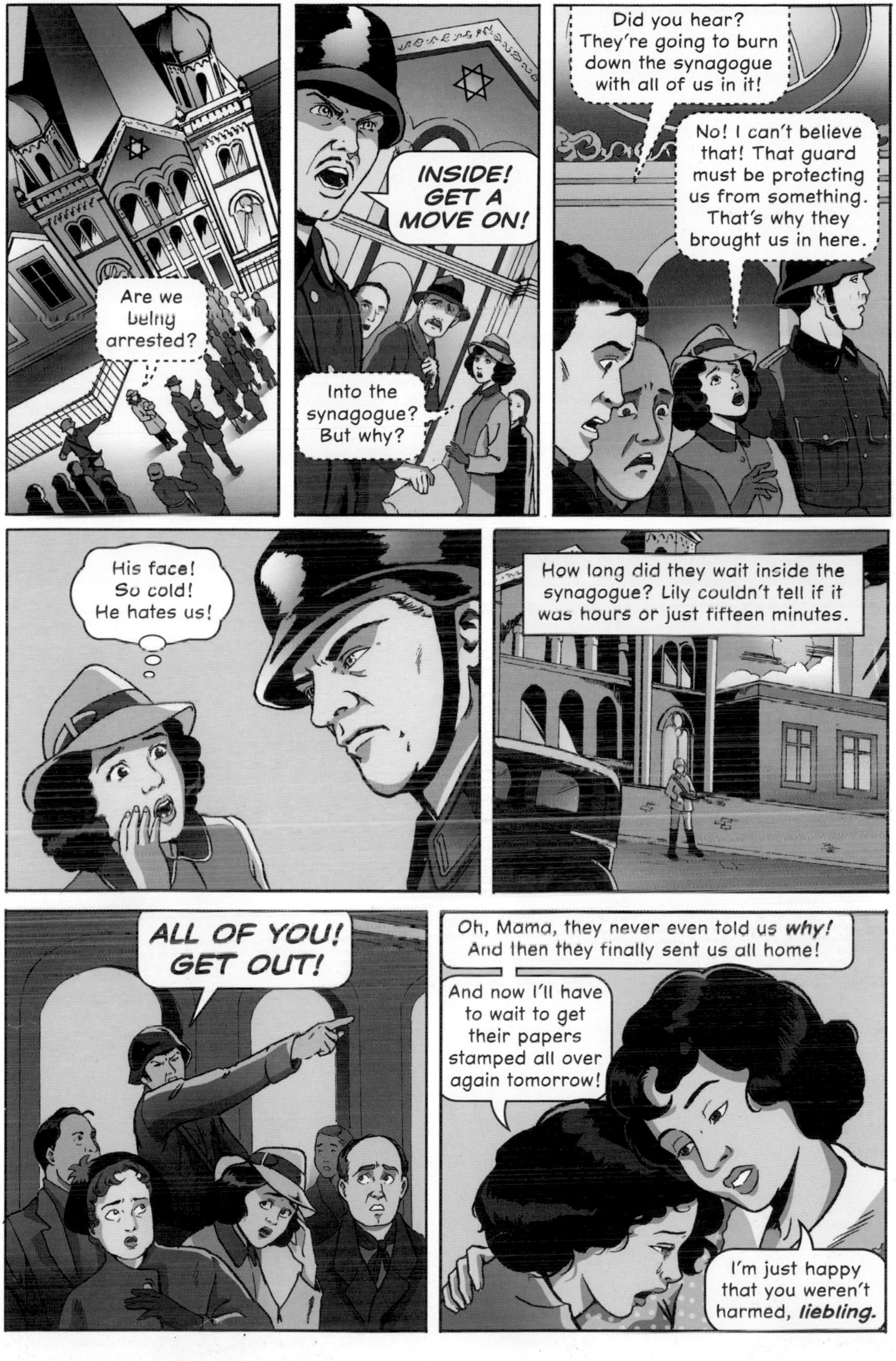

Are we being arrested?
INSIDE! GET A MOVE ON!
Into the synagogue? But why?
Did you hear? They're going to burn down the synagogue with all of us in it!
No! I can't believe that! That guard must be protecting us from something. That's why they brought us in here.
His face! So cold! He hates us!
How long did they wait inside the synagogue? Lily couldn't tell if it was hours or just fifteen minutes.
ALL OF YOU! GET OUT!
Oh, Mama, they never even told us *why!* And then they finally sent us all home!
And now I'll have to wait to get their papers stamped all over again tomorrow!
I'm just happy that you weren't harmed, ***liebling.***

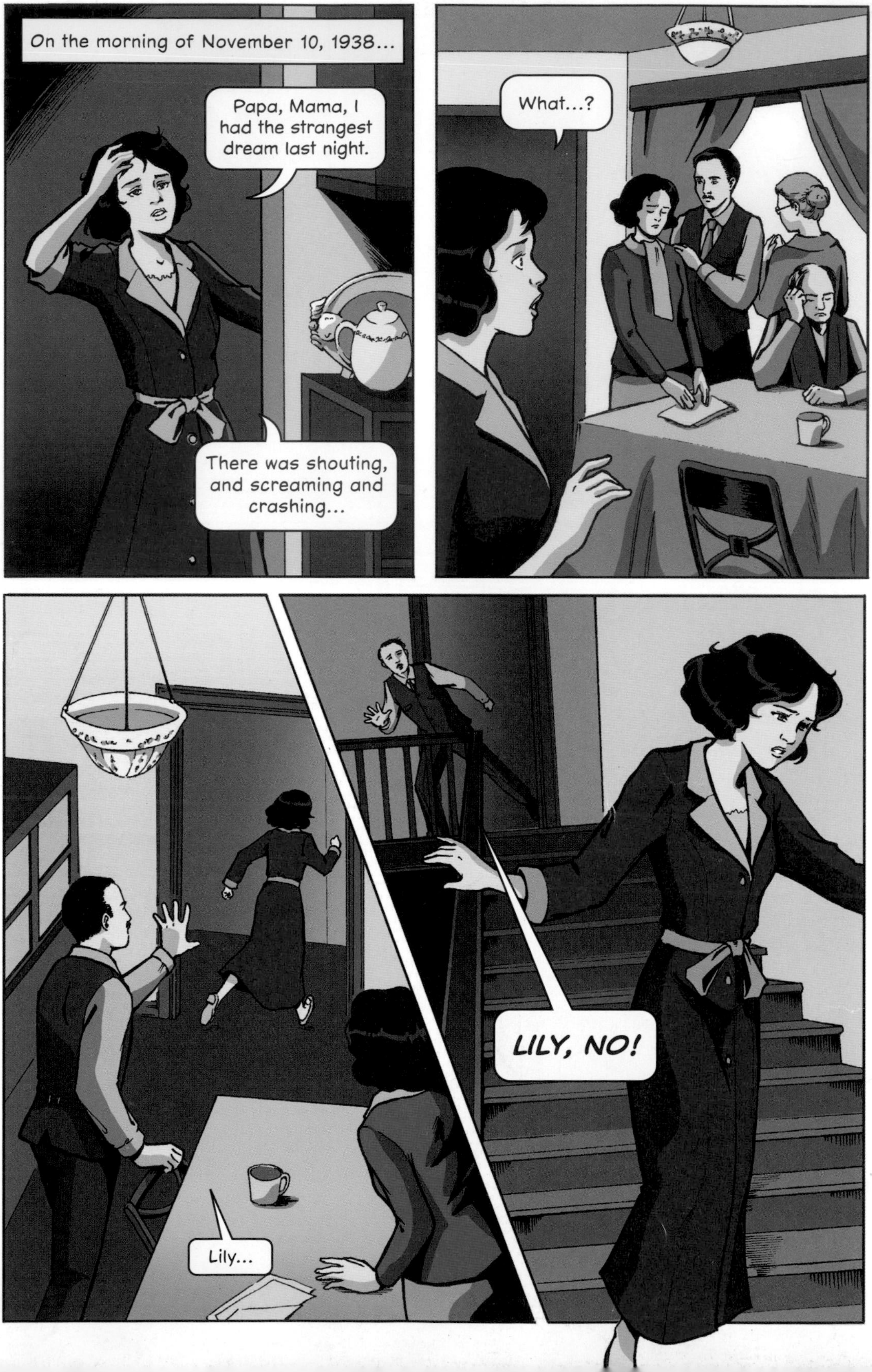
On the morning of November 10, 1938...
Papa, Mama, I had the strangest dream last night.
There was shouting, and screaming and crashing...
What...?
Lily...
LILY, NO!

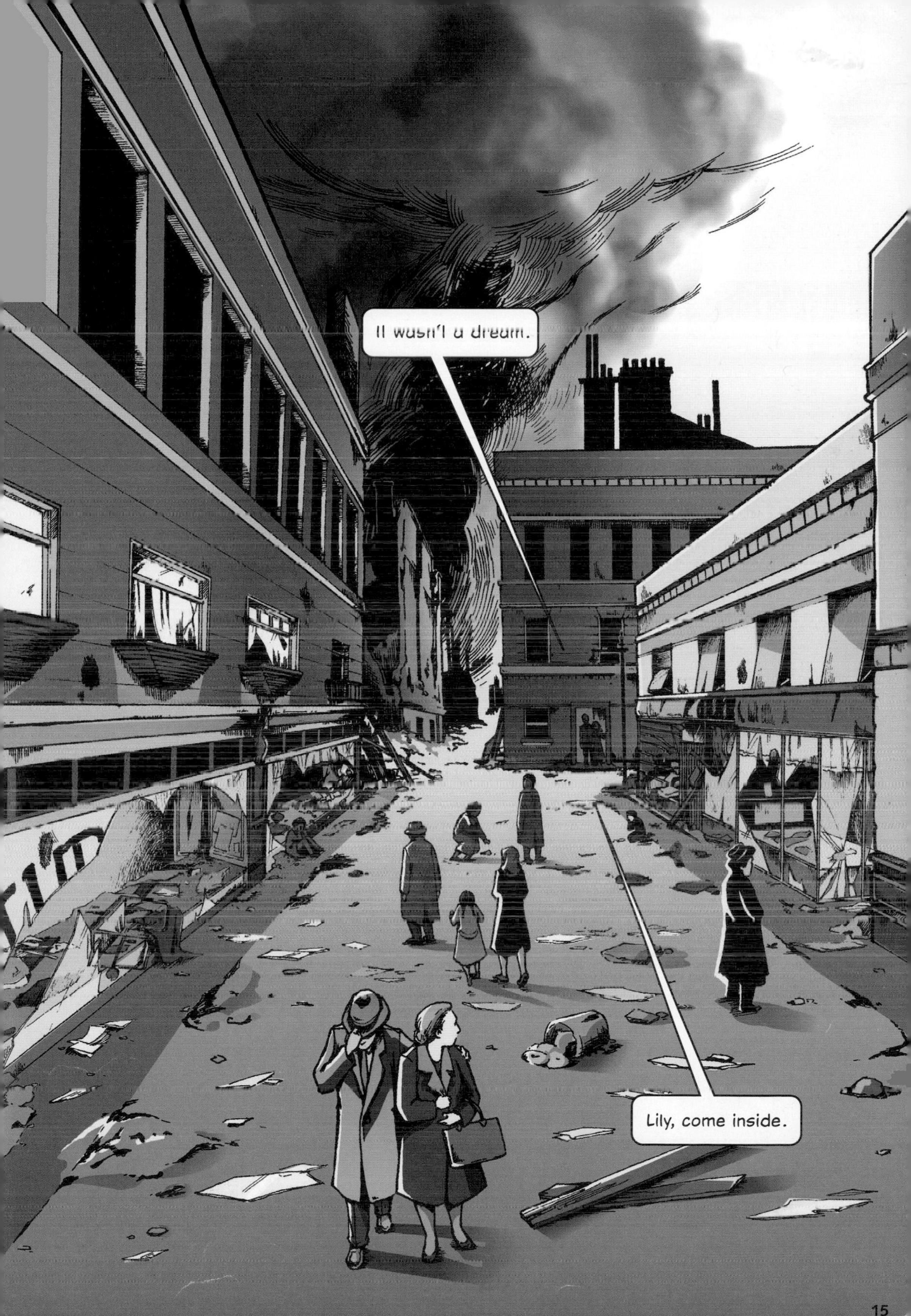
It wasn't a dream.
Lily, come inside.

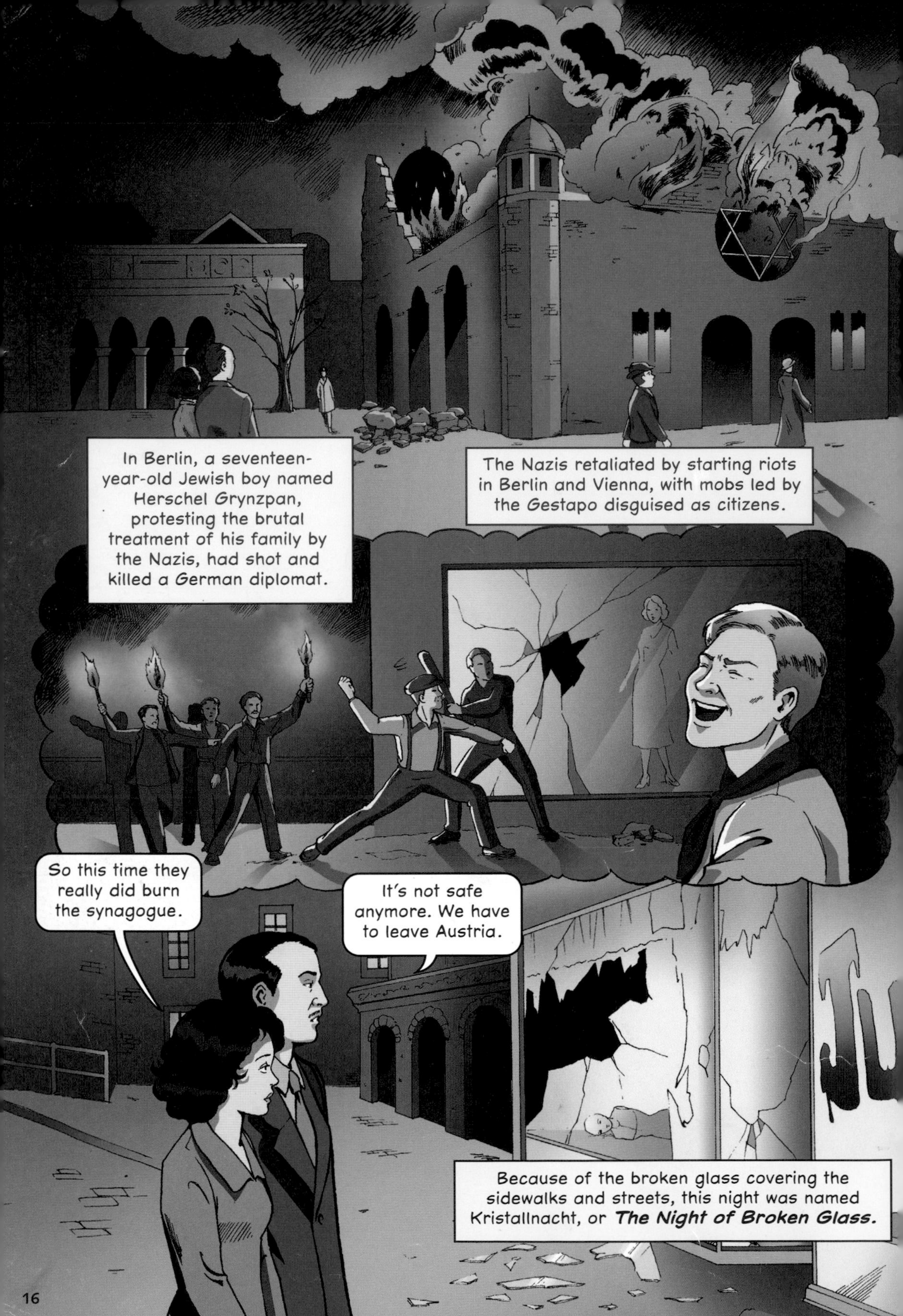

In Berlin, a seventeen-year-old Jewish boy named Herschel Grynzpan, protesting the brutal treatment of his family by the Nazis, had shot and killed a German diplomat.
The Nazis retaliated by starting riots in Berlin and Vienna, with mobs led by the *Gestapo* disguised as citizens.
So this time they really did burn the synagogue.
It's not safe anymore. We have to leave Austria.
Because of the broken glass covering the sidewalks and streets, this night was named Kristallnacht, or ***The Night of Broken Glass.***

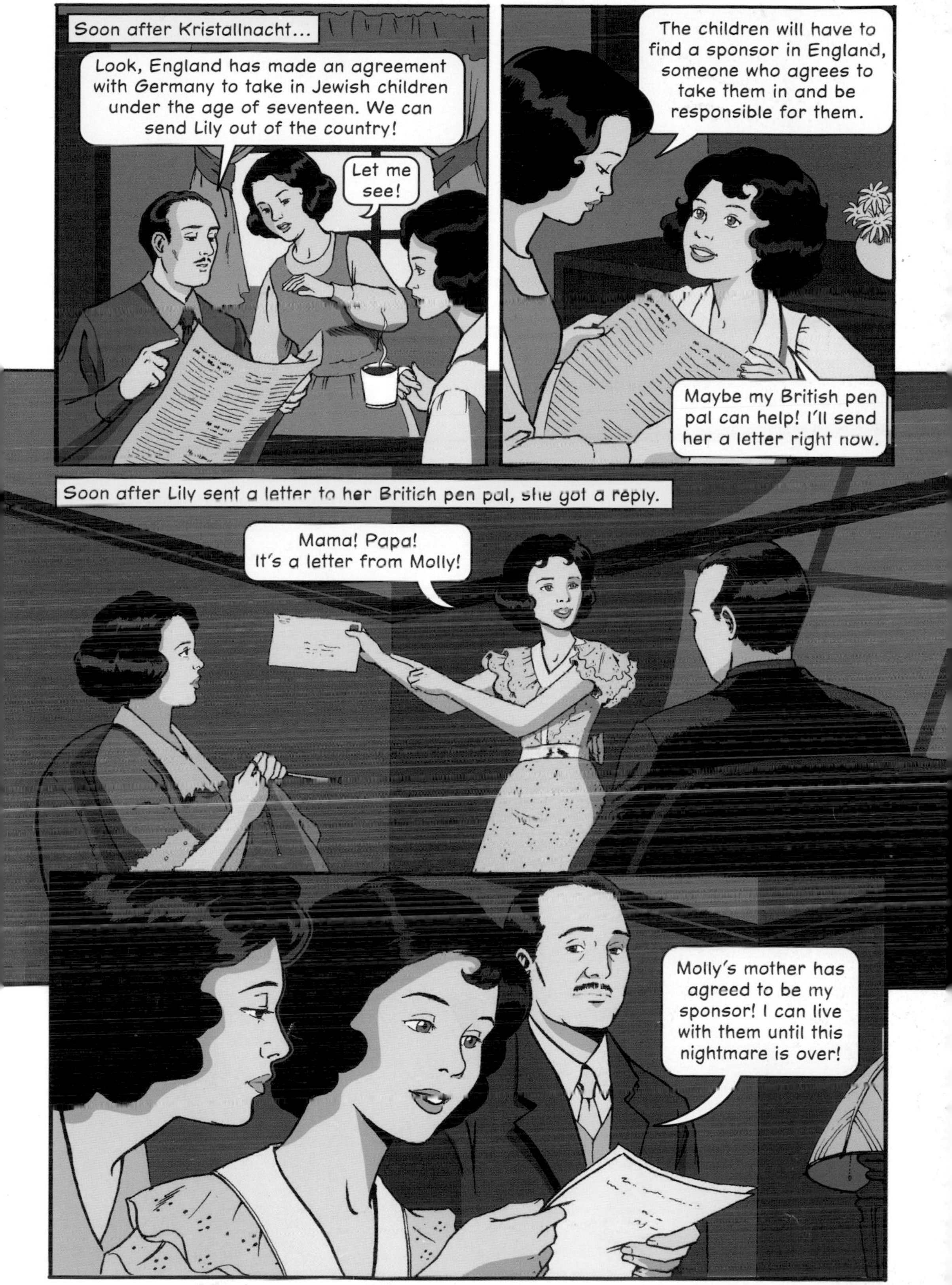
Soon after Kristallnacht...
Look, England has made an agreement with Germany to take in Jewish children under the age of seventeen. We can send Lily out of the country!
Let me see!
The children will have to find a sponsor in England, someone who agrees to take them in and be responsible for them.
Maybe my British pen pal can help! I'll send her a letter right now.
Soon after Lily sent a letter to her British pen pal, she got a reply.
Mama! Papa! It's a letter from Molly!
Molly's mother has agreed to be my sponsor! I can live with them until this nightmare is over!

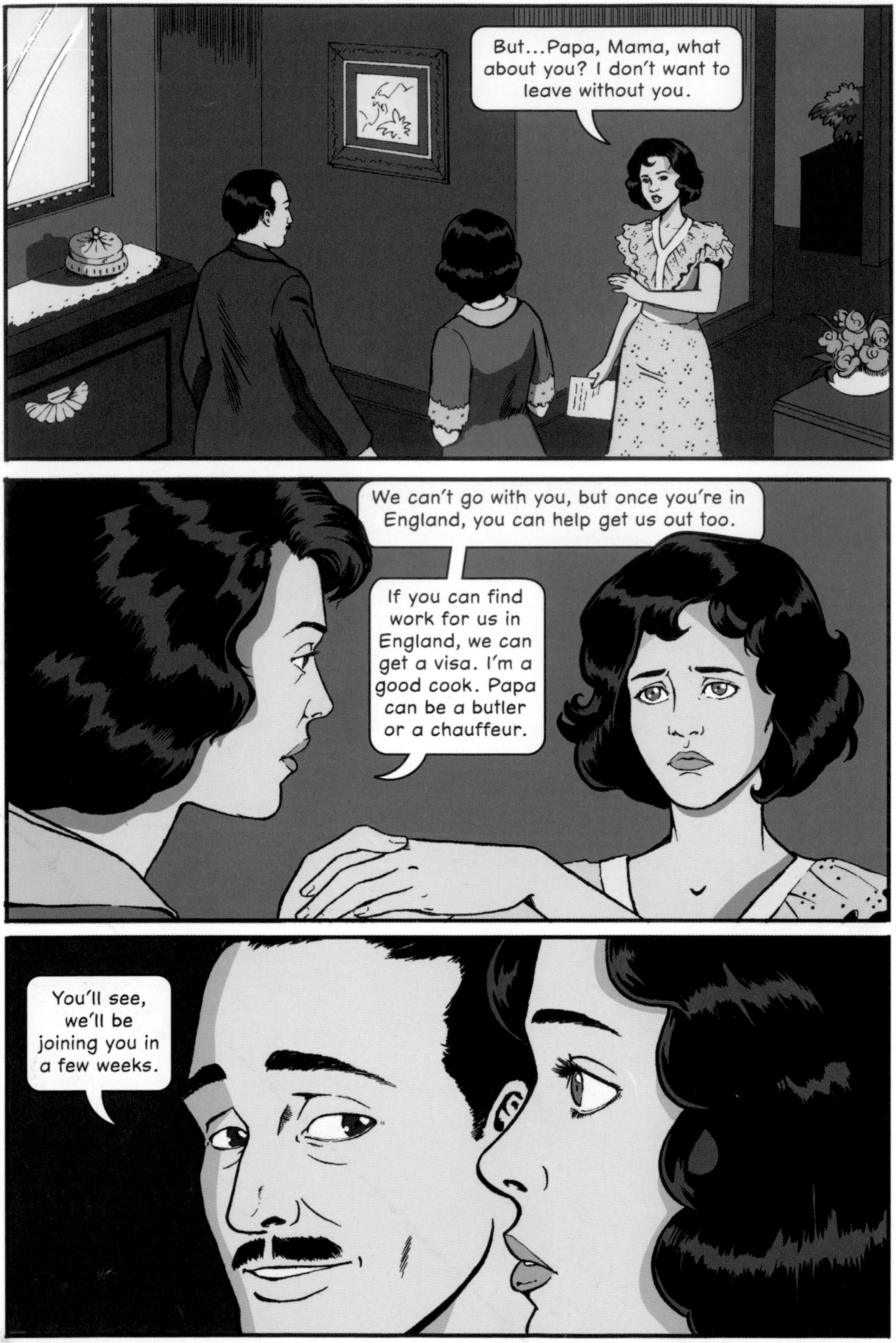

But...Papa, Mama, what about you? I don't want to leave without you.
We can't go with you, but once you're in England, you can help get us out too.
If you can find work for us in England, we can get a visa. I'm a good cook. Papa can be a butler or a chauffeur.
You'll see, we'll be joining you in a few weeks.

CHAPTER TWO: *Kindertransport, 1939*

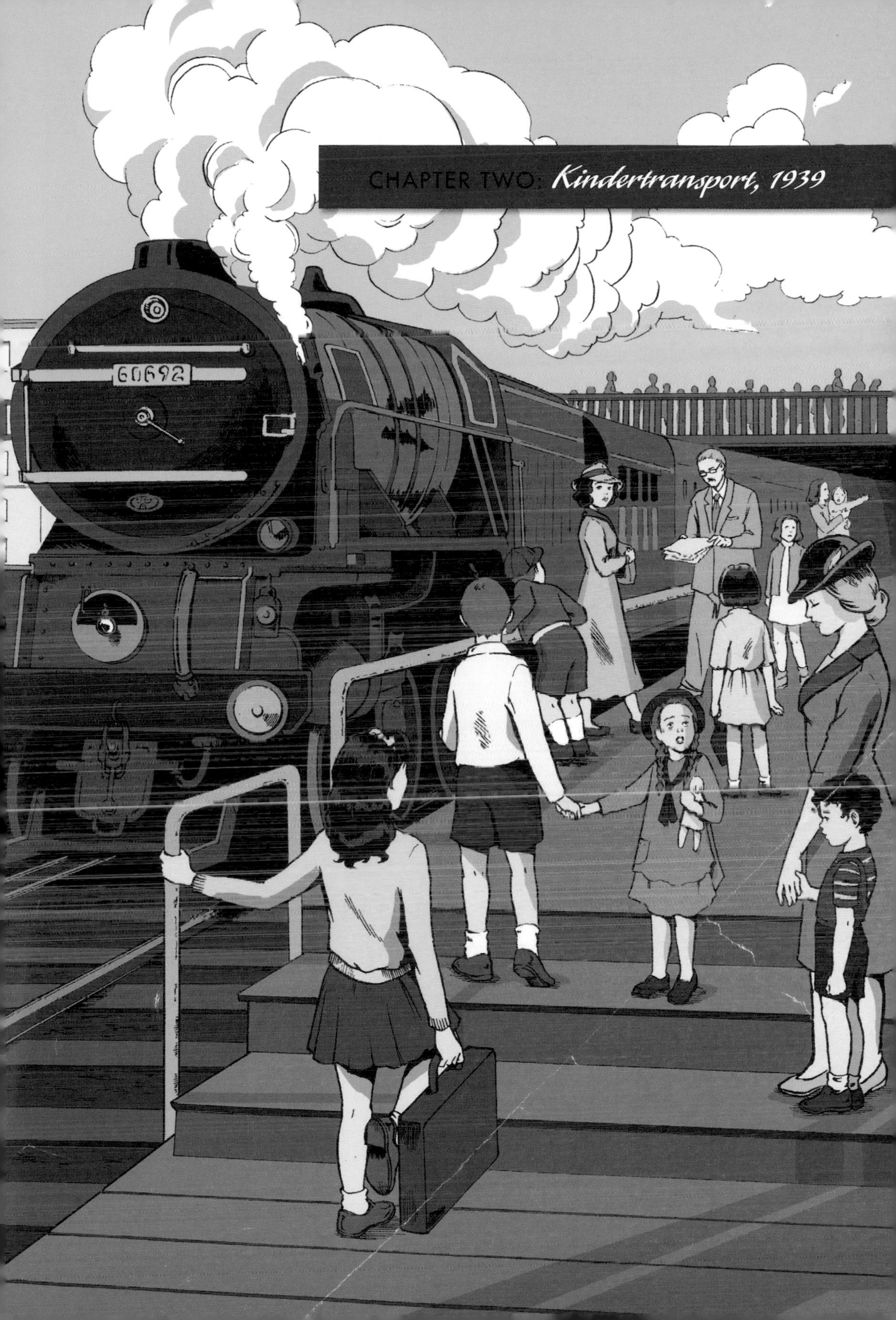
60692

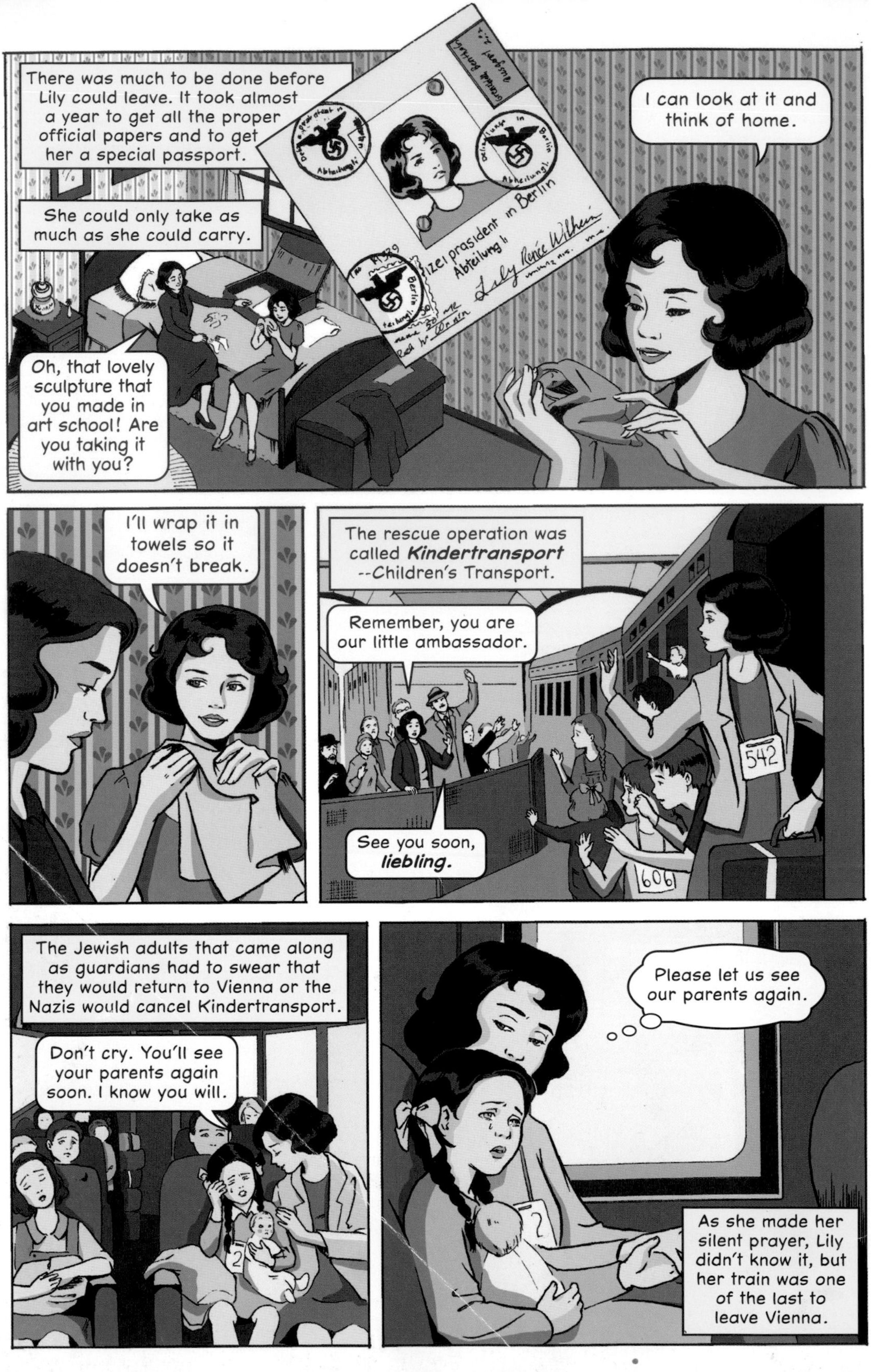

There was much to be done before Lily could leave. It took almost a year to get all the proper official papers and to get her a special passport.
She could only take as much as she could carry.
Oh, that lovely sculpture that you made in art school! Are you taking it with you?
I can look at it and think of home.
Berlin
Abteilung
I'll wrap it in towels so it doesn't break.
The rescue operation was called *Kindertransport* --Children's Transport.
Remember, you are our little ambassador.
See you soon, ***liebling.***
542
606
The Jewish adults that came along as guardians had to swear that they would return to Vienna or the Nazis would cancel Kindertransport.
Don't cry. You'll see your parents again soon. I know you will.
2
Please let us see our parents again.
2
As she made her silent prayer, Lily didn't know it, but her train was one of the last to leave Vienna.

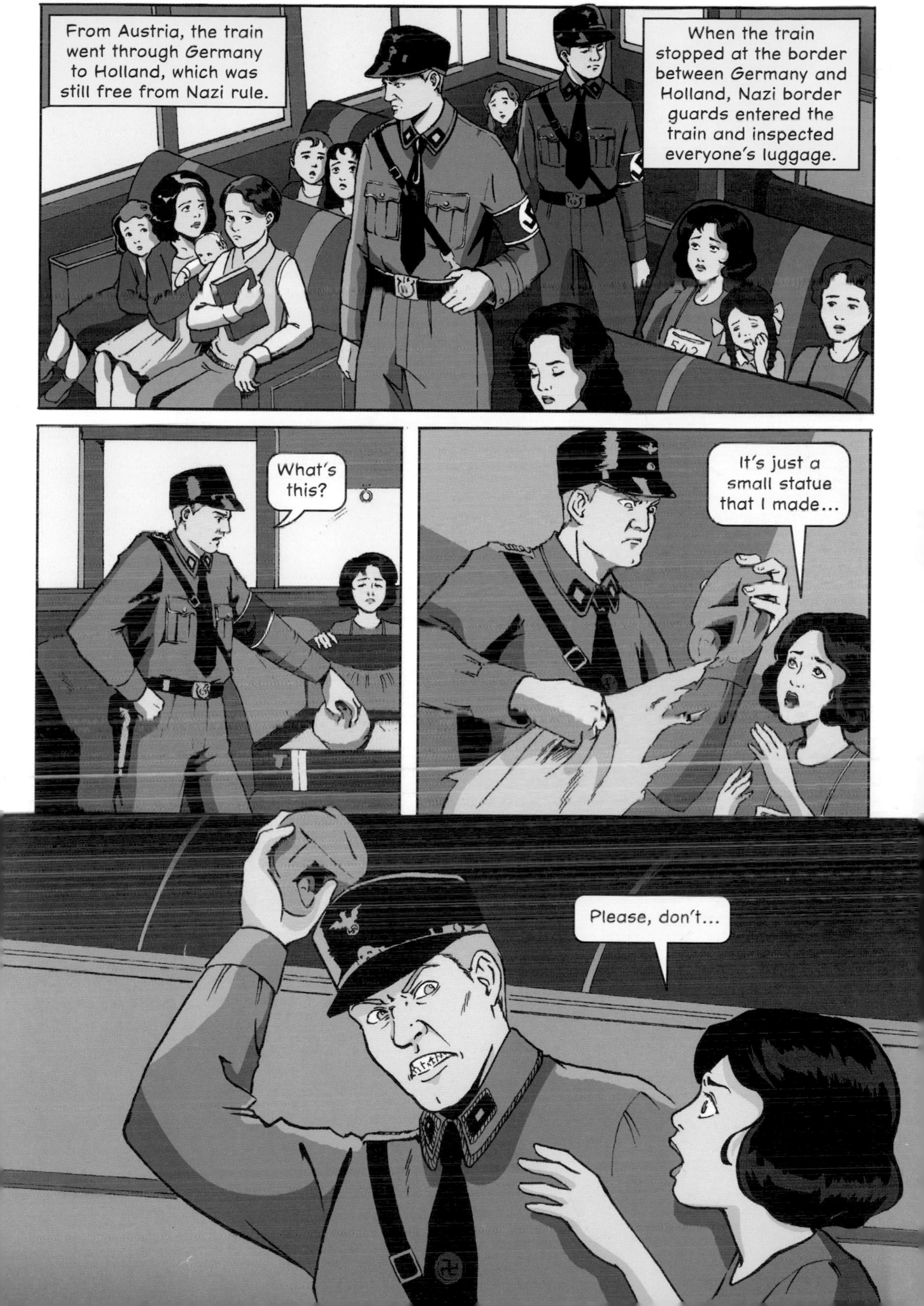
From Austria, the train went through Germany to Holland, which was still free from Nazi rule.
When the train stopped at the border between Germany and Holland, Nazi border guards entered the train and inspected everyone's luggage.
What's this?
It's just a small statue that I made...
Please, don't...

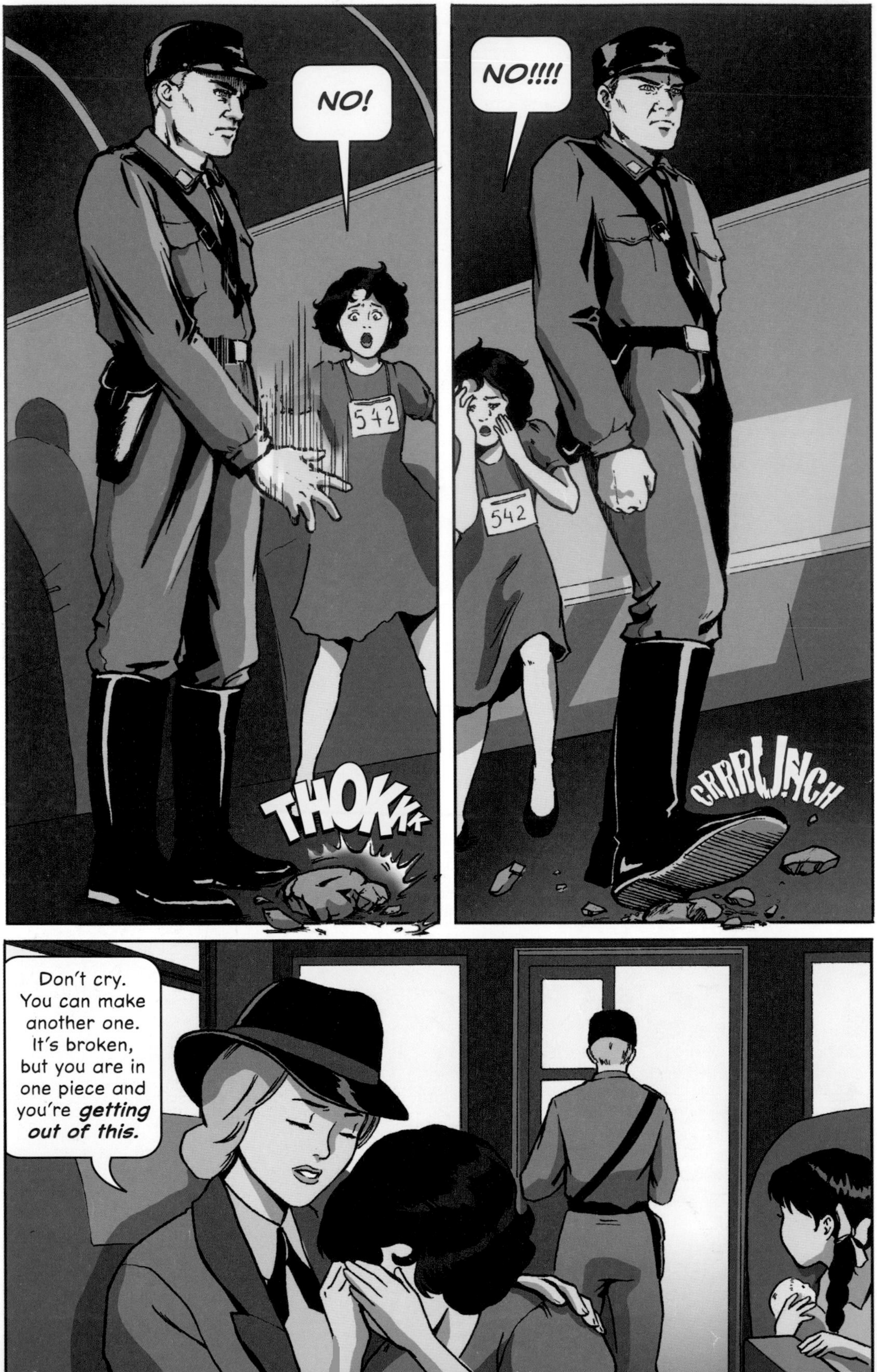
NO!
THOKKK
NO!!!!
CRRRUNCH
Don't cry. You can make another one. It's broken, but you are in one piece and you're **getting out of this.**

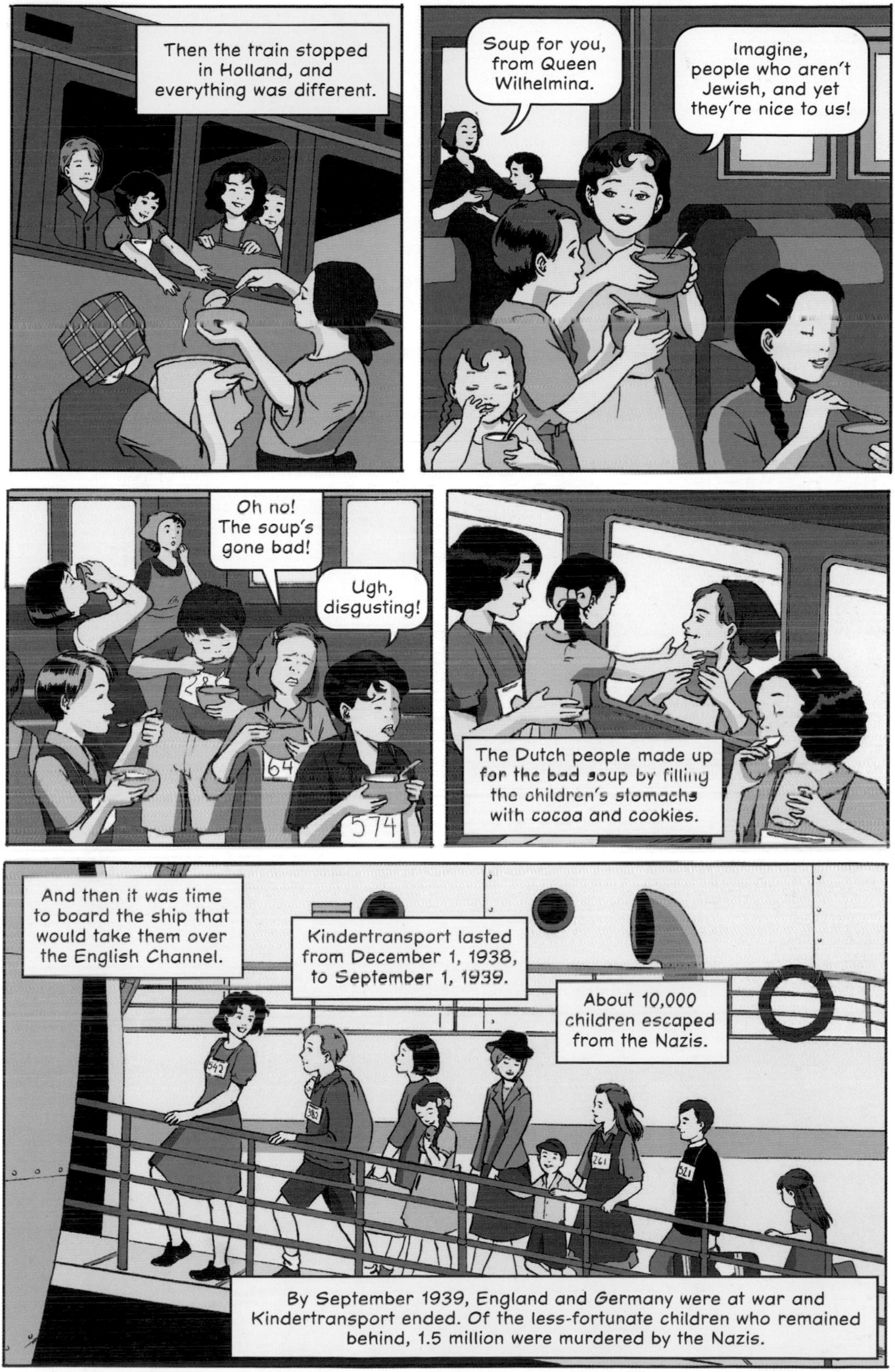
Then the train stopped in Holland, and everything was different.
Soup for you, from Queen Wilhelmina.
Imagine, people who aren't Jewish, and yet they're nice to us!
Oh no! The soup's gone bad!
Ugh, disgusting!
64
574
The Dutch people made up for the bad soup by filling the children's stomachs with cocoa and cookies.
And then it was time to board the ship that would take them over the English Channel.
Kindertransport lasted from December 1, 1938, to September 1, 1939.
About 10,000 children escaped from the Nazis.
By September 1939, England and Germany were at war and Kindertransport ended. Of the less-fortunate children who remained behind, 1.5 million were murdered by the Nazis.

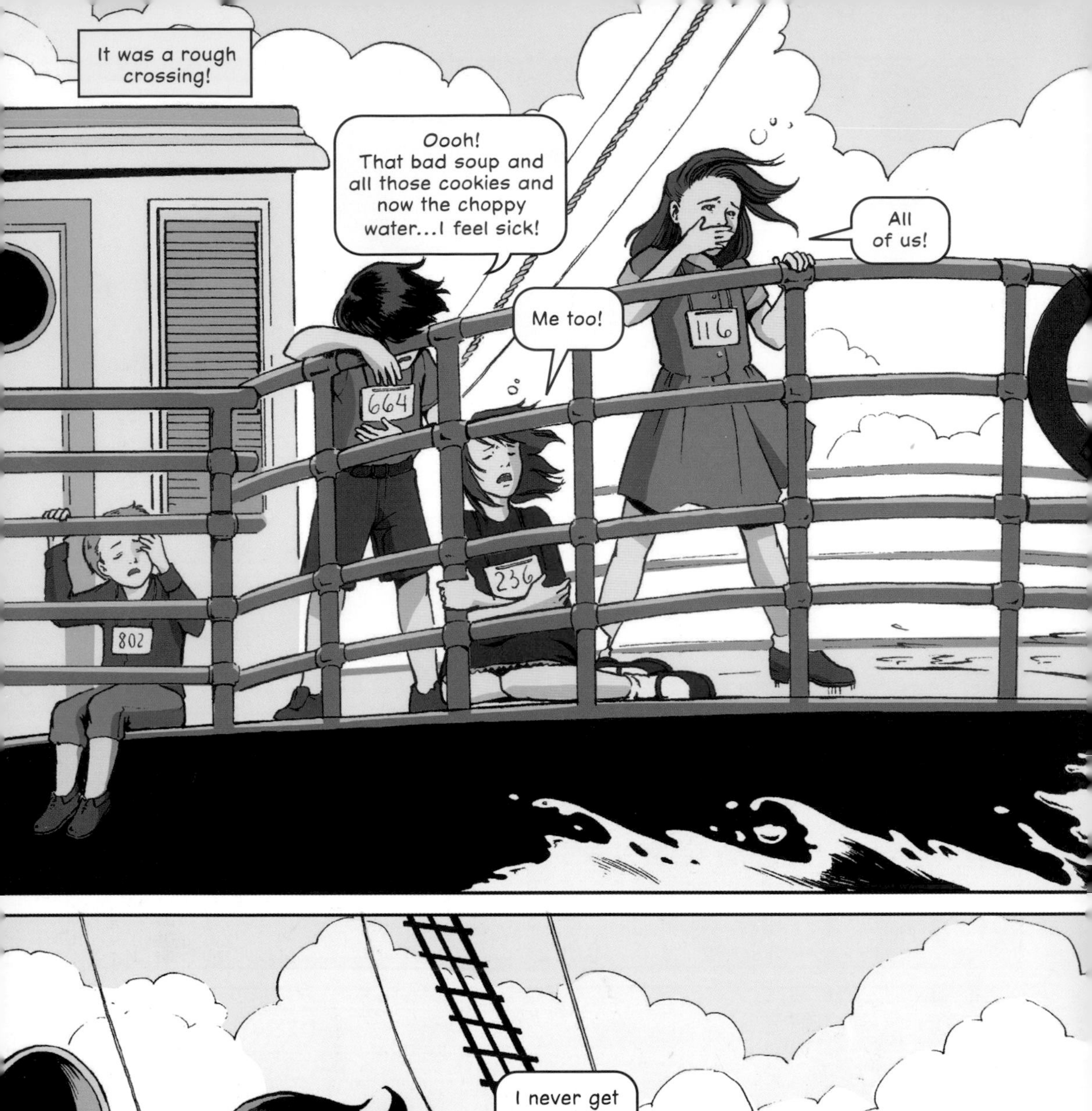
It was a rough crossing!
Oooh! That bad soup and all those cookies and now the choppy water...I feel sick!
Me too!
All of us!
664
802
236
116

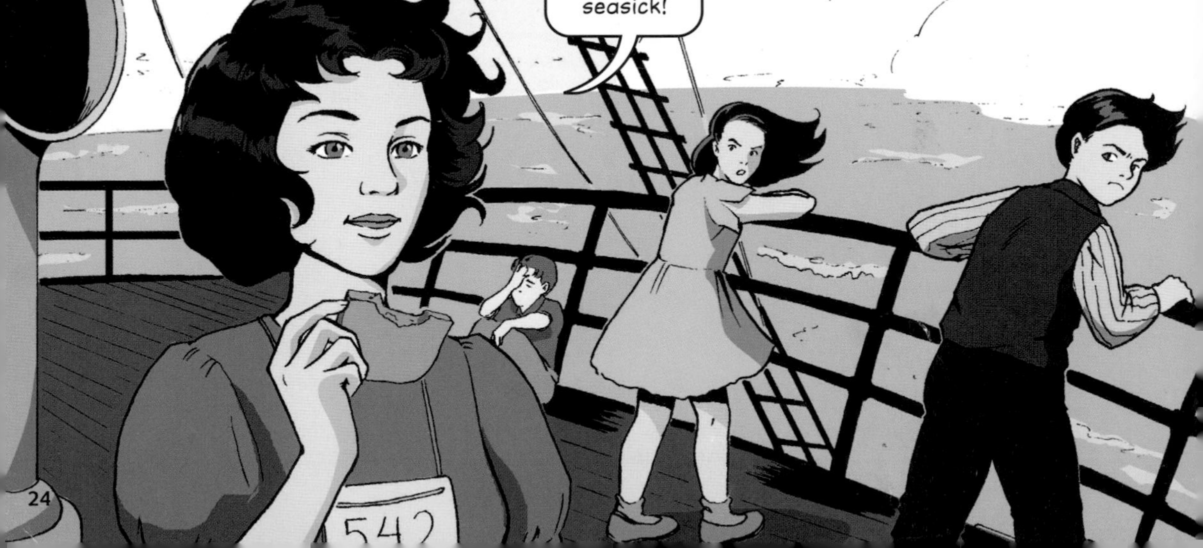
I never get seasick!
542

CHAPTER THREE: *England*

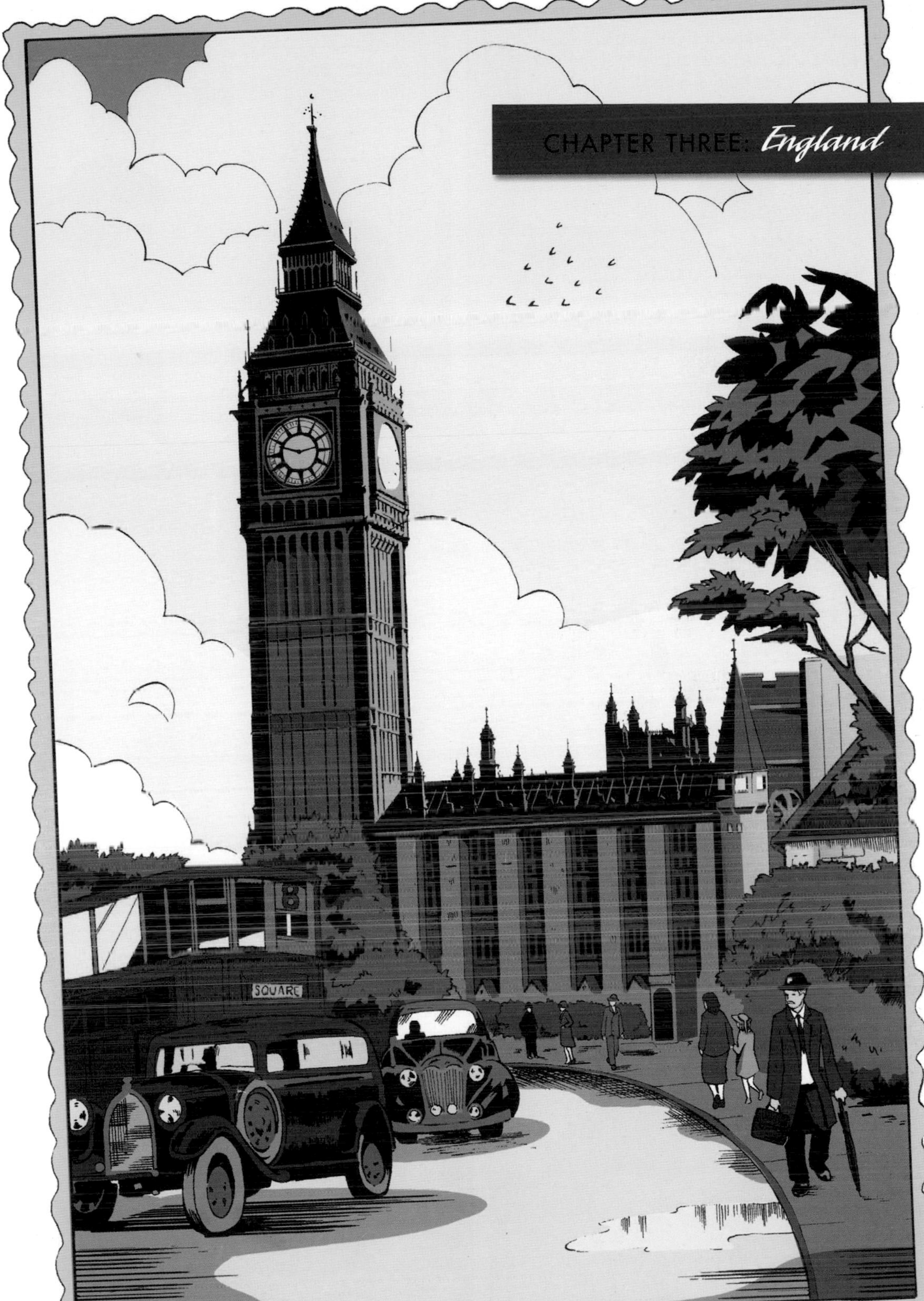

SQUARE

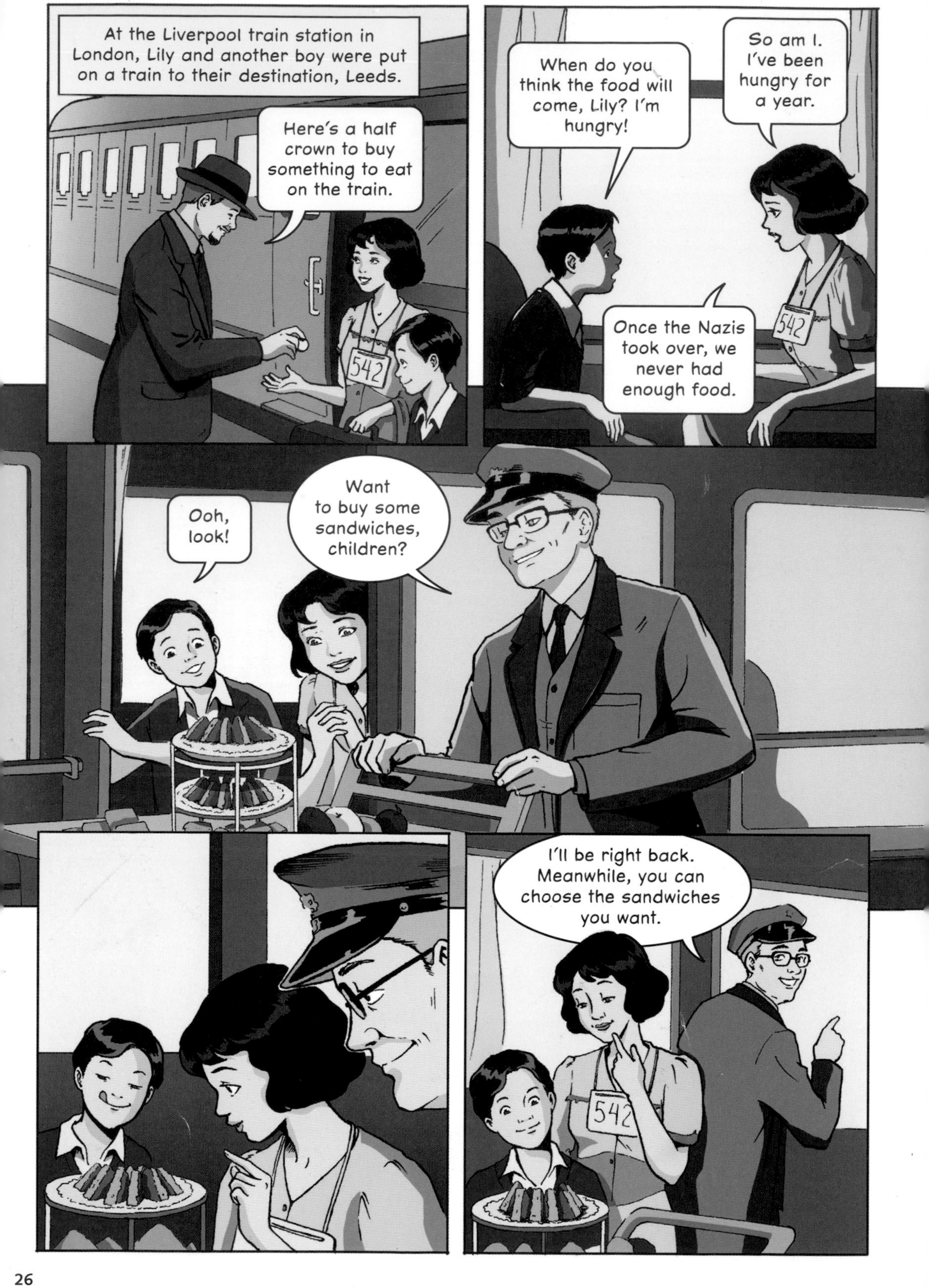
At the Liverpool train station in London, Lily and another boy were put on a train to their destination, Leeds.
Here's a half crown to buy something to eat on the train.
542
When do you think the food will come, Lily? I'm hungry!
So am I. I've been hungry for a year.
Once the Nazis took over, we never had enough food.
542
Ooh, look!
Want to buy some sandwiches, children?
I'll be right back. Meanwhile, you can choose the sandwiches you want.
542

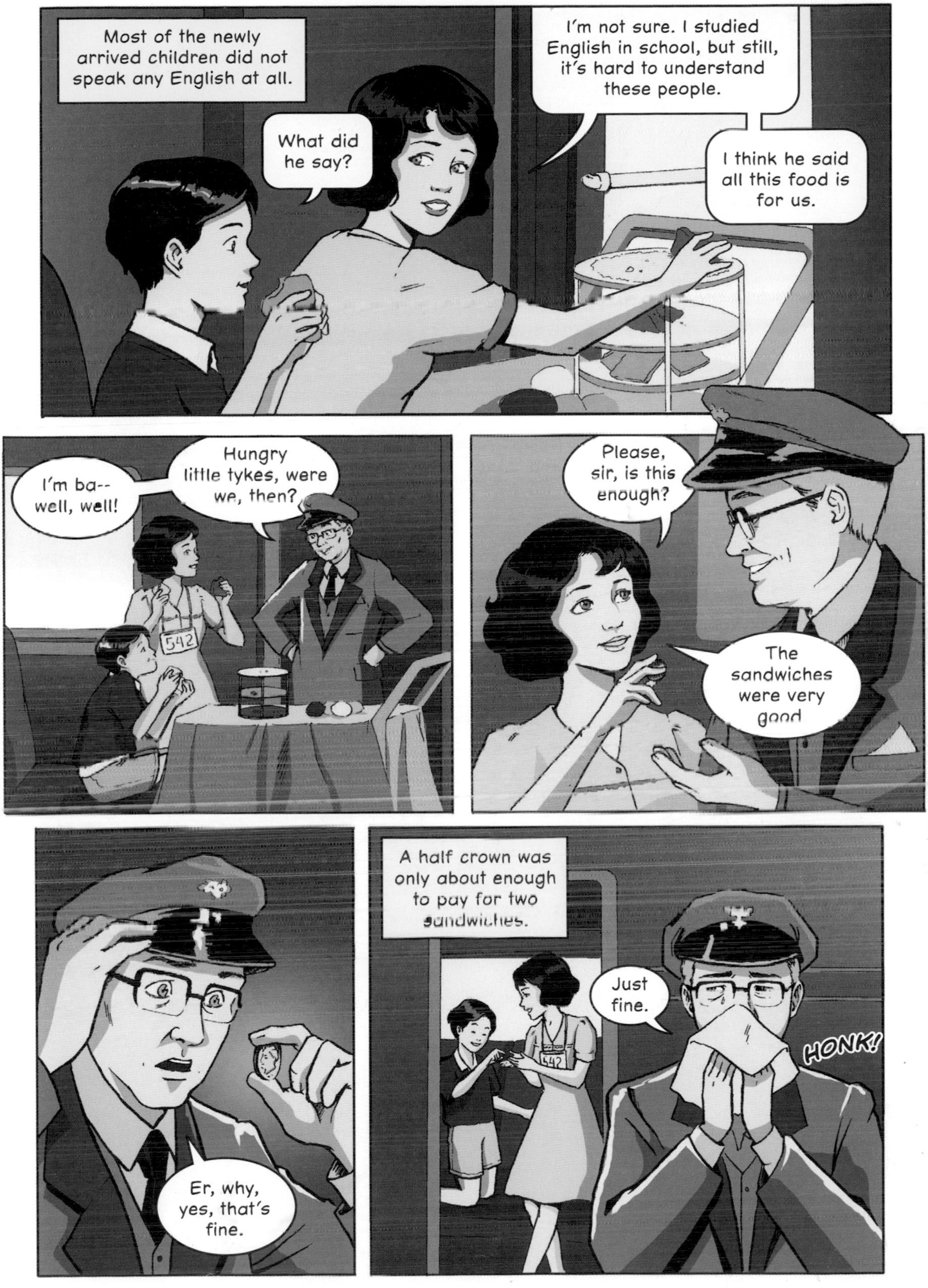

Most of the newly arrived children did not speak any English at all.
What did he say?
I'm not sure. I studied English in school, but still, it's hard to understand these people.
I think he said all this food is for us.
I'm ba-- well, well!
Hungry little tykes, were we, then?
542
Please, sir, is this enough?
The sandwiches were very good
Er, why, yes, that's fine.
A half crown was only about enough to pay for two sandwiches.
Just fine.
HONK!
542

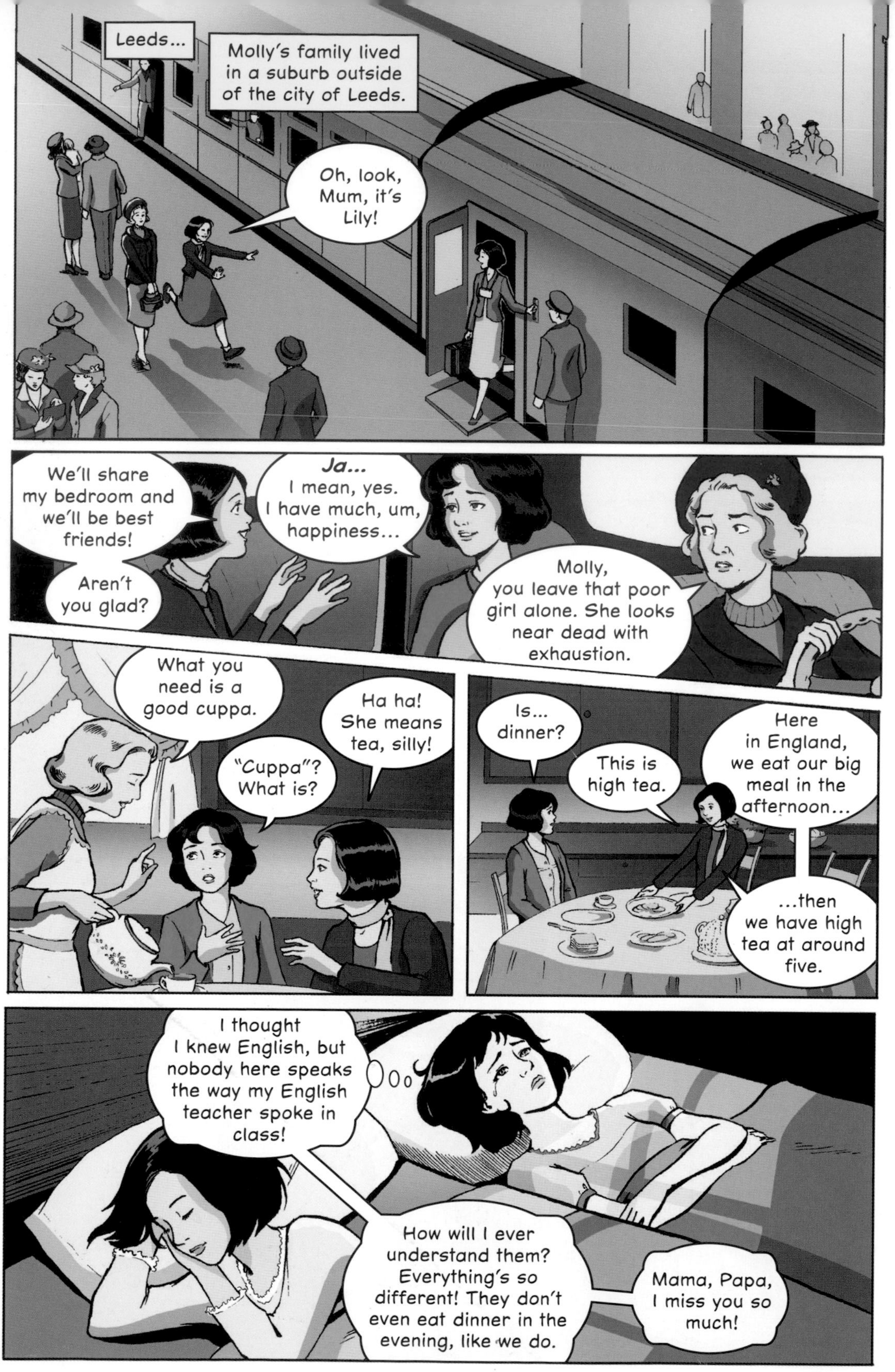

Leeds...
Molly's family lived in a suburb outside of the city of Leeds.
Oh, look, Mum, it's Lily!
We'll share my bedroom and we'll be best friends!
Aren't you glad?
Ja... I mean, yes. I have much, um, happiness...
Molly, you leave that poor girl alone. She looks near dead with exhaustion.
What you need is a good cuppa.
"Cuppa"? What is?
Ha ha! She means tea, silly!
Is... dinner?
This is high tea.
Here in England, we eat our big meal in the afternoon...
...then we have high tea at around five.
I thought I knew English, but nobody here speaks the way my English teacher spoke in class!
How will I ever understand them? Everything's so different! They don't even eat dinner in the evening, like we do.
Mama, Papa, I miss you so much!

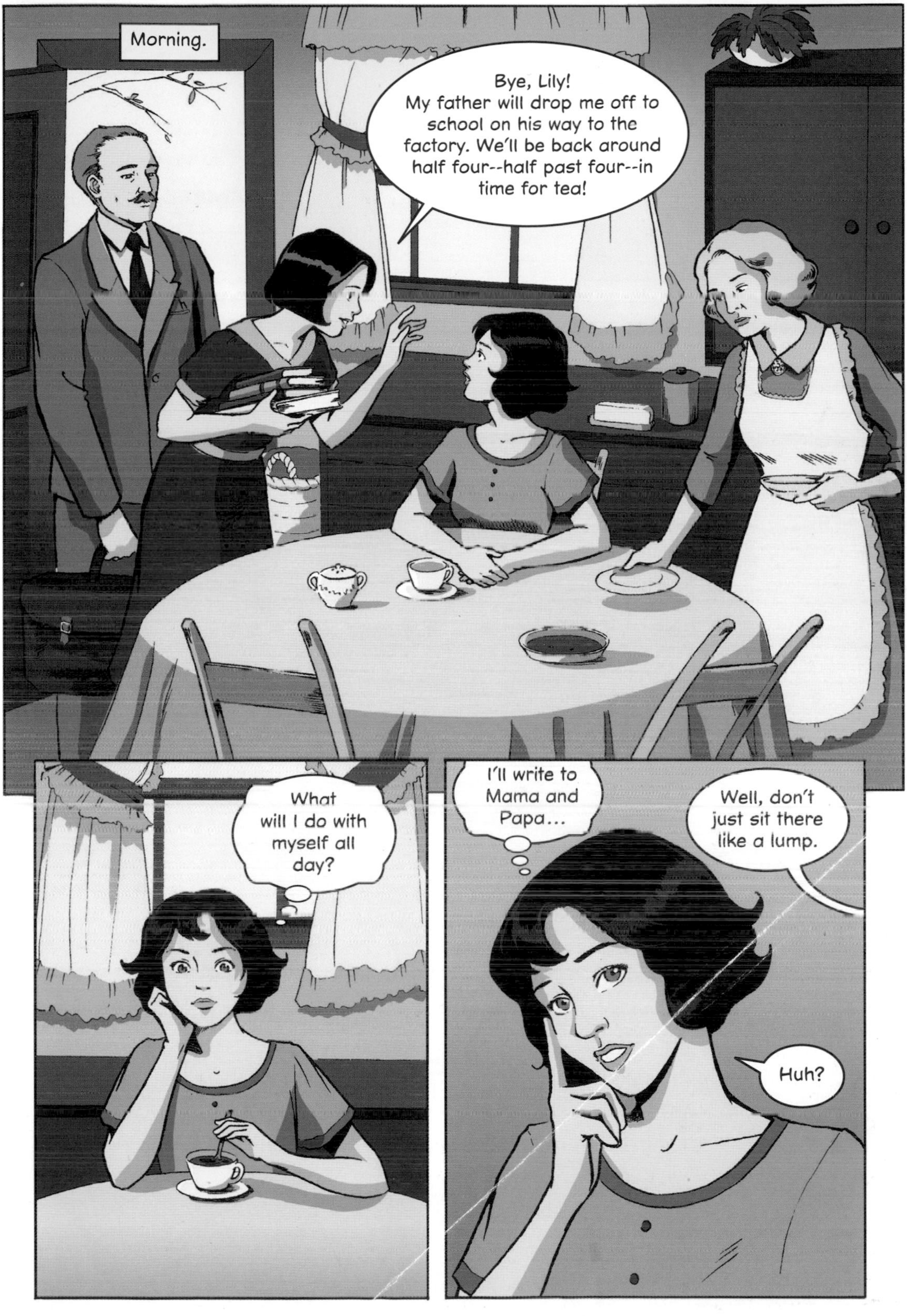
Morning.
Bye, Lily! My father will drop me off to school on his way to the factory. We'll be back around half four--half past four--in time for tea!
What will I do with myself all day?
I'll write to Mama and Papa...
Well, don't just sit there like a lump.
Huh?

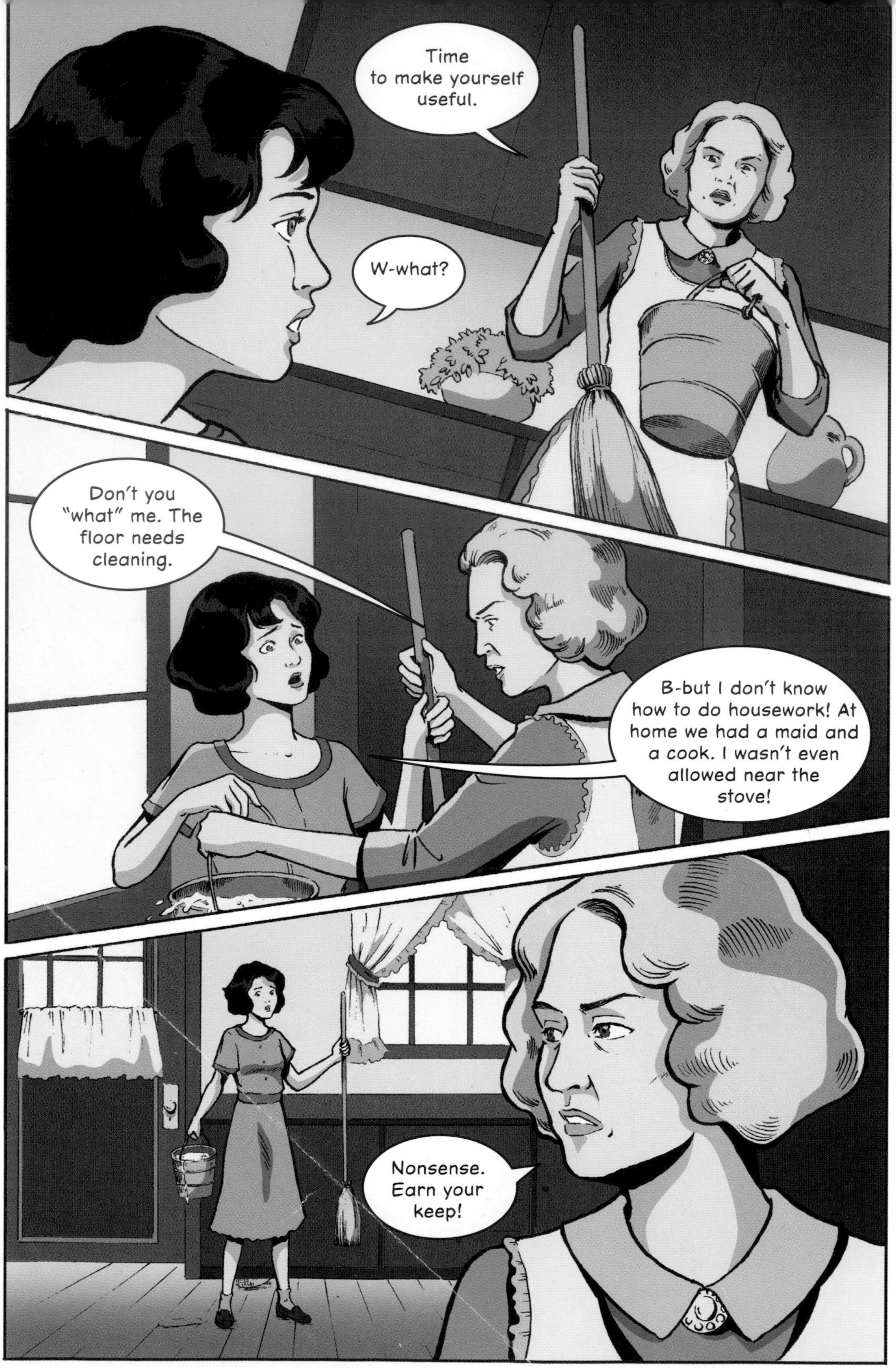
Time to make yourself useful.
W-what?
Don't you "what" me. The floor needs cleaning.
B-but I don't know how to do housework! At home we had a maid and a cook. I wasn't even allowed near the stove!
Nonsense. Earn your keep!

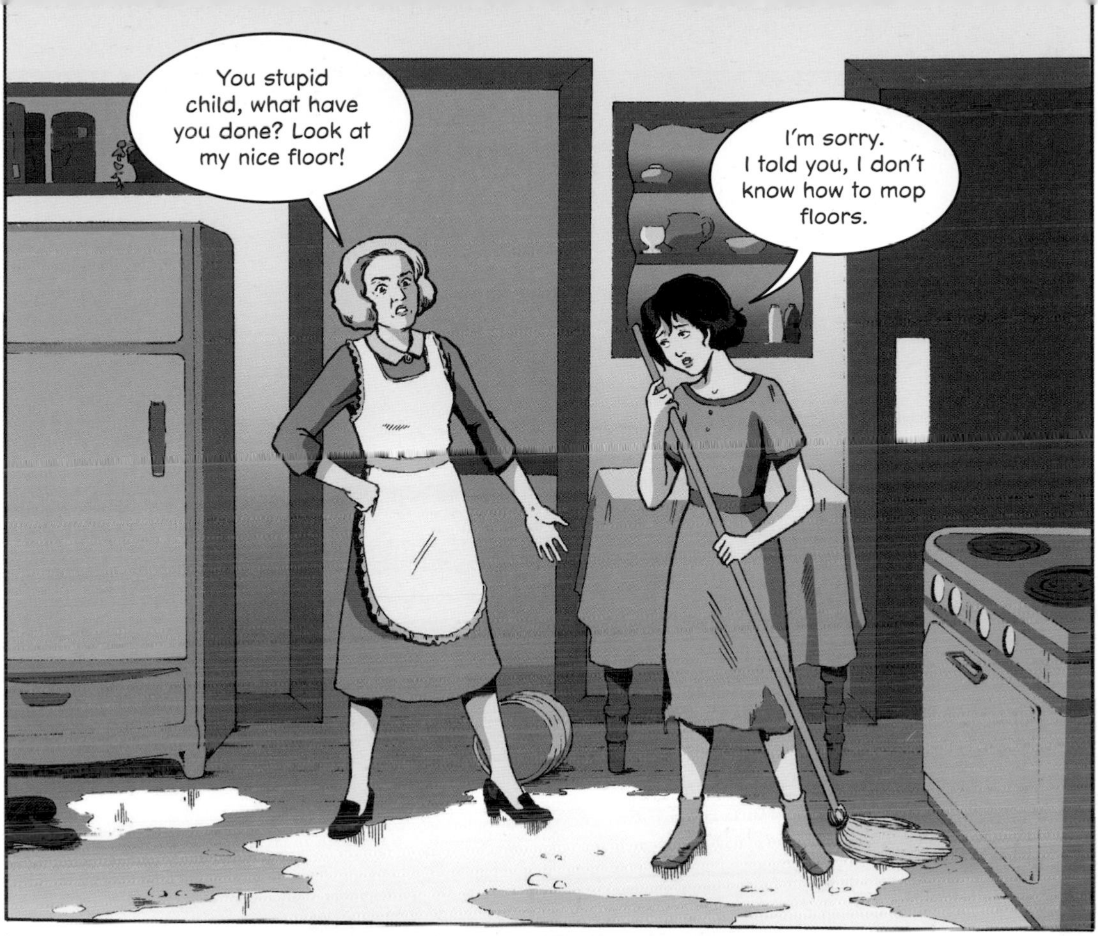
You stupid child, what have you done? Look at my nice floor!
I'm sorry. I told you, I don't know how to mop floors.

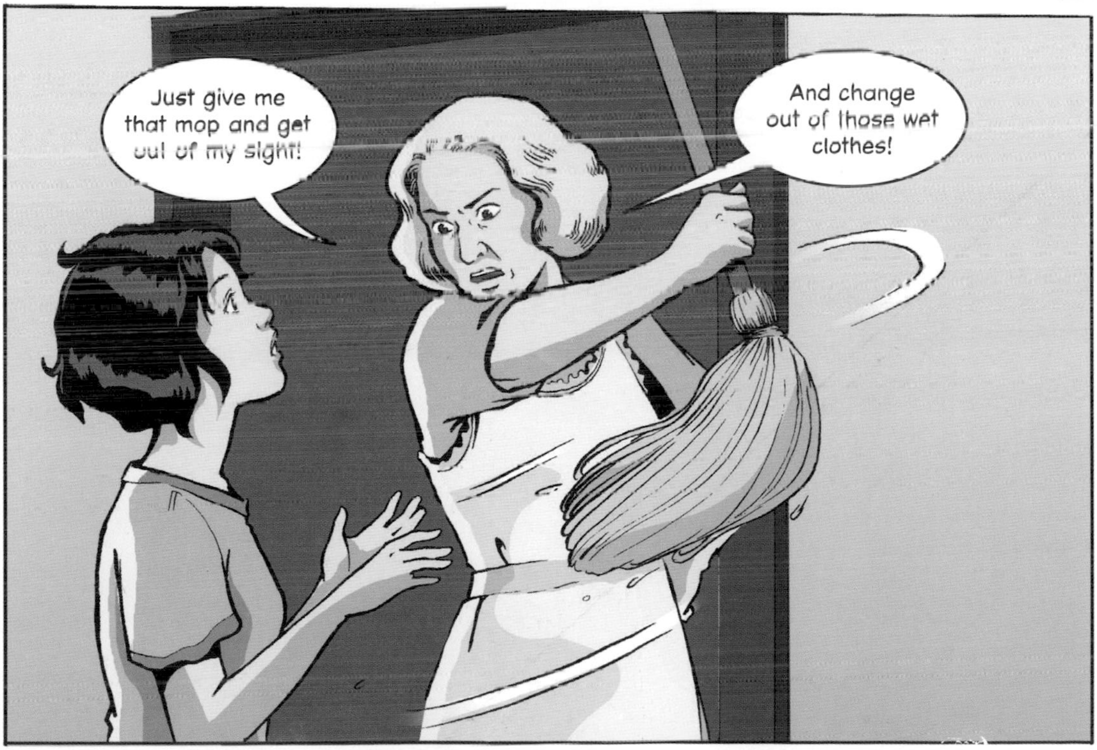
Just give me that mop and get out of my sight!
And change out of those wet clothes!

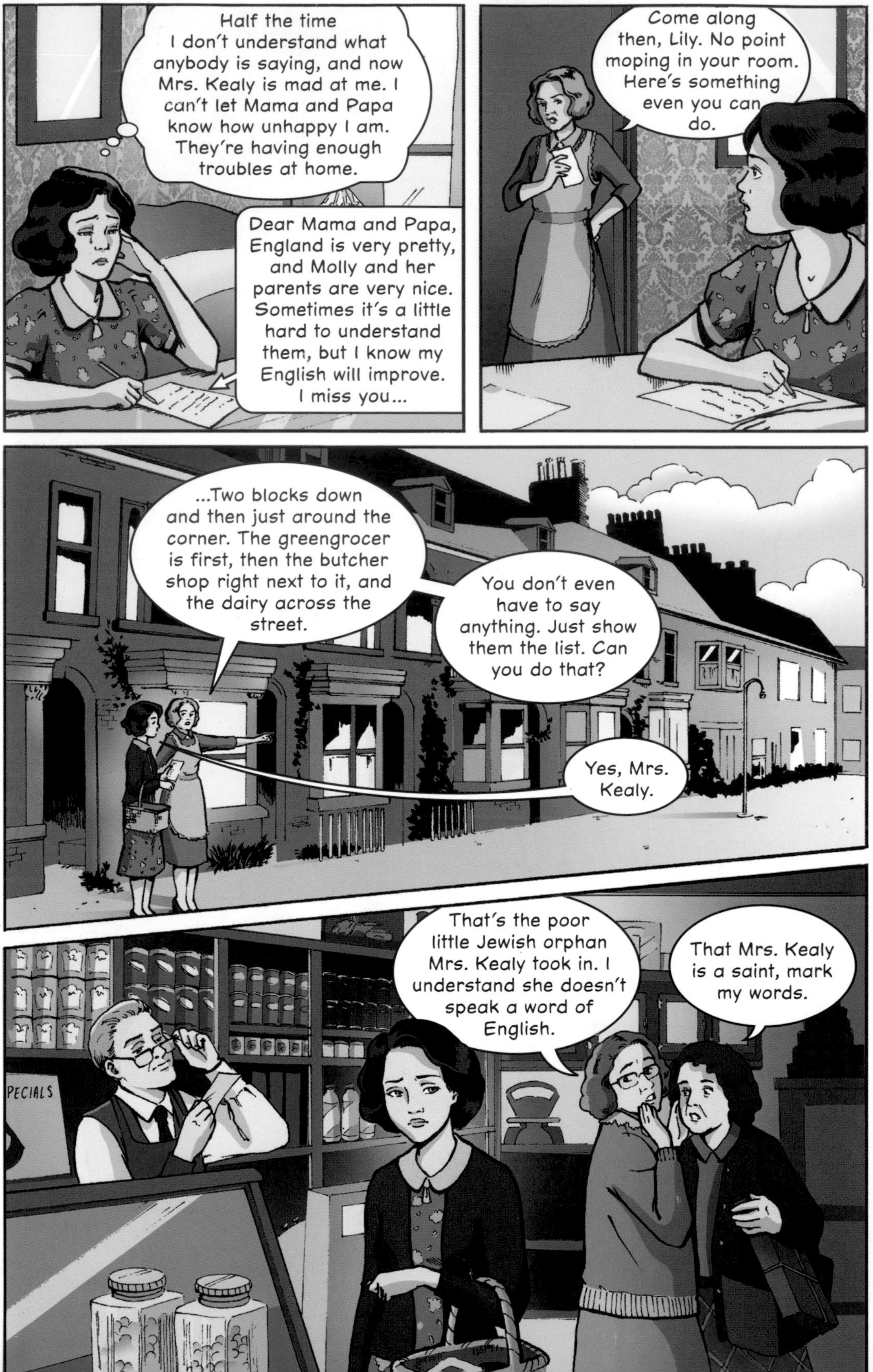
Half the time I don't understand what anybody is saying, and now Mrs. Kealy is mad at me. I can't let Mama and Papa know how unhappy I am. They're having enough troubles at home.
Dear Mama and Papa, England is very pretty, and Molly and her parents are very nice. Sometimes it's a little hard to understand them, but I know my English will improve. I miss you...
Come along then, Lily. No point moping in your room. Here's something even you can do.
...Two blocks down and then just around the corner. The greengrocer is first, then the butcher shop right next to it, and the dairy across the street.
You don't even have to say anything. Just show them the list. Can you do that?
Yes, Mrs. Kealy.
That's the poor little Jewish orphan Mrs. Kealy took in. I understand she doesn't speak a word of English.
That Mrs. Kealy is a saint, mark my words.
PECIALS

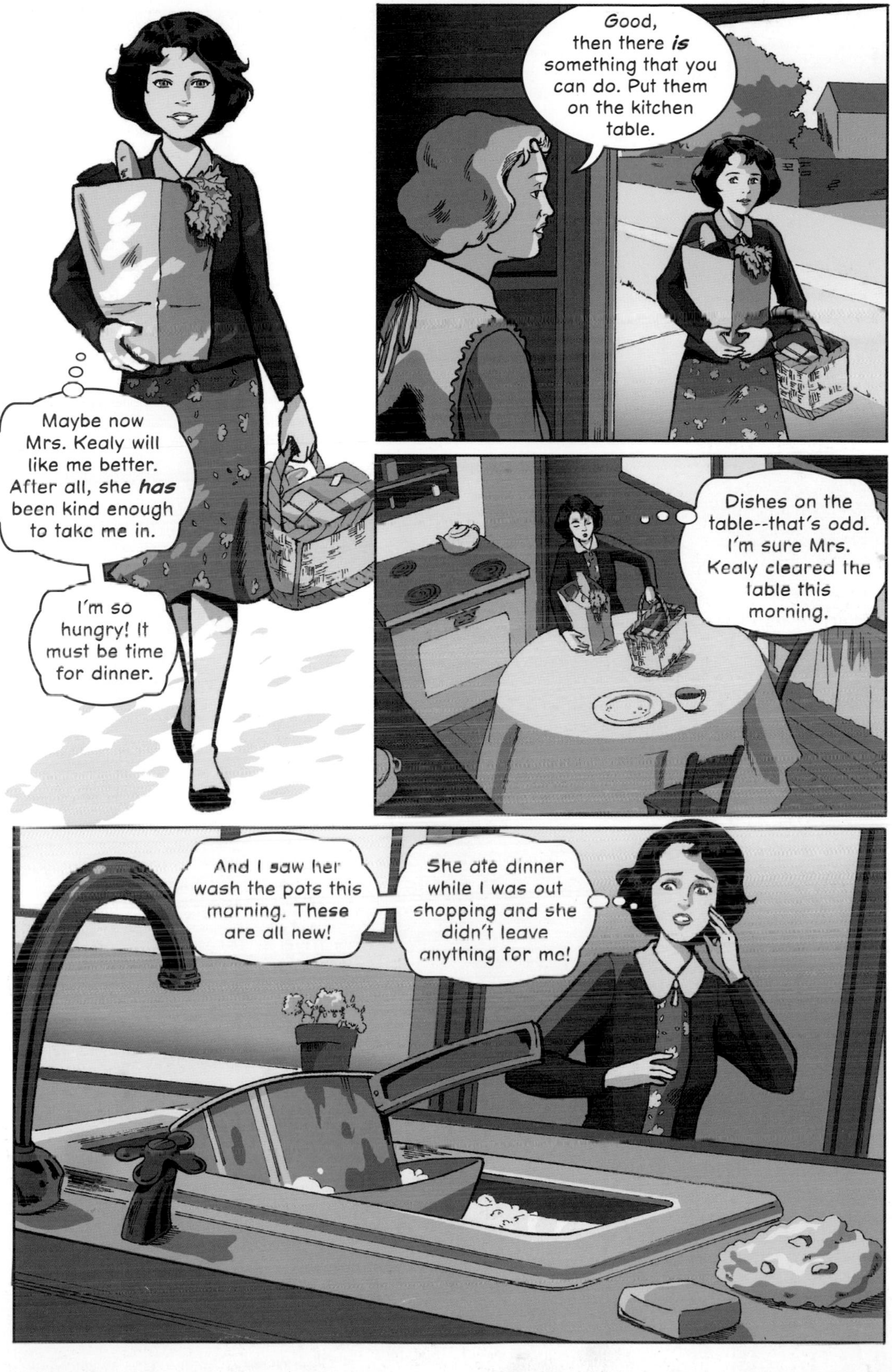
Maybe now Mrs. Kealy will like me better. After all, she *has* been kind enough to take me in.
I'm so hungry! It must be time for dinner.
Good, then there *is* something that you can do. Put them on the kitchen table.
Dishes on the table--that's odd. I'm sure Mrs. Kealy cleared the table this morning.
And I saw her wash the pots this morning. These are all new!
She ate dinner while I was out shopping and she didn't leave anything for me!

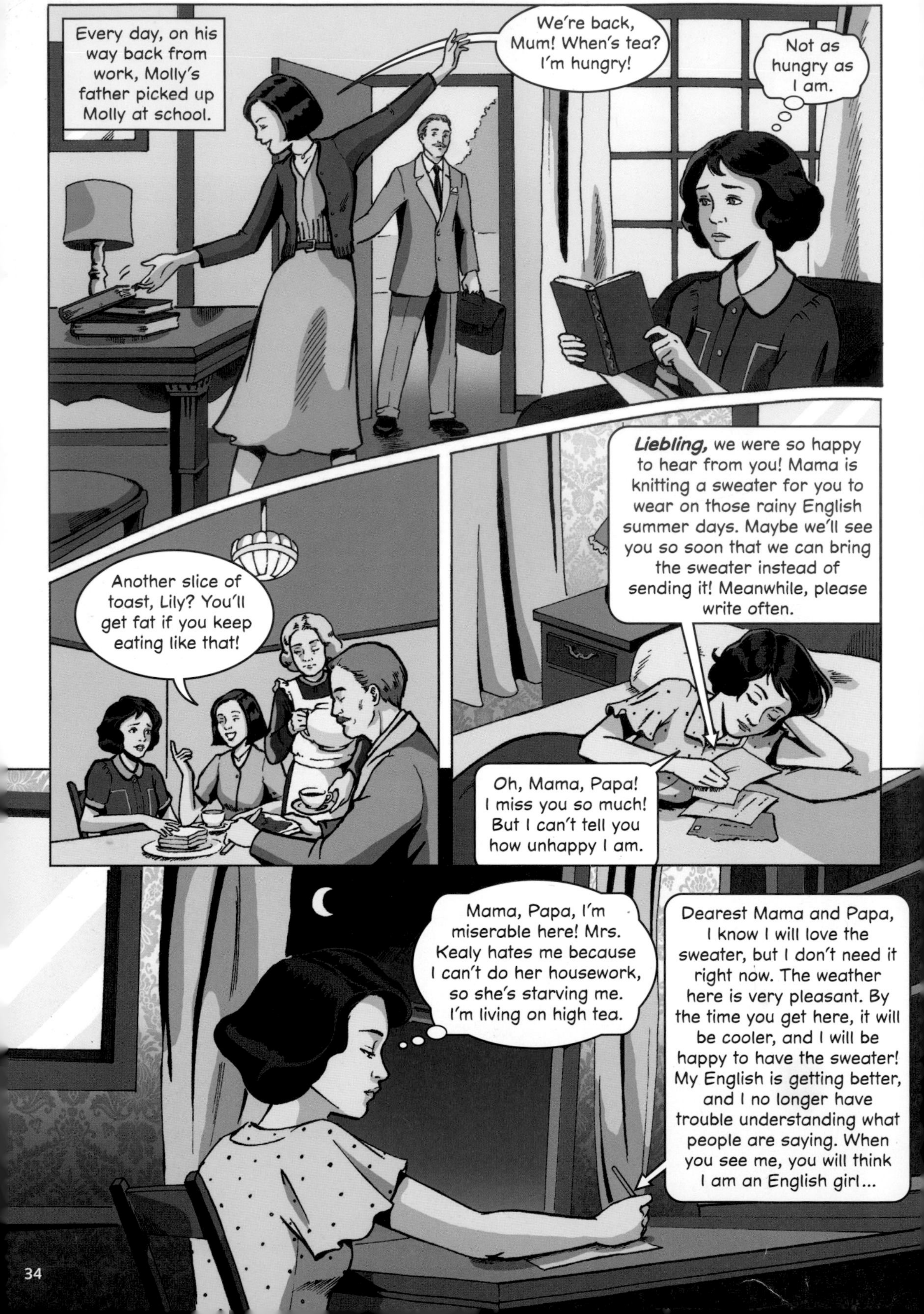
Every day, on his way back from work, Molly's father picked up Molly at school.
We're back, Mum! When's tea? I'm hungry!
Not as hungry as I am.
Another slice of toast, Lily? You'll get fat if you keep eating like that!
Liebling, we were so happy to hear from you! Mama is knitting a sweater for you to wear on those rainy English summer days. Maybe we'll see you so soon that we can bring the sweater instead of sending it! Meanwhile, please write often.
Oh, Mama, Papa! I miss you so much! But I can't tell you how unhappy I am.
Mama, Papa, I'm miserable here! Mrs. Kealy hates me because I can't do her housework, so she's starving me. I'm living on high tea.
Dearest Mama and Papa, I know I will love the sweater, but I don't need it right now. The weather here is very pleasant. By the time you get here, it will be cooler, and I will be happy to have the sweater! My English is getting better, and I no longer have trouble understanding what people are saying. When you see me, you will think I am an English girl...

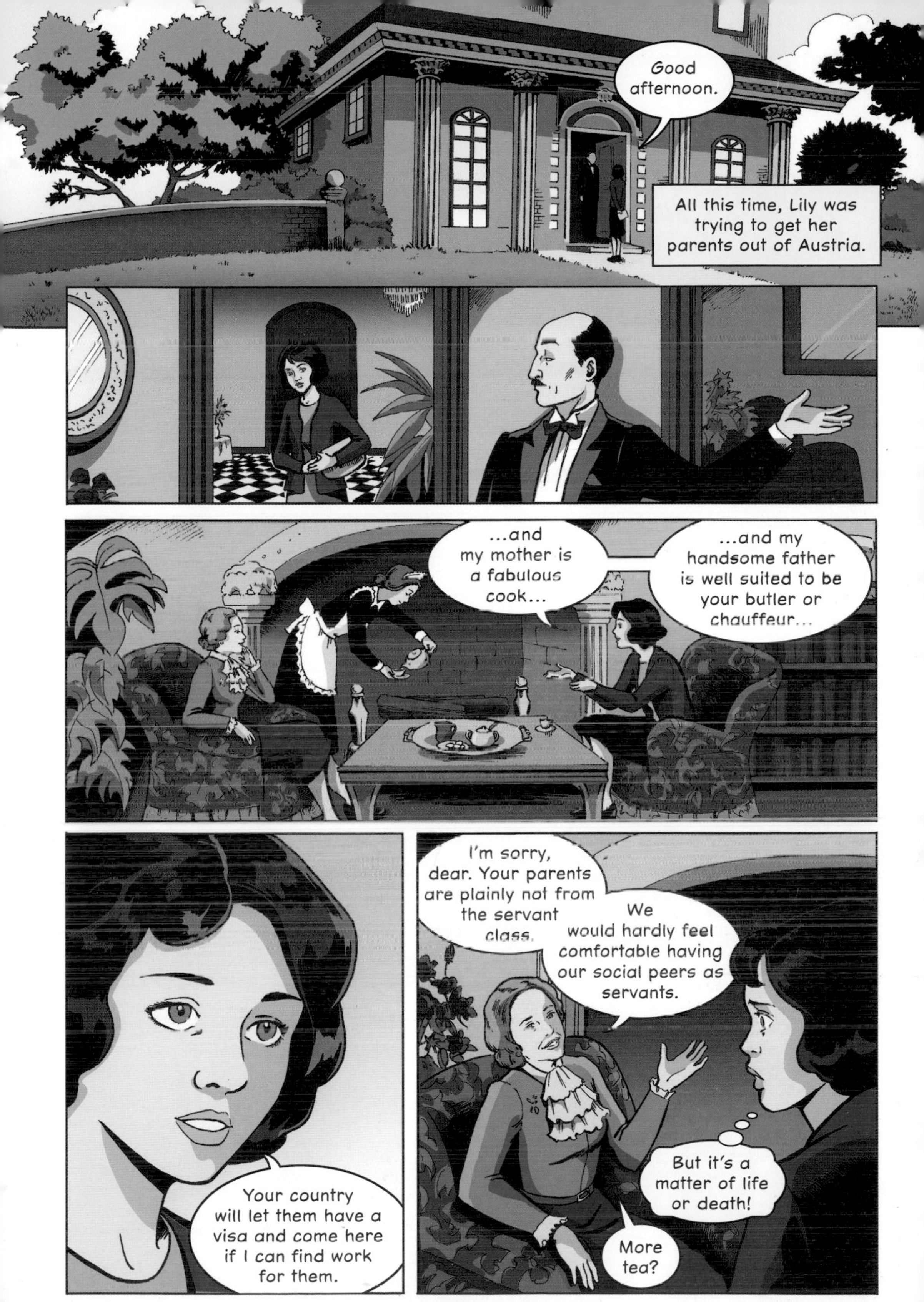
Good afternoon.
All this time, Lily was trying to get her parents out of Austria.
...and my mother is a fabulous cook...
...and my handsome father is well suited to be your butler or chauffeur...
Your country will let them have a visa and come here if I can find work for them.
I'm sorry, dear. Your parents are plainly not from the servant class.
We would hardly feel comfortable having our social peers as servants.
But it's a matter of life or death!
More tea?

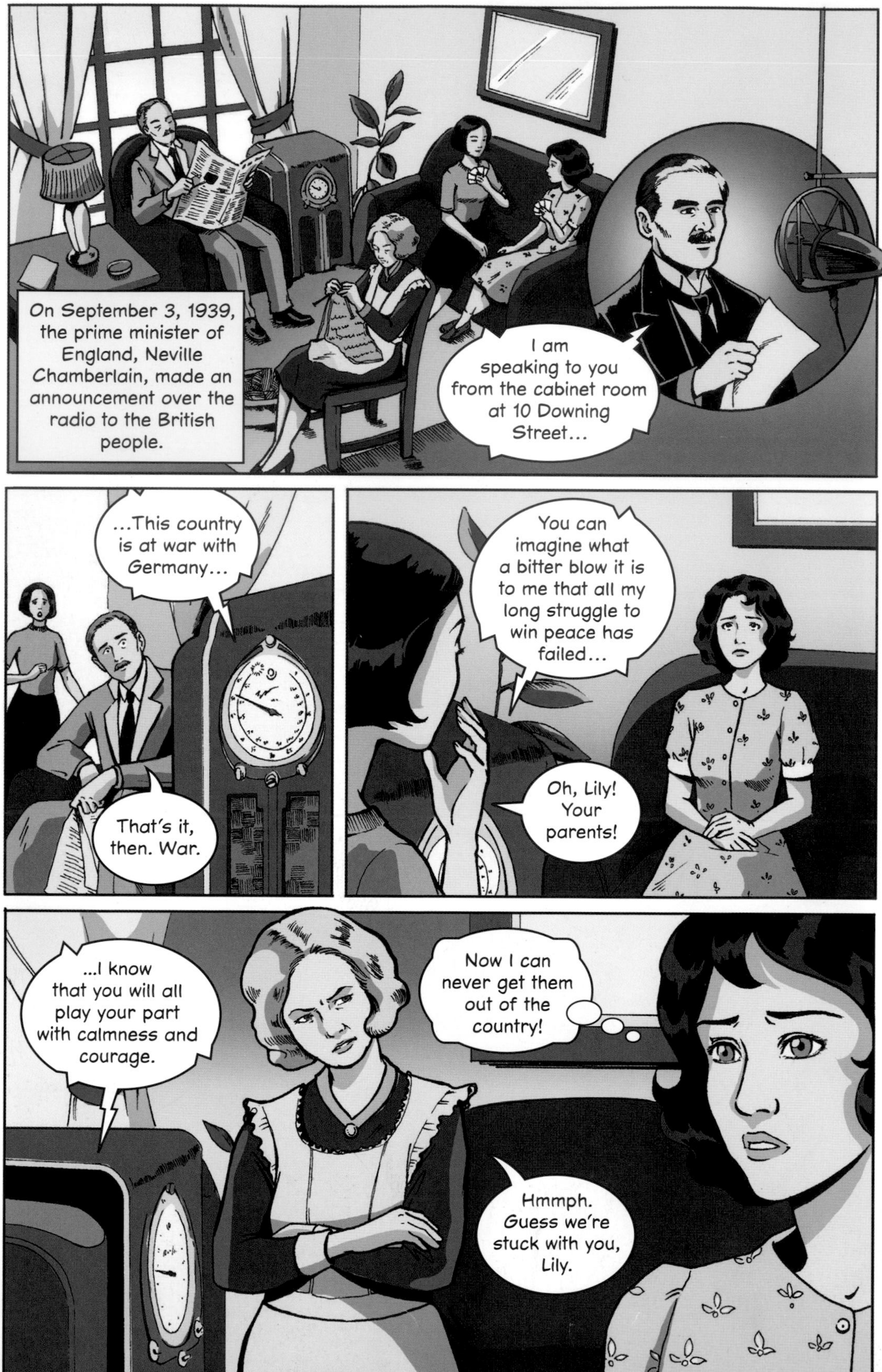

On September 3, 1939, the prime minister of England, Neville Chamberlain, made an announcement over the radio to the British people.
I am speaking to you from the cabinet room at 10 Downing Street...
...This country is at war with Germany...
That's it, then. War.
You can imagine what a bitter blow it is to me that all my long struggle to win peace has failed...
Oh, Lily! Your parents!
...I know that you will all play your part with calmness and courage.
Now I can never get them out of the country!
Hmmph. Guess we're stuck with you, Lily.

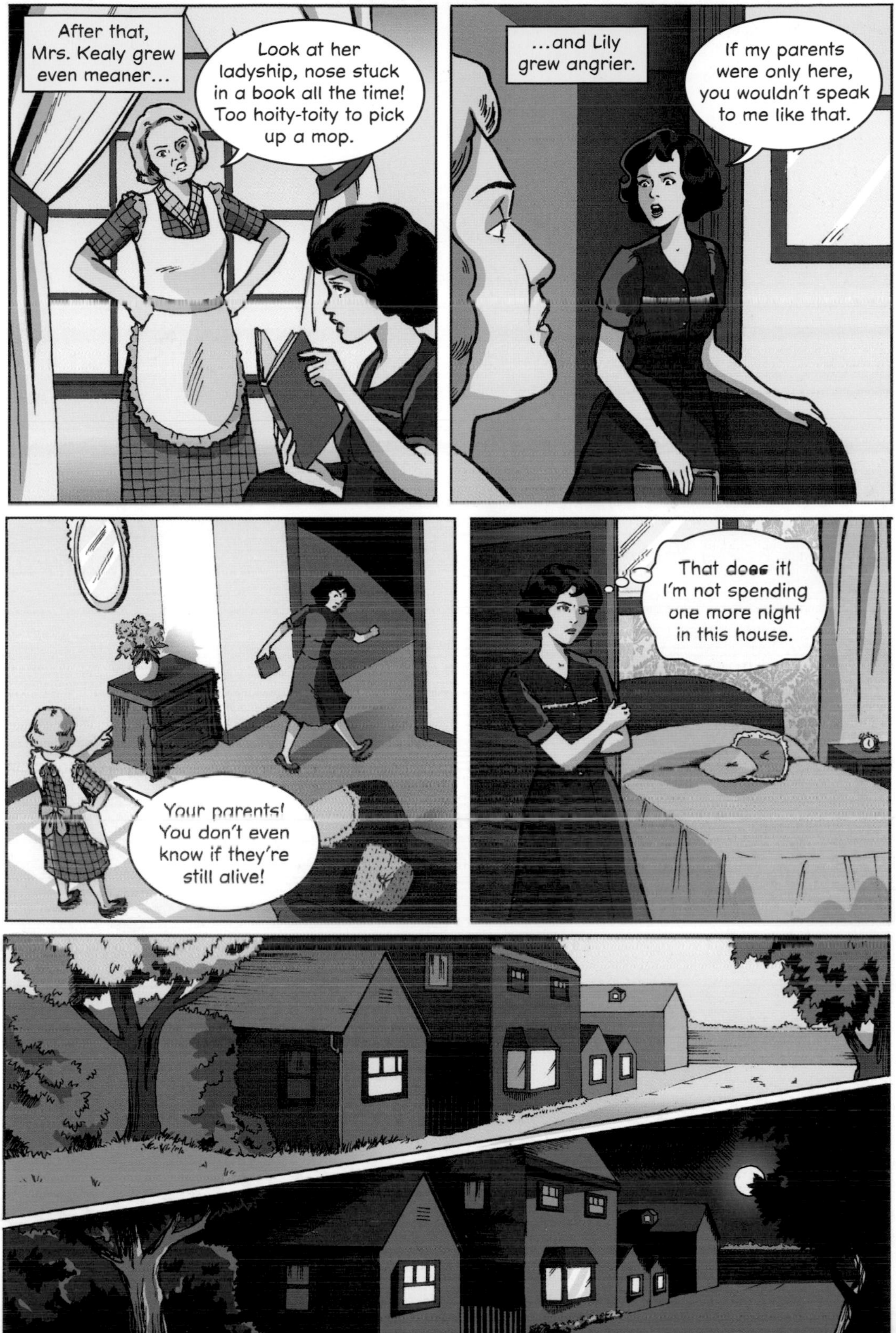

After that, Mrs. Kealy grew even meaner...
Look at her ladyship, nose stuck in a book all the time! Too hoity-toity to pick up a mop.
...and Lily grew angrier.
If my parents were only here, you wouldn't speak to me like that.
Your parents! You don't even know if they're still alive!
That does it! I'm not spending one more night in this house.

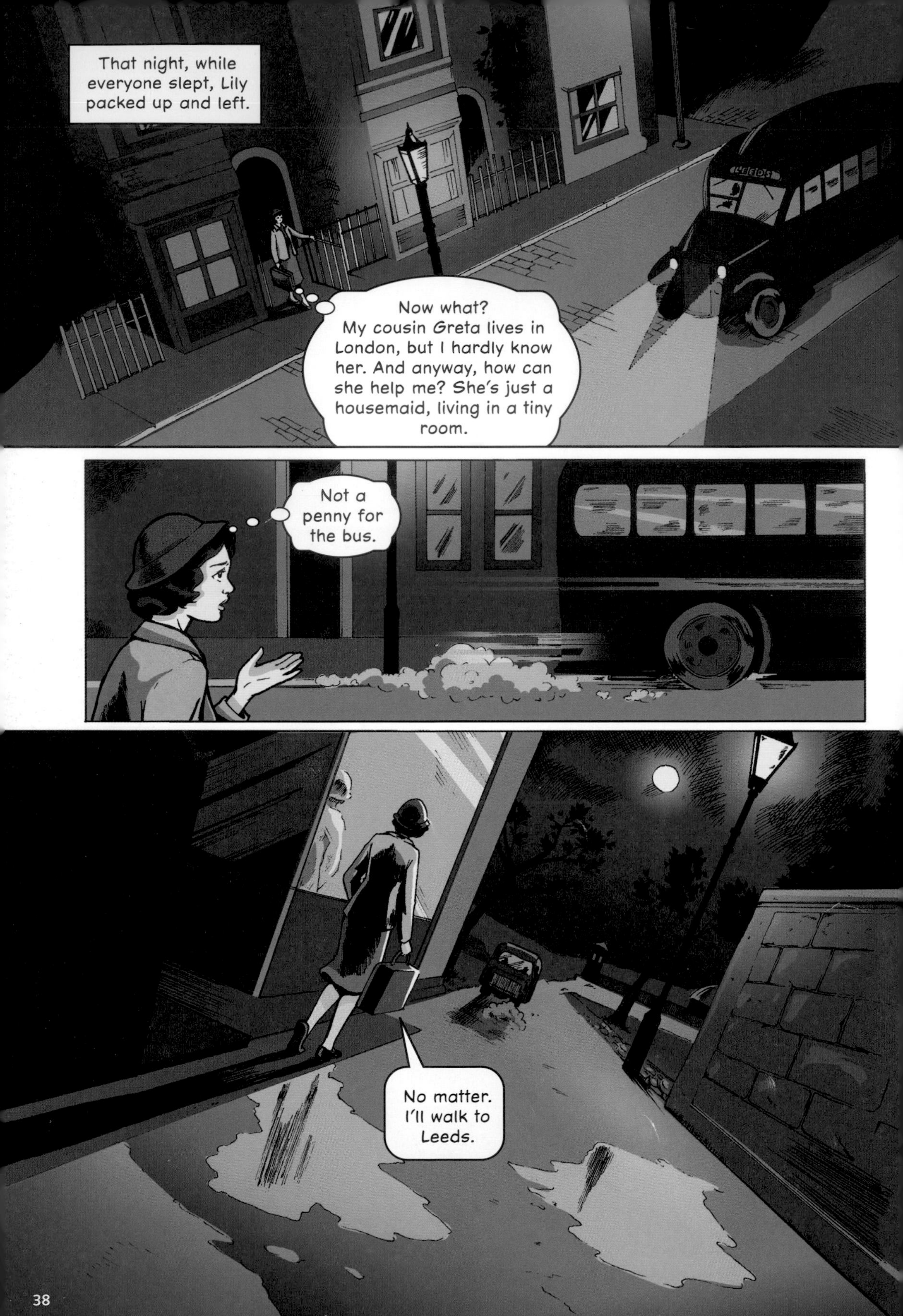
That night, while everyone slept, Lily packed up and left.
Now what? My cousin Greta lives in London, but I hardly know her. And anyway, how can she help me? She's just a housemaid, living in a tiny room.
LEEDS
Not a penny for the bus.
No matter. I'll walk to Leeds.

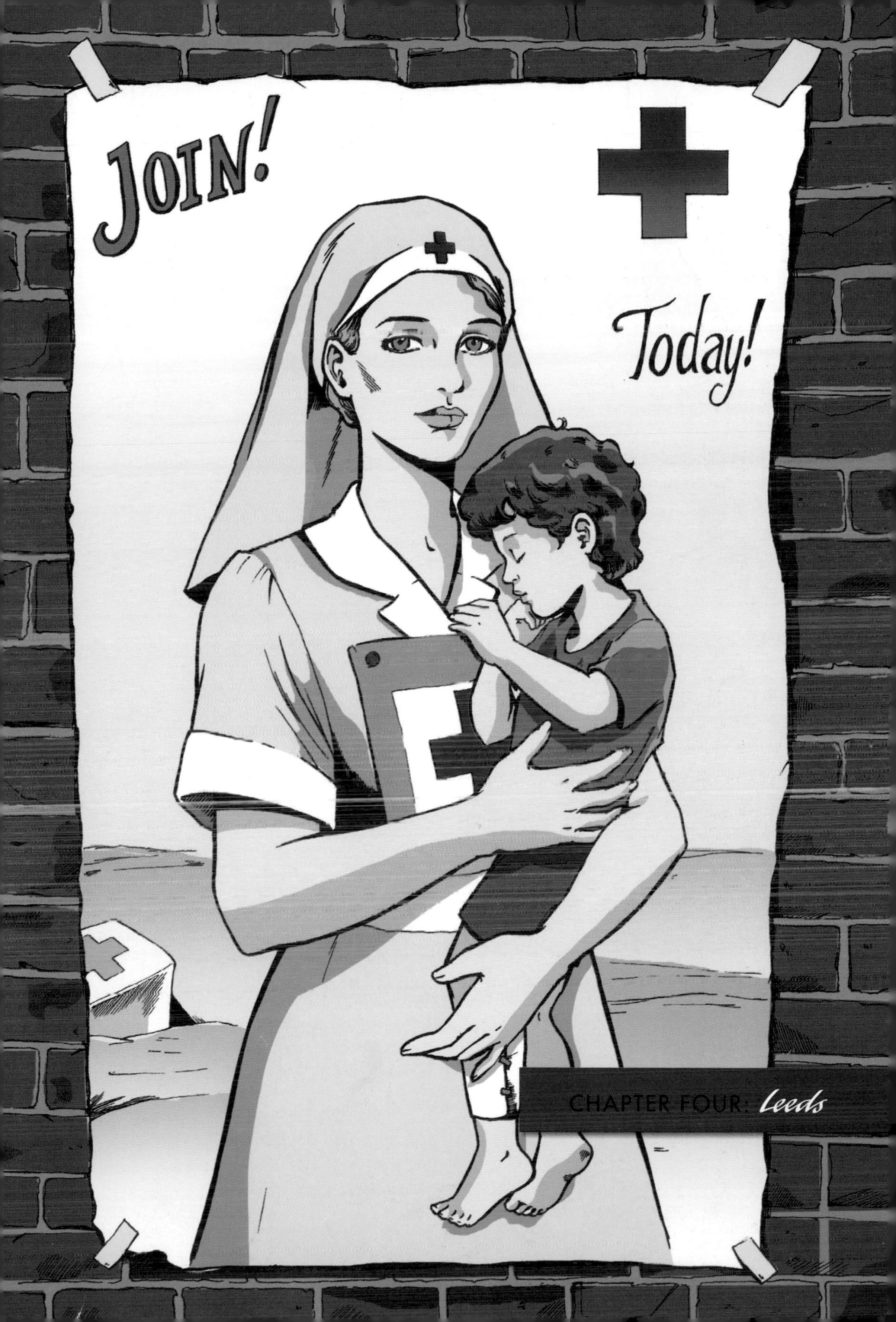
JOIN!
Today!
CHAPTER FOUR: Leeds

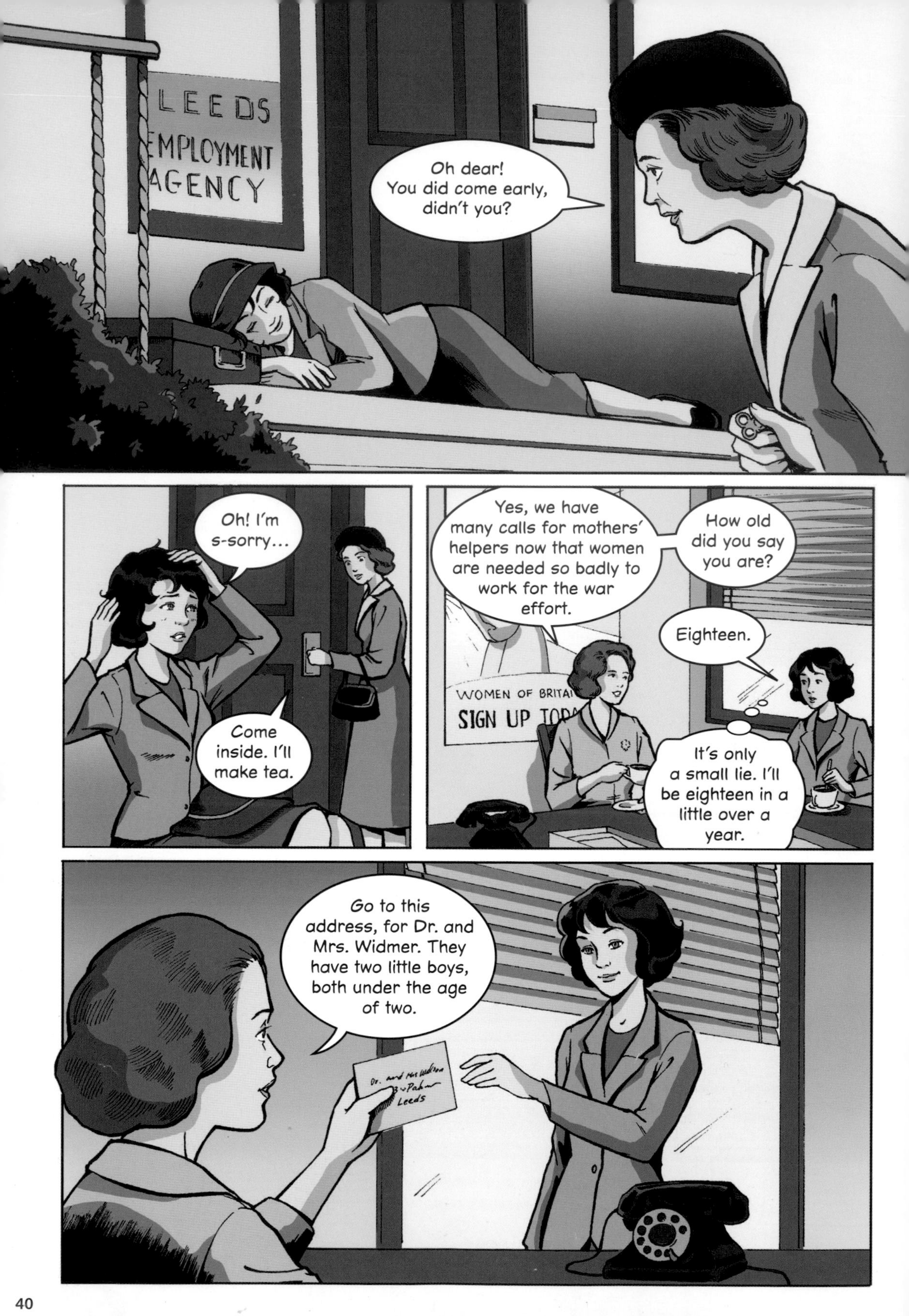
LEEDS
EMPLOYMENT
AGENCY
Oh dear! You did come early, didn't you?
Oh! I'm s-sorry...
Come inside. I'll make tea.
Yes, we have many calls for mothers' helpers now that women are needed so badly to work for the war effort.
WOMEN OF BRITAI
SIGN UP TO
How old did you say you are?
Eighteen.
It's only a small lie. I'll be eighteen in a little over a year.
Go to this address, for Dr. and Mrs. Widmer. They have two little boys, both under the age of two.

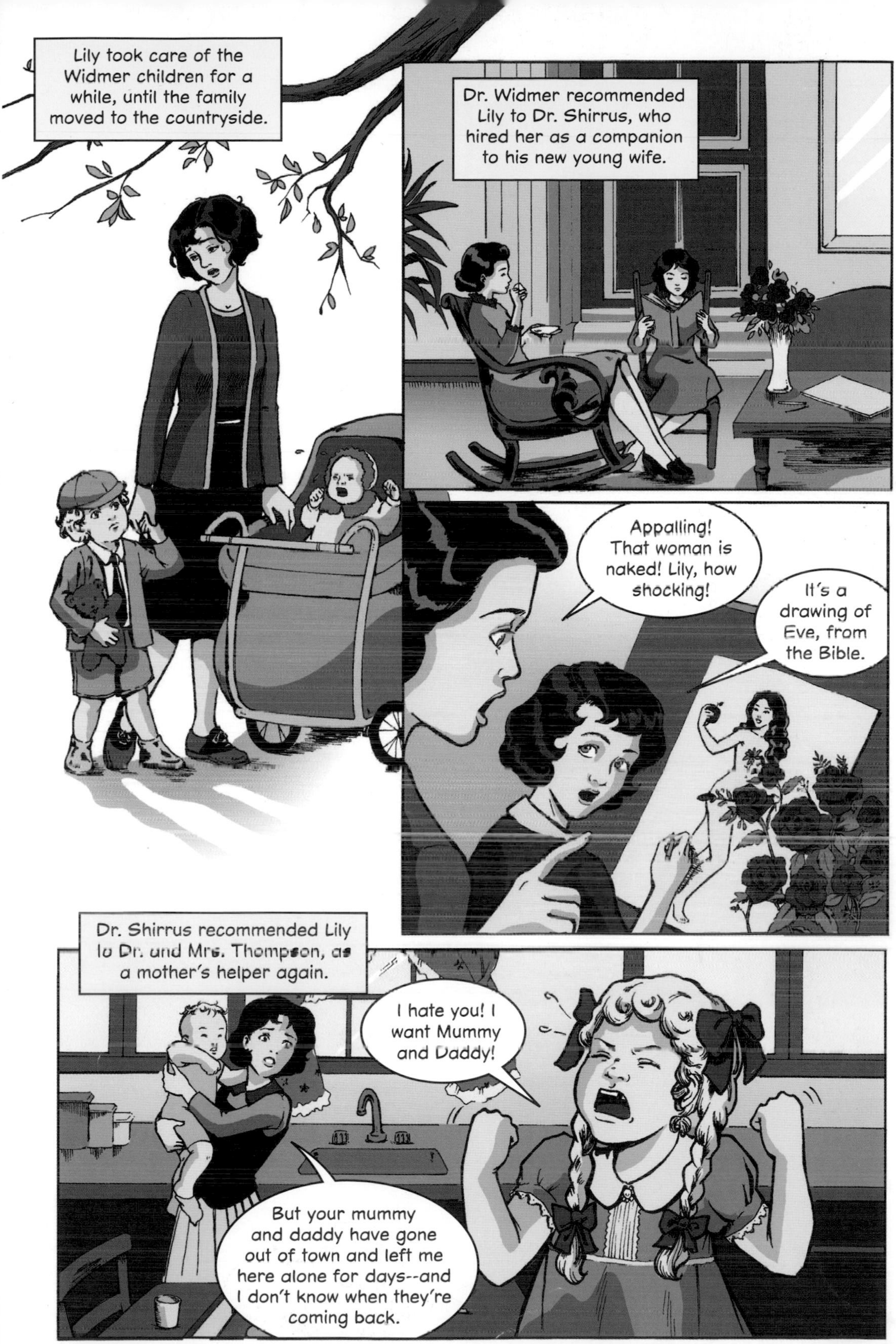

Lily took care of the Widmer children for a while, until the family moved to the countryside.
Dr. Widmer recommended Lily to Dr. Shirrus, who hired her as a companion to his new young wife.
Appalling! That woman is naked! Lily, how shocking!
It's a drawing of Eve, from the Bible.
Dr. Shirrus recommended Lily to Dr. and Mrs. Thompson, as a mother's helper again.
I hate you! I want Mummy and Daddy!
But your mummy and daddy have gone out of town and left me here alone for days--and I don't know when they're coming back.

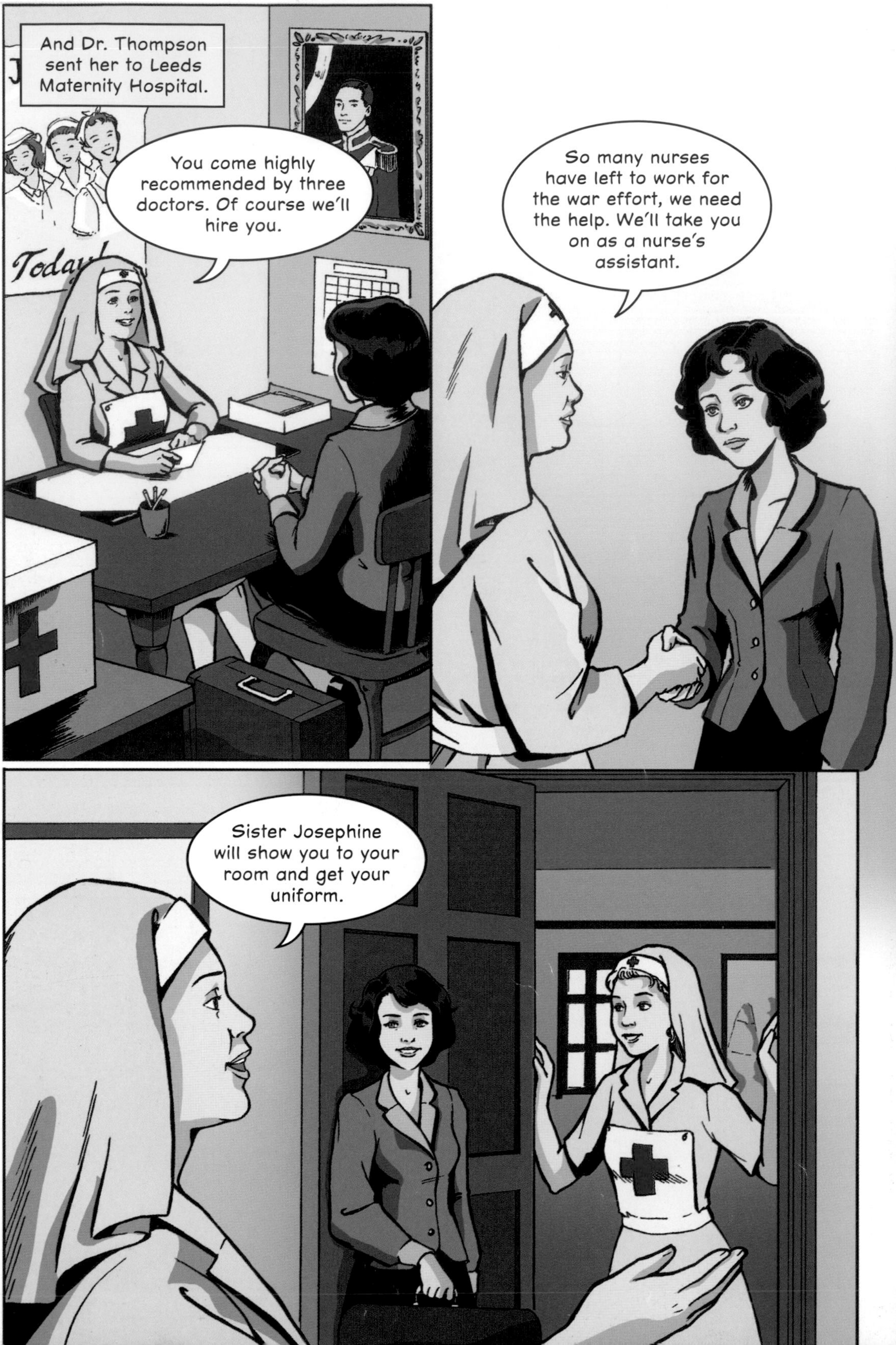
And Dr. Thompson sent her to Leeds Maternity Hospital.
You come highly recommended by three doctors. Of course we'll hire you.
So many nurses have left to work for the war effort, we need the help. We'll take you on as a nurse's assistant.
Sister Josephine will show you to your room and get your uniform.

CHAPTER FIVE: *The Blitz*

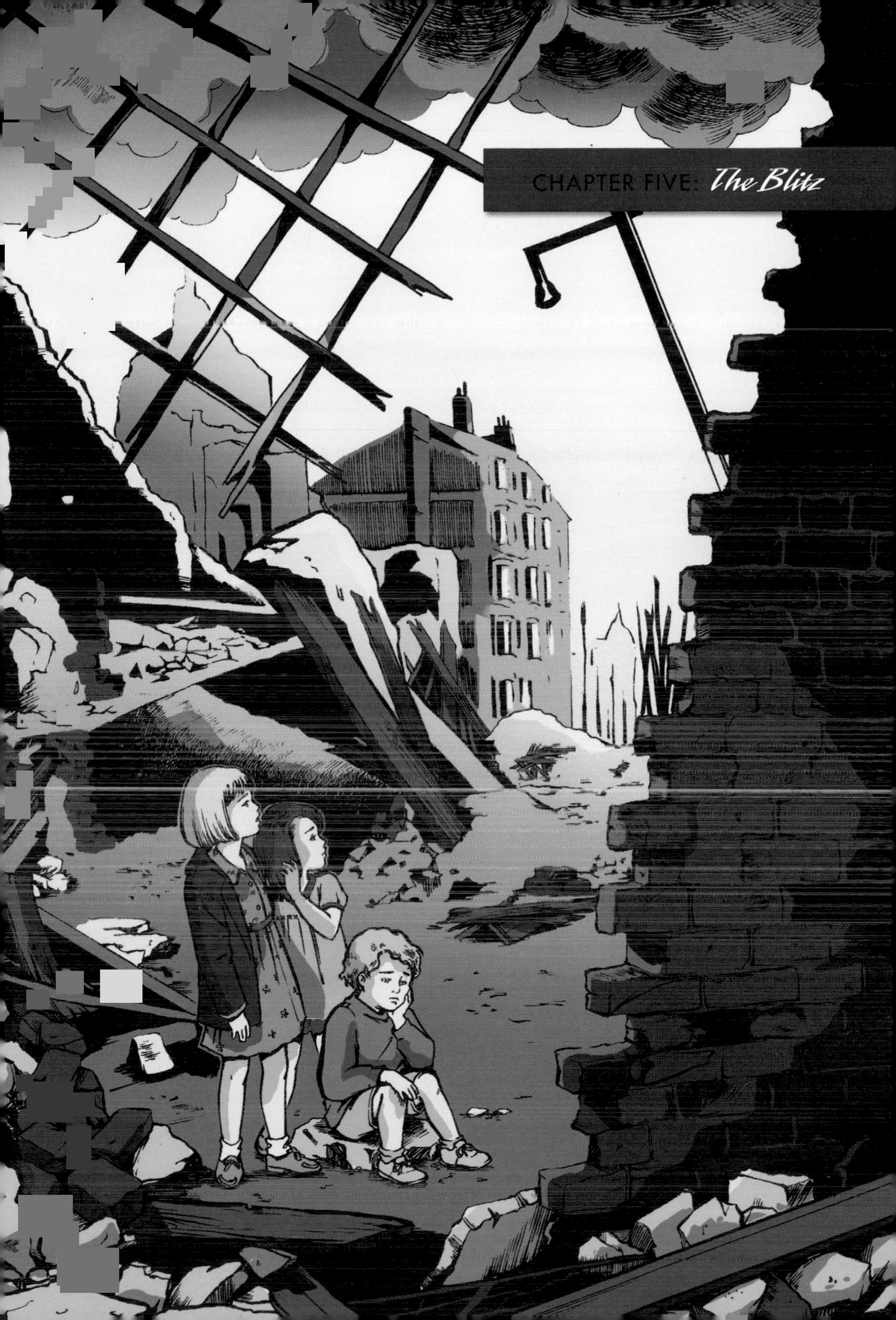

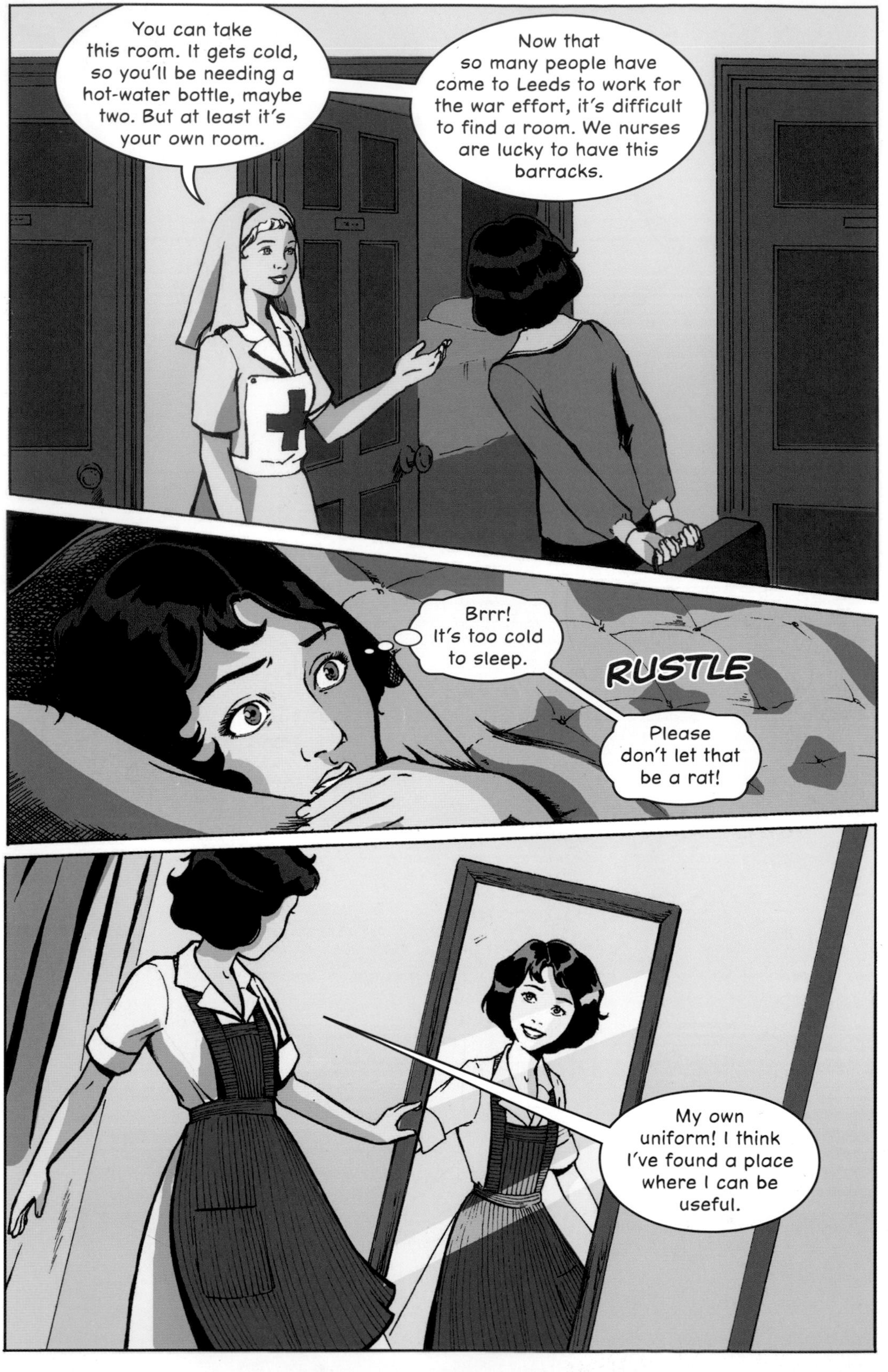
You can take this room. It gets cold, so you'll be needing a hot-water bottle, maybe two. But at least it's your own room.
Now that so many people have come to Leeds to work for the war effort, it's difficult to find a room. We nurses are lucky to have this barracks.
Brrr! It's too cold to sleep.
RUSTLE
Please don't let that be a rat!
My own uniform! I think I've found a place where I can be useful.

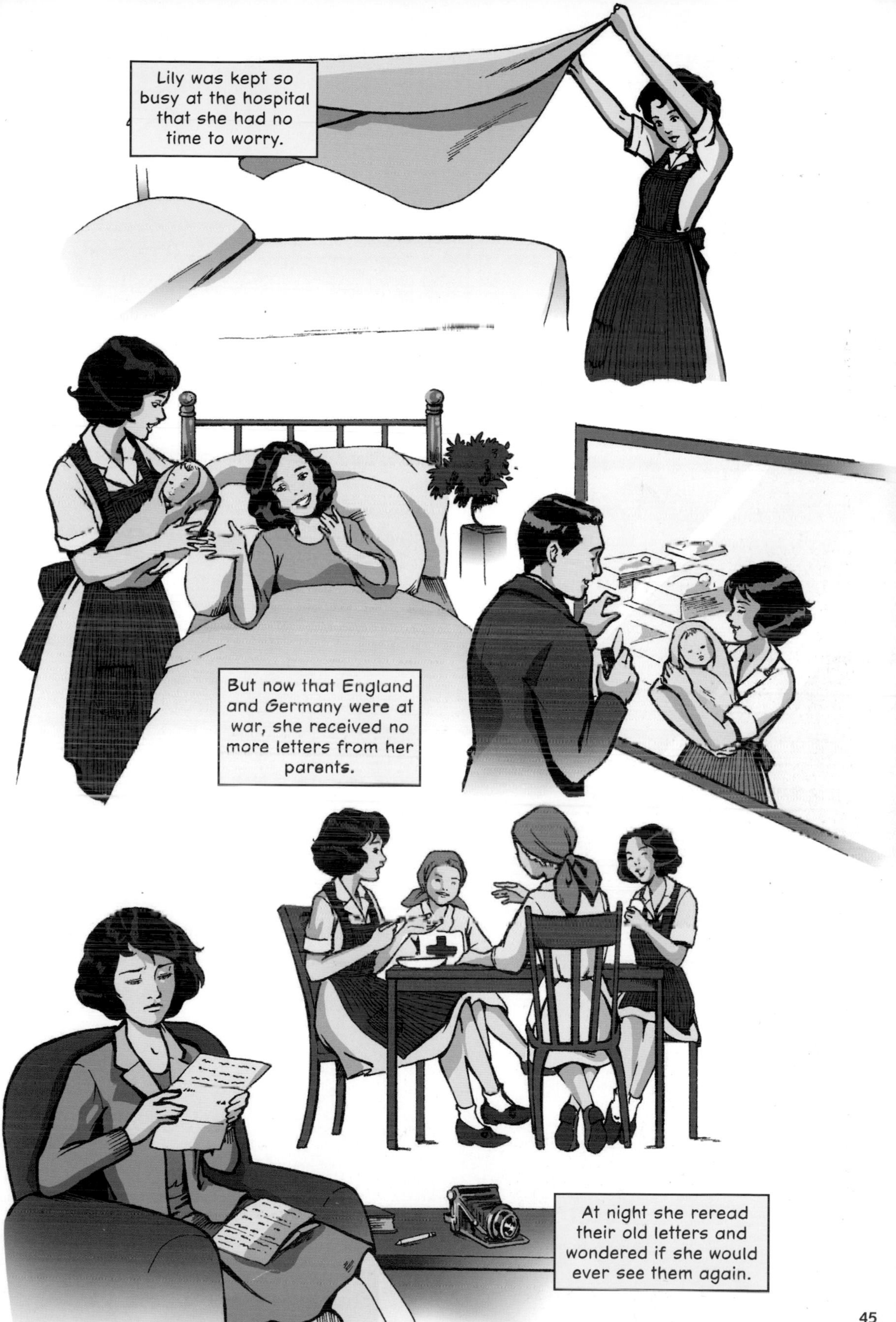
Lily was kept so busy at the hospital that she had no time to worry.
But now that England and Germany were at war, she received no more letters from her parents.
At night she reread their old letters and wondered if she would ever see them again.

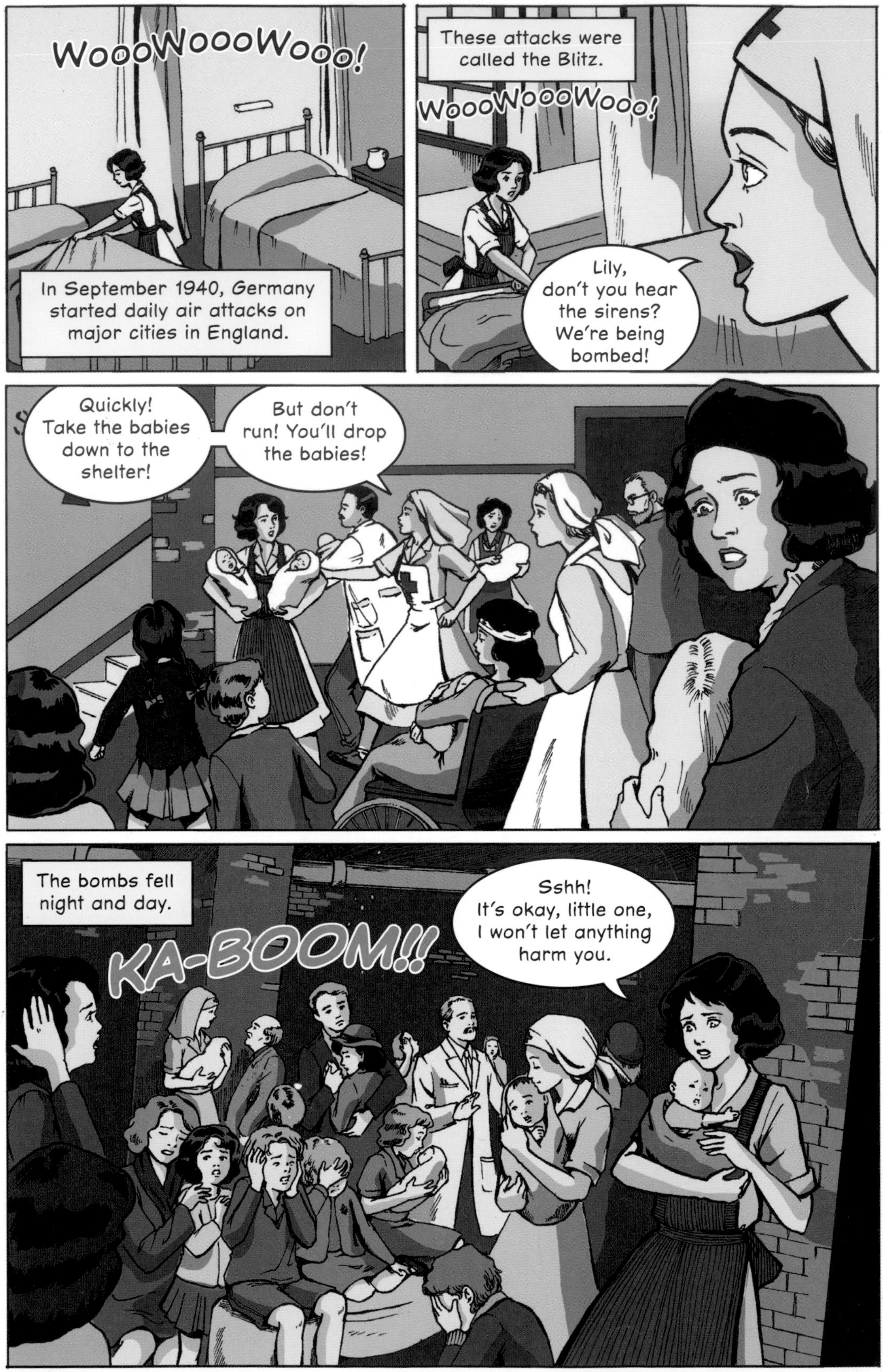
WoooWoooWooo!
In September 1940, Germany started daily air attacks on major cities in England.
These attacks were called the Blitz.
WoooWoooWooo!
Lily, don't you hear the sirens? We're being bombed!
Quickly! Take the babies down to the shelter!
But don't run! You'll drop the babies!
The bombs fell night and day.
KA-BOOM!!
Sshh! It's okay, little one, I won't let anything harm you.

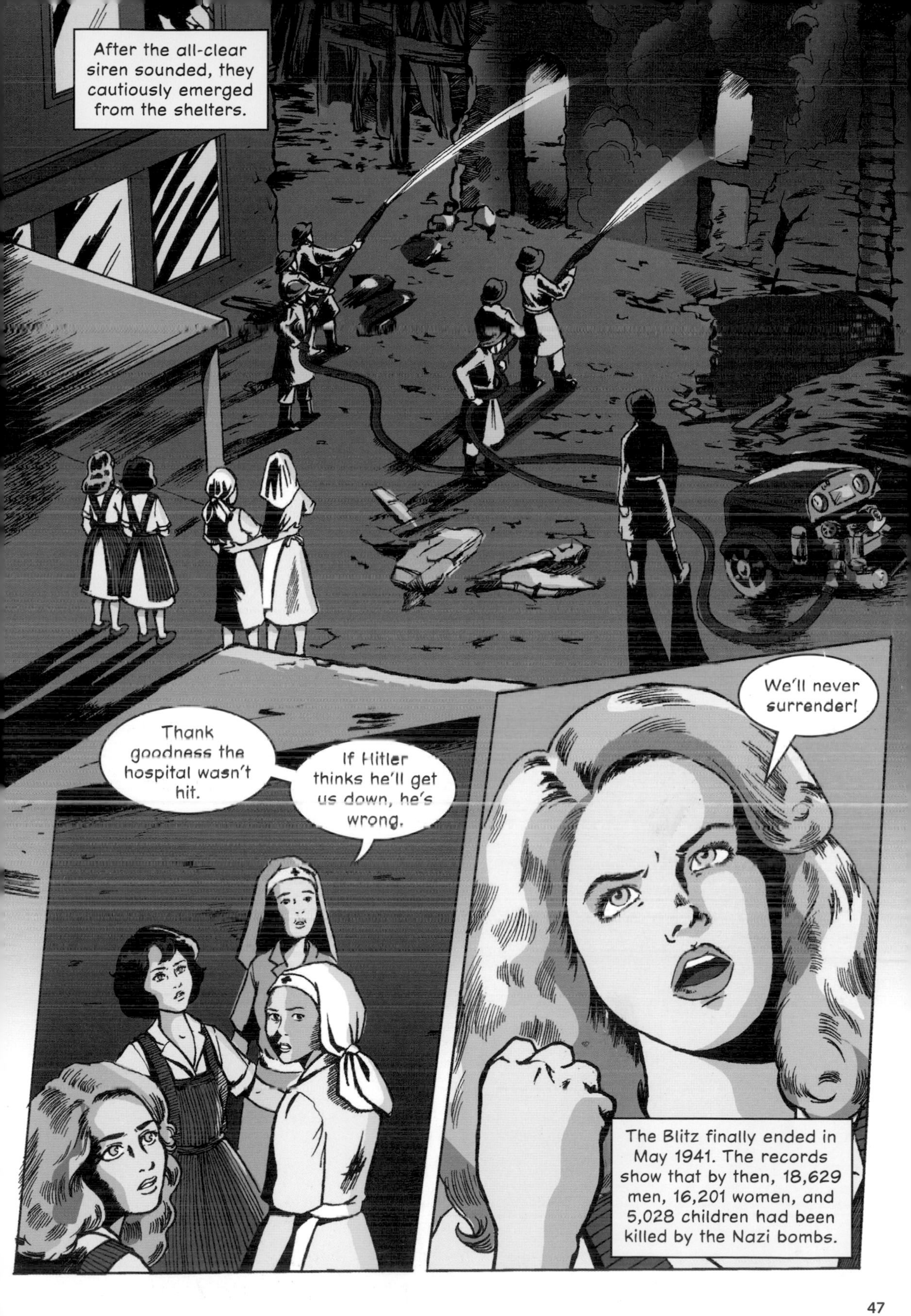

After the all-clear siren sounded, they cautiously emerged from the shelters.
Thank goodness the hospital wasn't hit.
If Hitler thinks he'll get us down, he's wrong.
We'll never surrender!
The Blitz finally ended in May 1941. The records show that by then, 18,629 men, 16,201 women, and 5,028 children had been killed by the Nazi bombs.

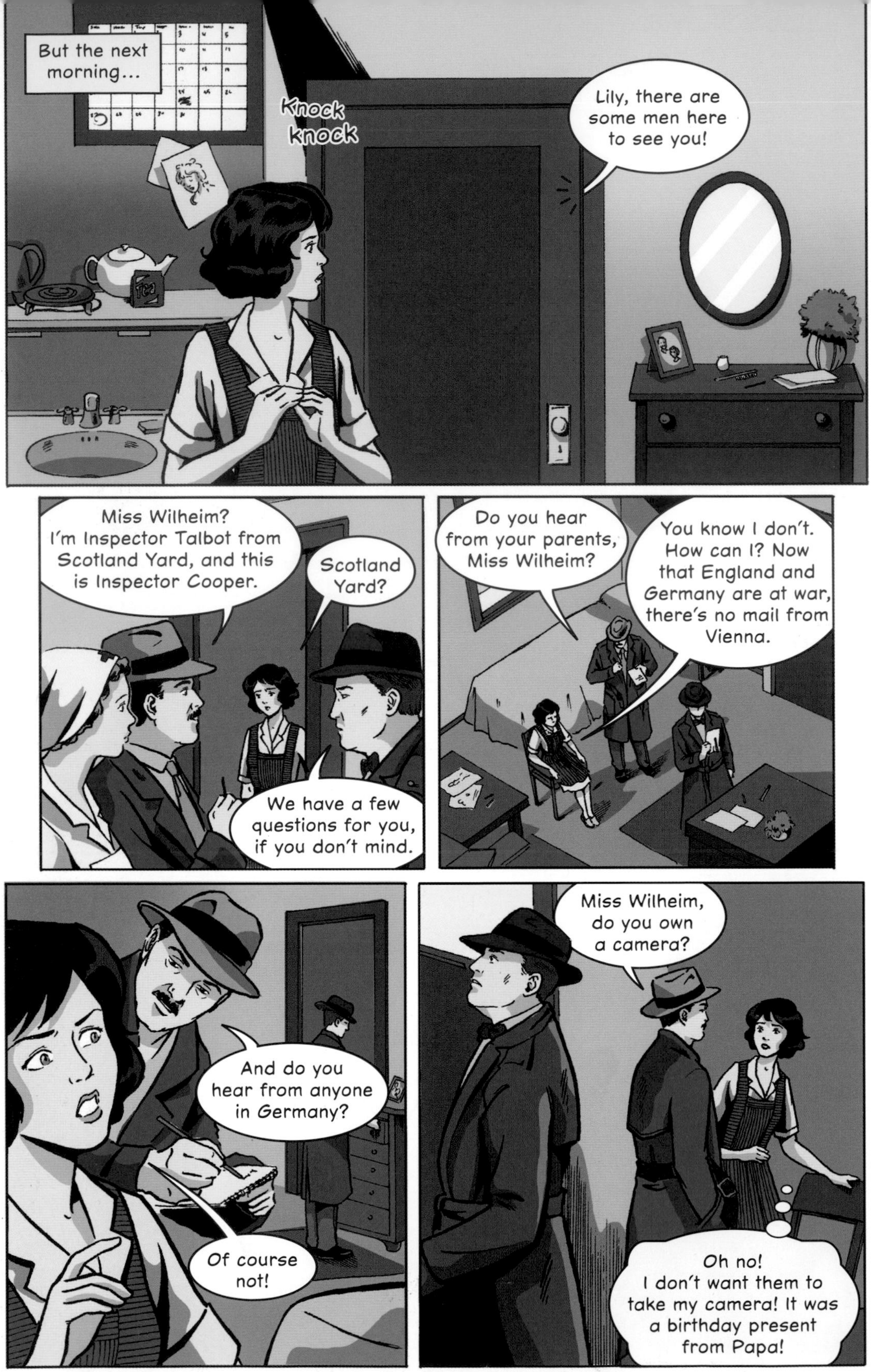
But the next morning...
Knock knock
Lily, there are some men here to see you!
Miss Wilheim? I'm Inspector Talbot from Scotland Yard, and this is Inspector Cooper.
Scotland Yard?
We have a few questions for you, if you don't mind.
Do you hear from your parents, Miss Wilheim?
You know I don't. How can I? Now that England and Germany are at war, there's no mail from Vienna.
And do you hear from anyone in Germany?
Of course not!
Miss Wilheim, do you own a camera?
Oh no! I don't want them to take my camera! It was a birthday present from Papa!

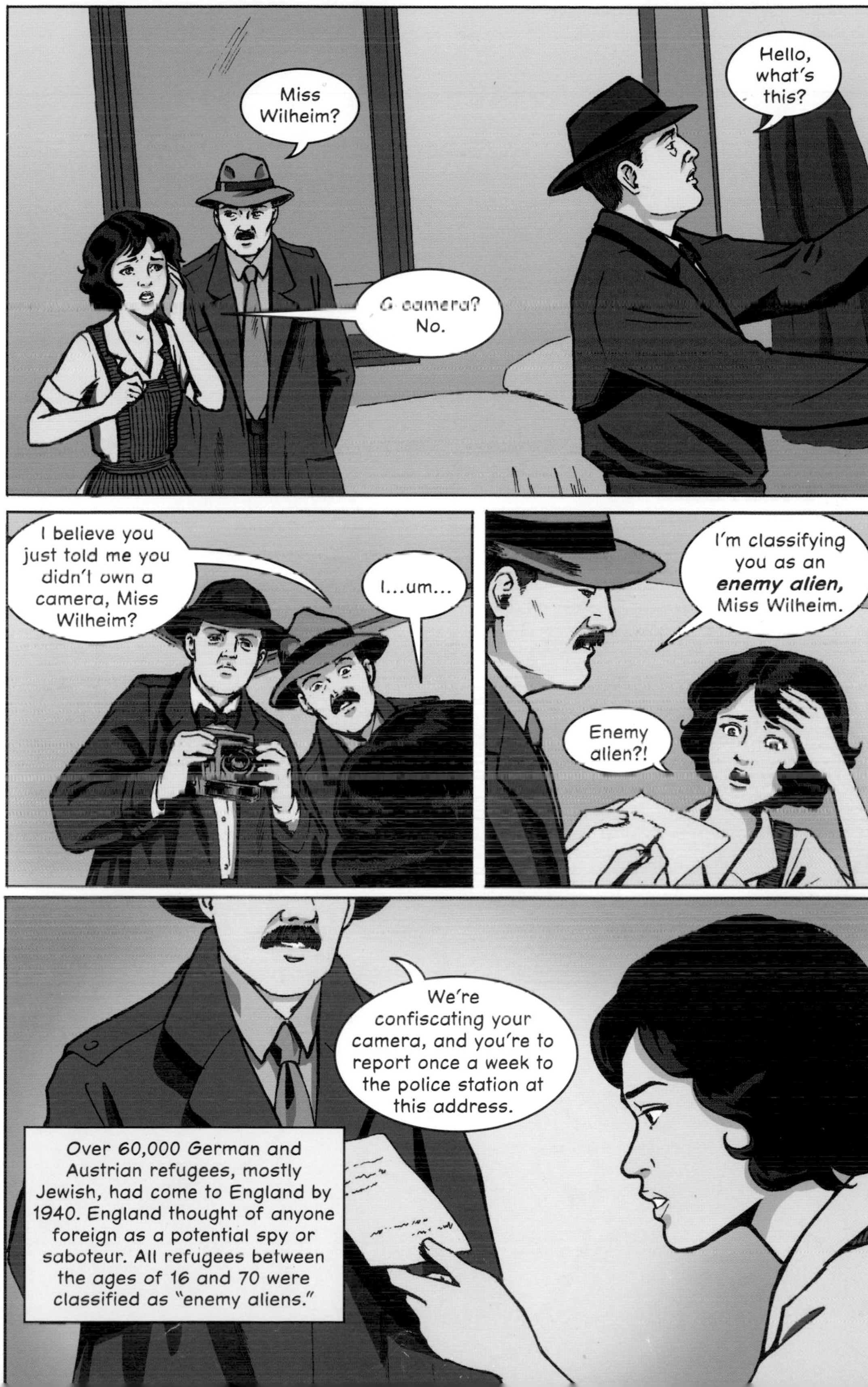
Miss Wilheim?
A camera? No.
Hello, what's this?
I believe you just told me you didn't own a camera, Miss Wilheim?
I...um...
I'm classifying you as an ***enemy alien,*** Miss Wilheim.
Enemy alien?!
We're confiscating your camera, and you're to report once a week to the police station at this address.
Over 60,000 German and Austrian refugees, mostly Jewish, had come to England by 1940. England thought of anyone foreign as a potential spy or saboteur. All refugees between the ages of 16 and 70 were classified as "enemy aliens."

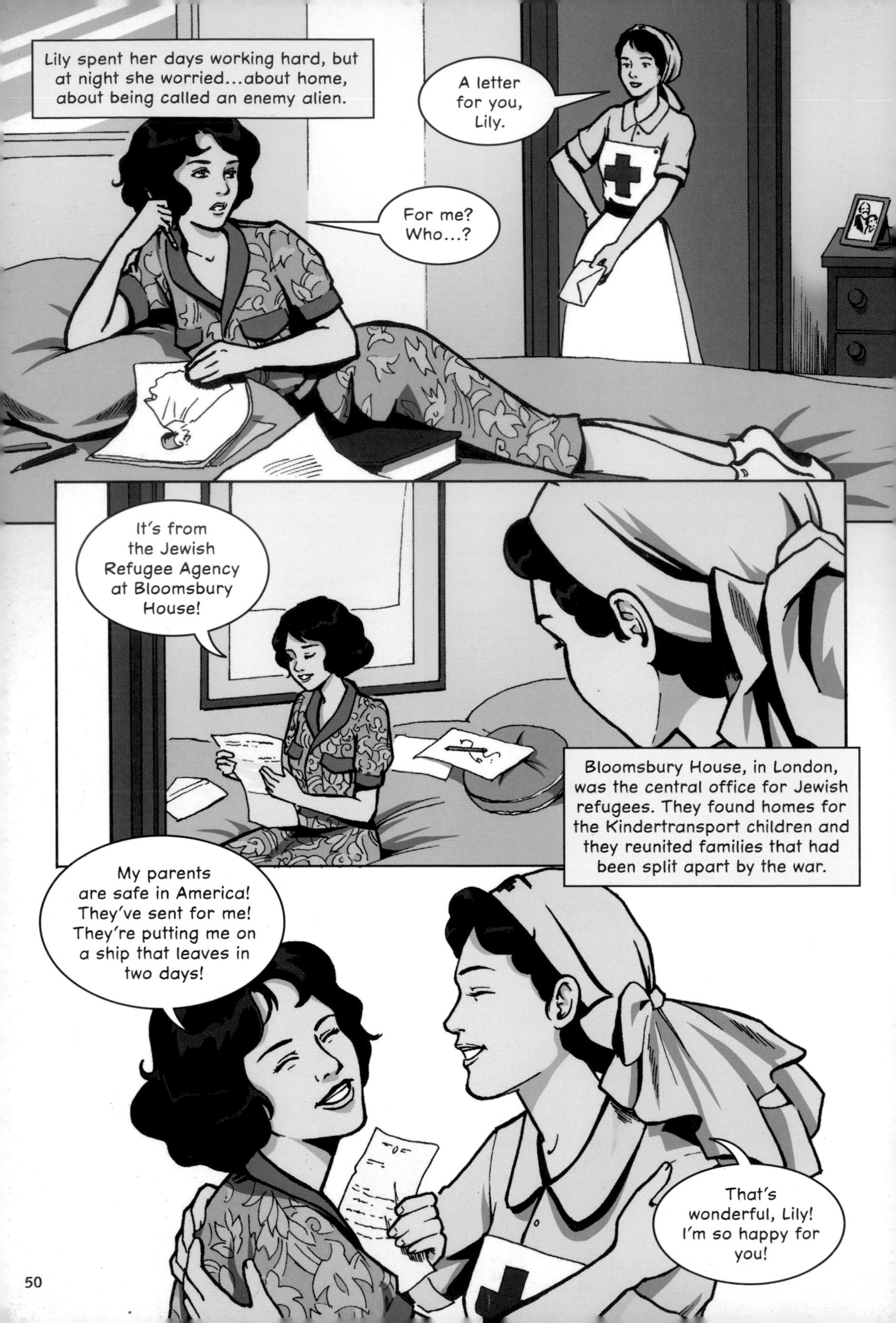

Lily spent her days working hard, but at night she worried...about home, about being called an enemy alien.
A letter for you, Lily.
For me? Who...?
It's from the Jewish Refugee Agency at Bloomsbury House!
Bloomsbury House, in London, was the central office for Jewish refugees. They found homes for the Kindertransport children and they reunited families that had been split apart by the war.
My parents are safe in America! They've sent for me! They're putting me on a ship that leaves in two days!
That's wonderful, Lily! I'm so happy for you!

CHAPTER SIX: *"Enemy Alien"*

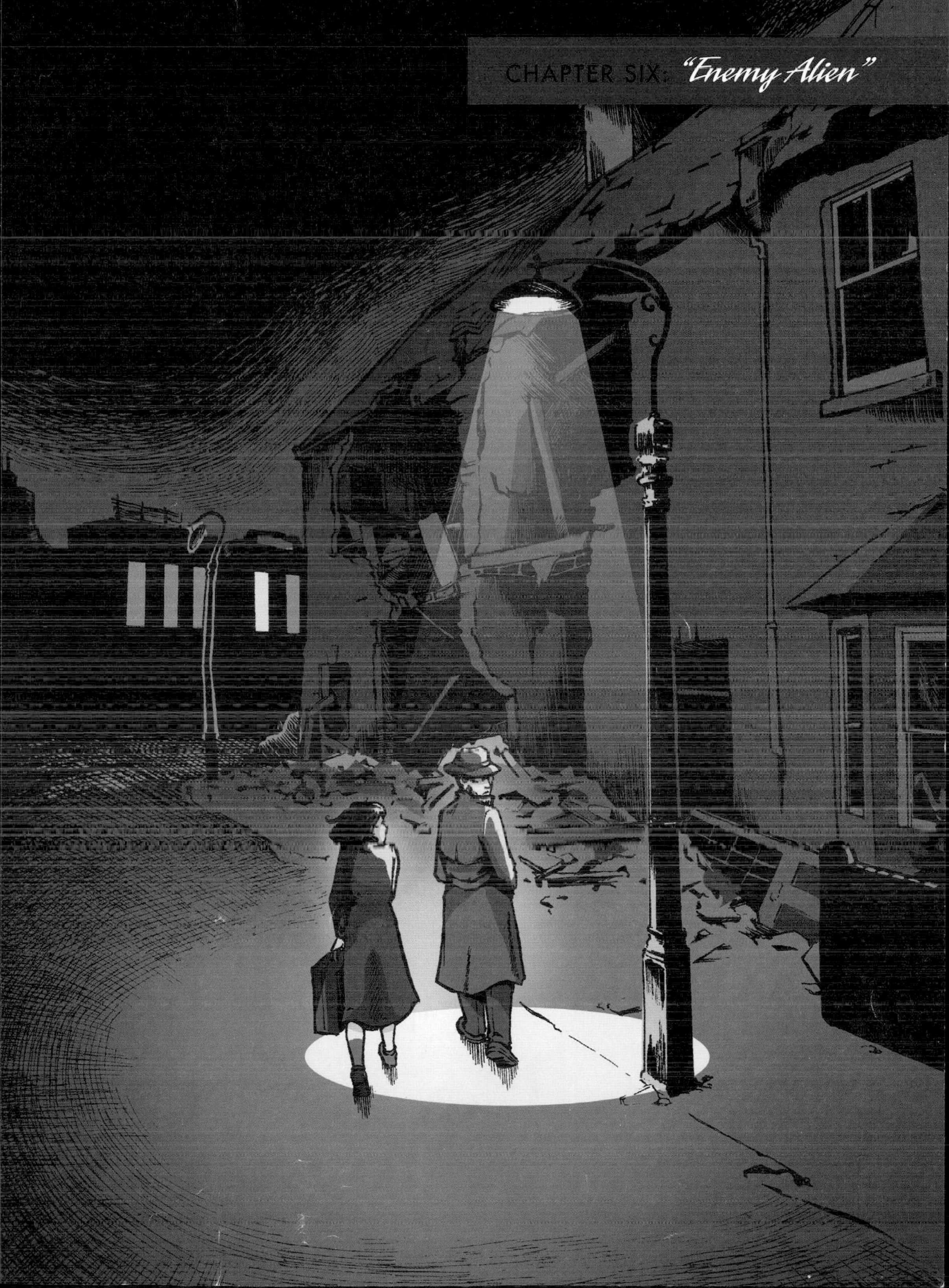

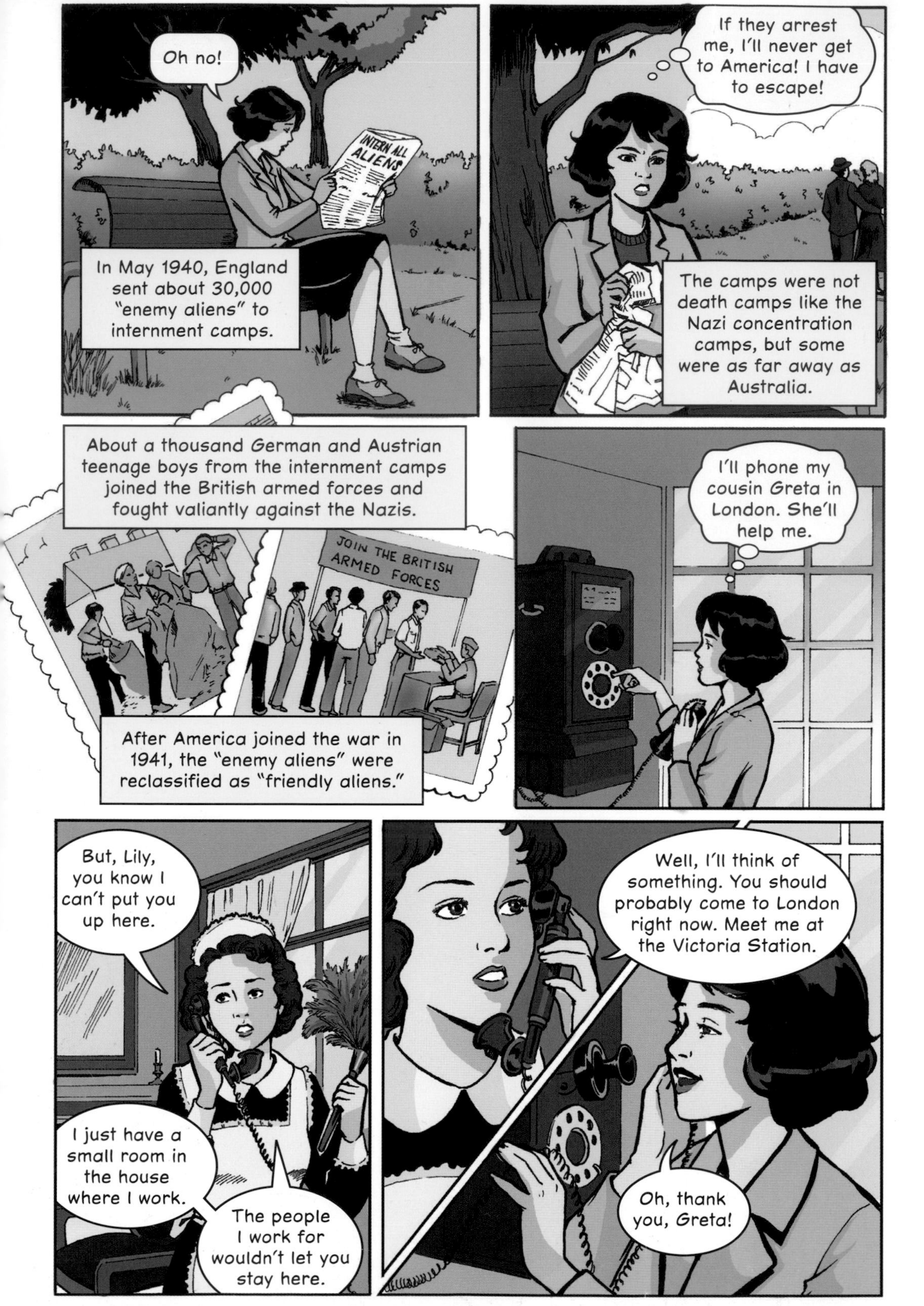

Oh no!
INTERN ALL ALIENS
In May 1940, England sent about 30,000 "enemy aliens" to internment camps.
If they arrest me, I'll never get to America! I have to escape!
The camps were not death camps like the Nazi concentration camps, but some were as far away as Australia.
About a thousand German and Austrian teenage boys from the internment camps joined the British armed forces and fought valiantly against the Nazis.
JOIN THE BRITISH ARMED FORCES
After America joined the war in 1941, the "enemy aliens" were reclassified as "friendly aliens."
I'll phone my cousin Greta in London. She'll help me.
But, Lily, you know I can't put you up here.
I just have a small room in the house where I work.
The people I work for wouldn't let you stay here.
Well, I'll think of something. You should probably come to London right now. Meet me at the Victoria Station.
Oh, thank you, Greta!

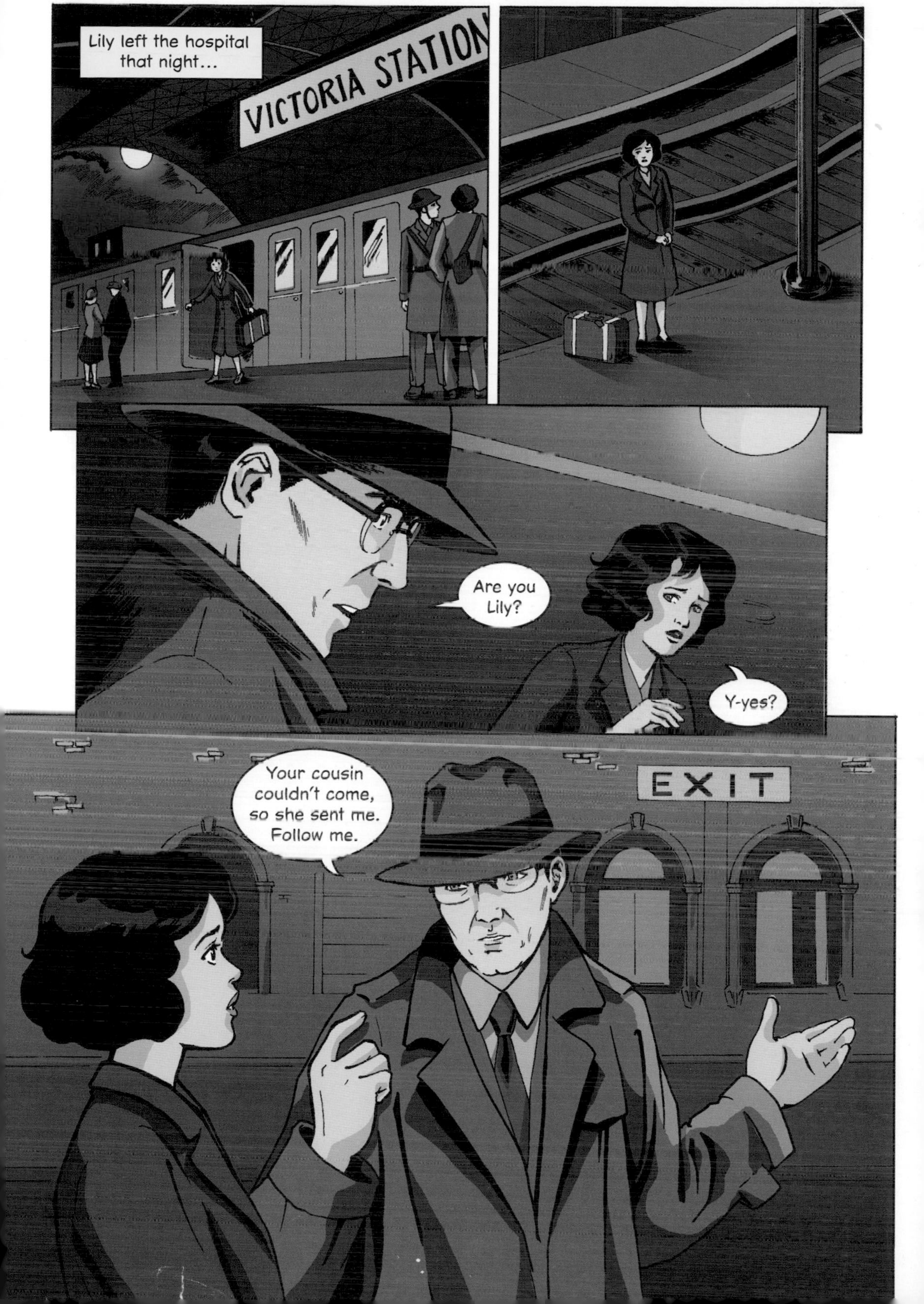
Lily left the hospital that night...
VICTORIA STATION
Are you Lily?
Y-yes?
Your cousin couldn't come, so she sent me. Follow me.
EXIT

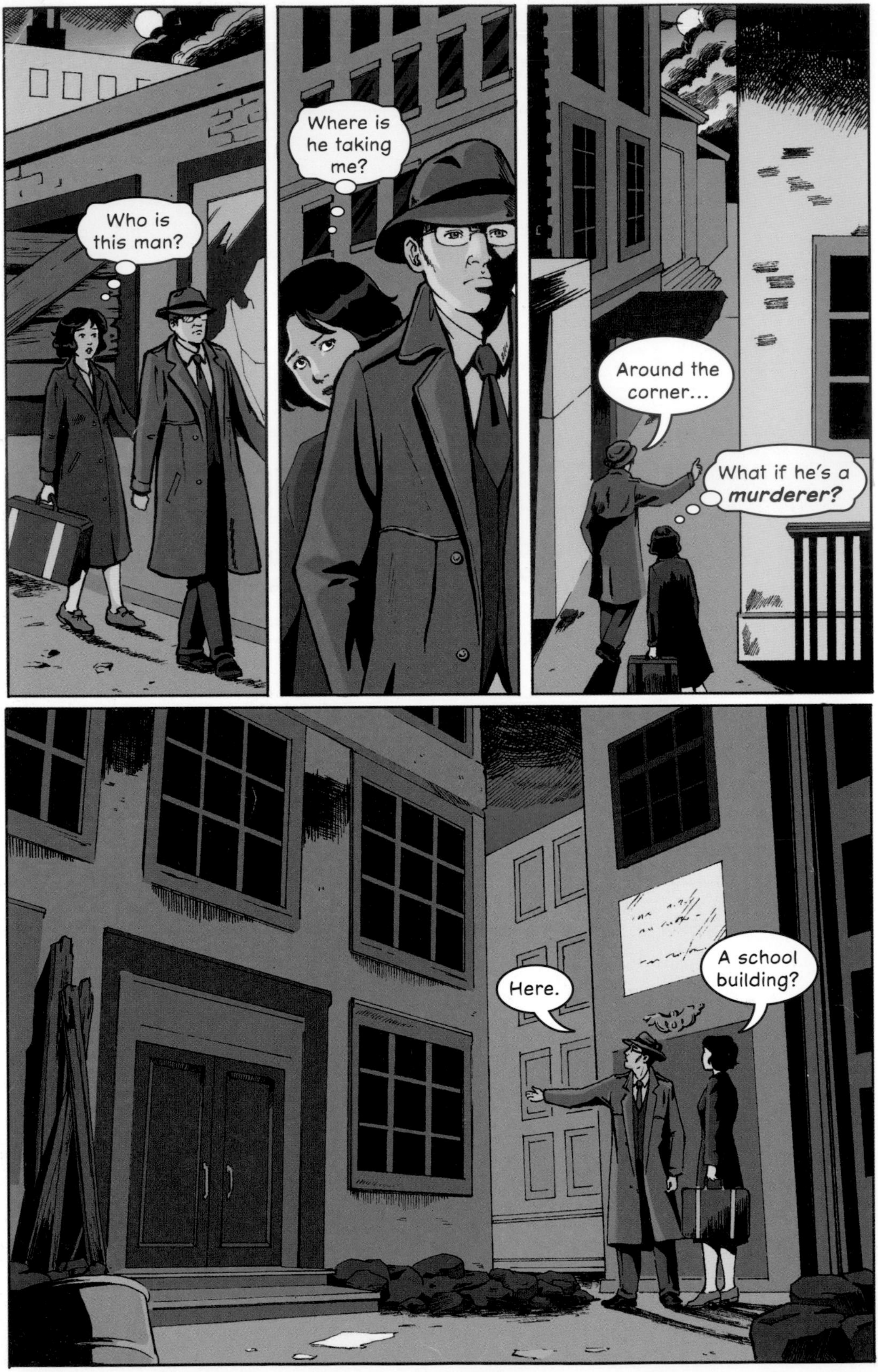

Who is this man?
Where is he taking me?
Around the corner...
What if he's a *murderer?*
Here.
A school building?

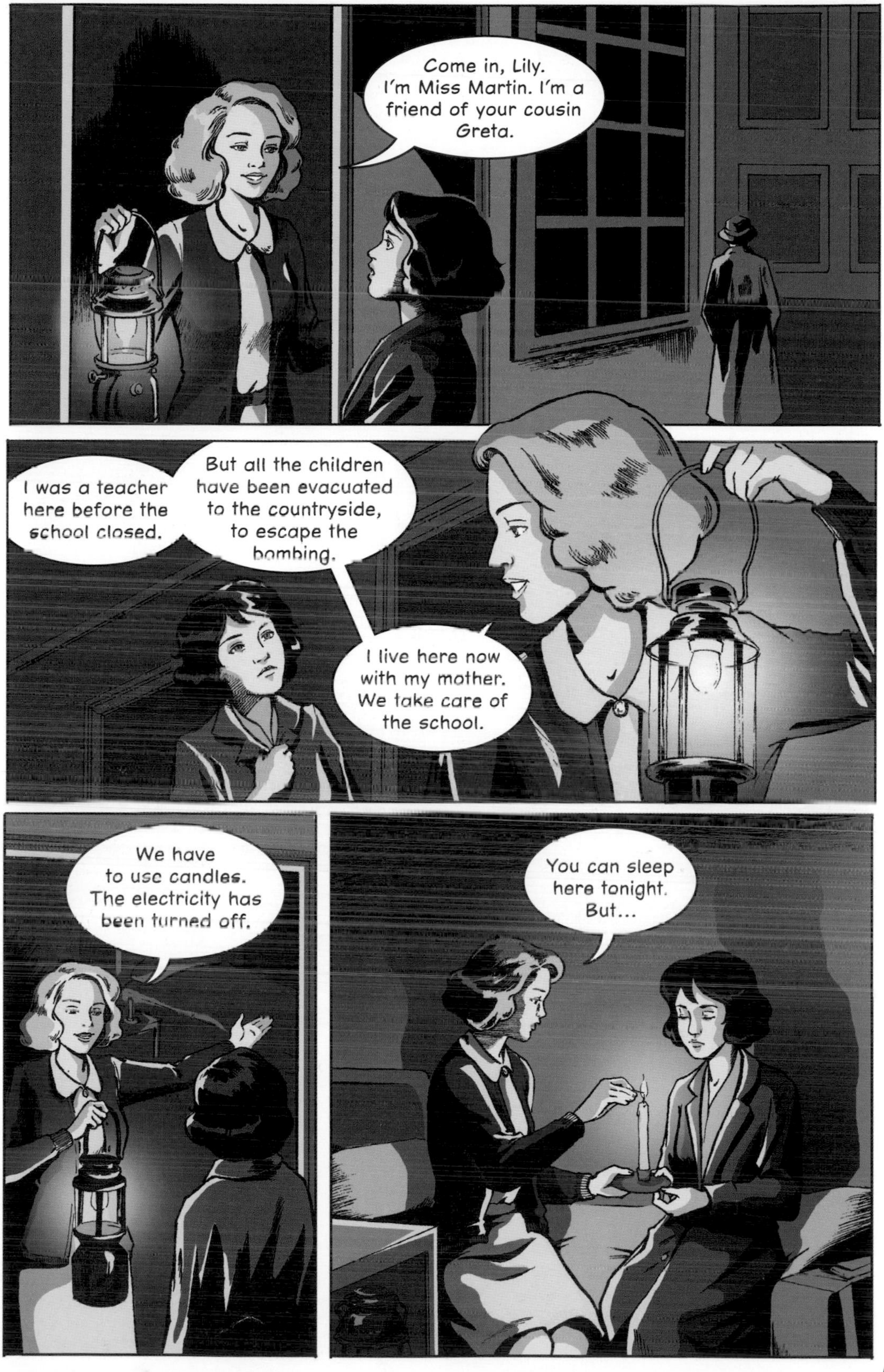
Come in, Lily. I'm Miss Martin. I'm a friend of your cousin Greta.
I was a teacher here before the school closed.
But all the children have been evacuated to the countryside, to escape the bombing.
I live here now with my mother. We take care of the school.
We have to use candles. The electricity has been turned off.
You can sleep here tonight. But...

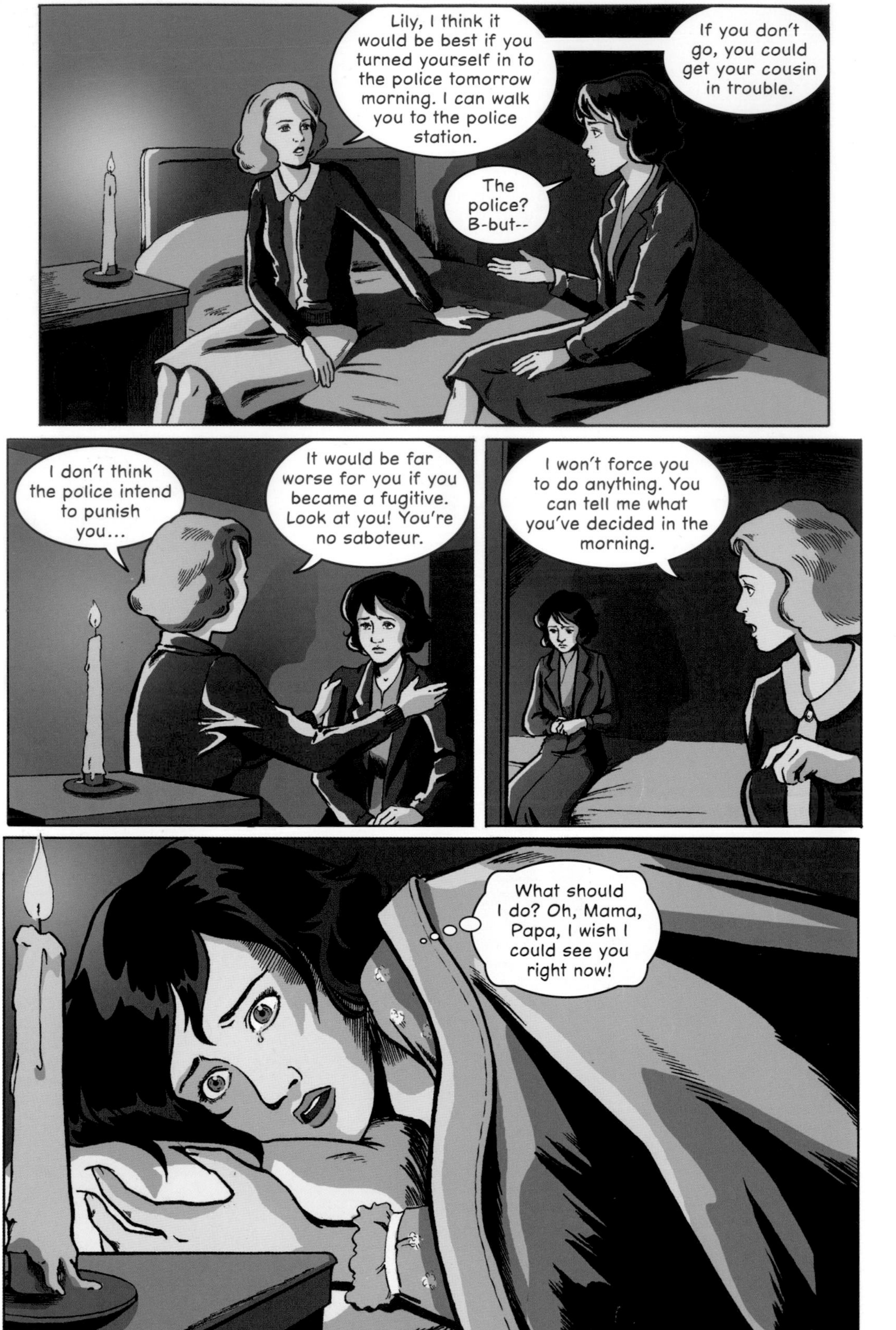
Lily, I think it would be best if you turned yourself in to the police tomorrow morning. I can walk you to the police station.
If you don't go, you could get your cousin in trouble.
The police? B-but--
I don't think the police intend to punish you...
It would be far worse for you if you became a fugitive. Look at you! You're no saboteur.
I won't force you to do anything. You can tell me what you've decided in the morning.
What should I do? Oh, Mama, Papa, I wish I could see you right now!

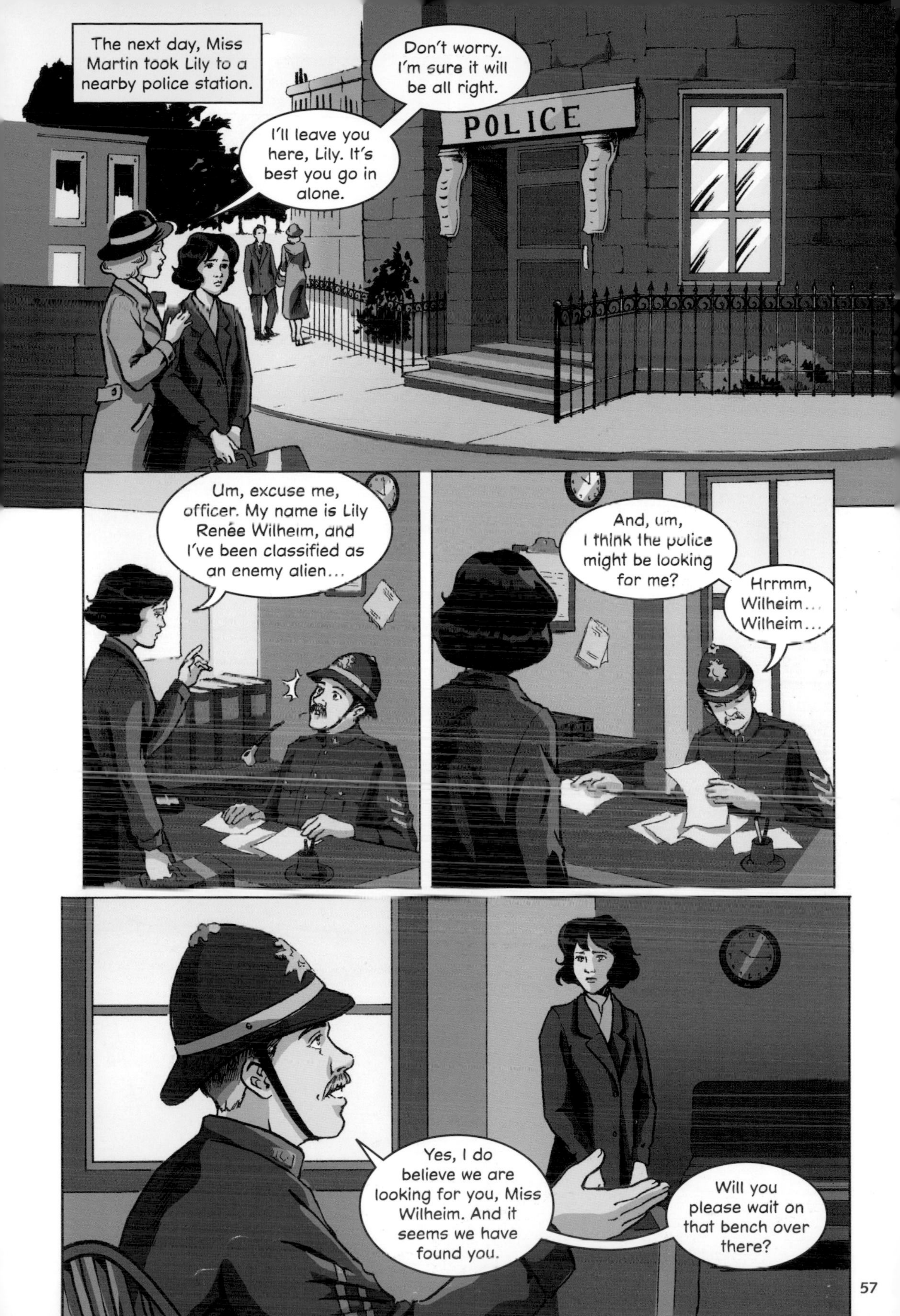
The next day, Miss Martin took Lily to a nearby police station.
Don't worry. I'm sure it will be all right.
I'll leave you here, Lily. It's best you go in alone.
POLICE
Um, excuse me, officer. My name is Lily Renée Wilheim, and I've been classified as an enemy alien...
And, um, I think the police might be looking for me?
Hrrmm, Wilheim... Wilheim...
Yes, I do believe we are looking for you, Miss Wilheim. And it seems we have found you.
Will you please wait on that bench over there?

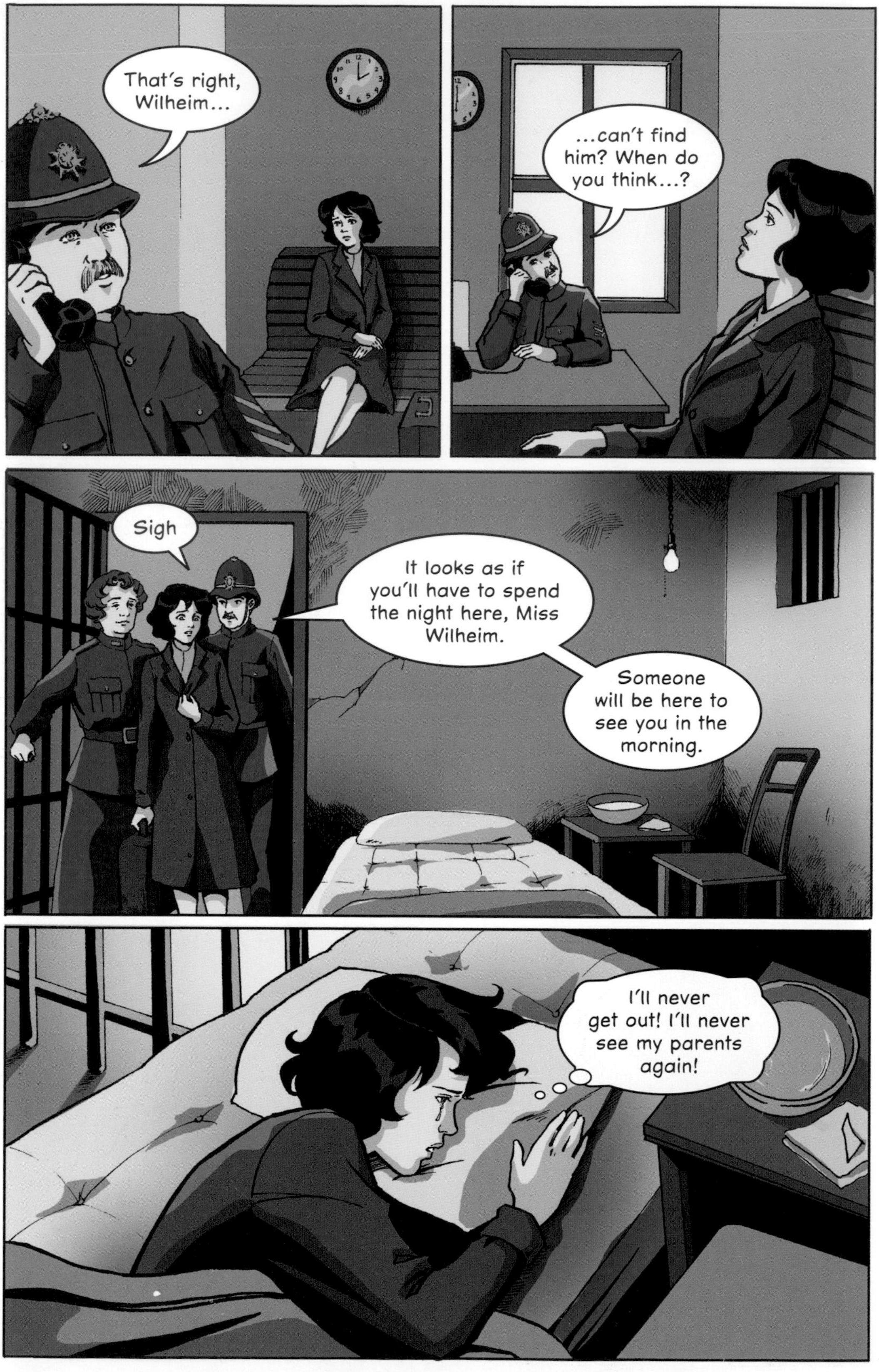

That's right, Wilheim...
...can't find him? When do you think...?
Sigh
It looks as if you'll have to spend the night here, Miss Wilheim.
Someone will be here to see you in the morning.
I'll never get out! I'll never see my parents again!

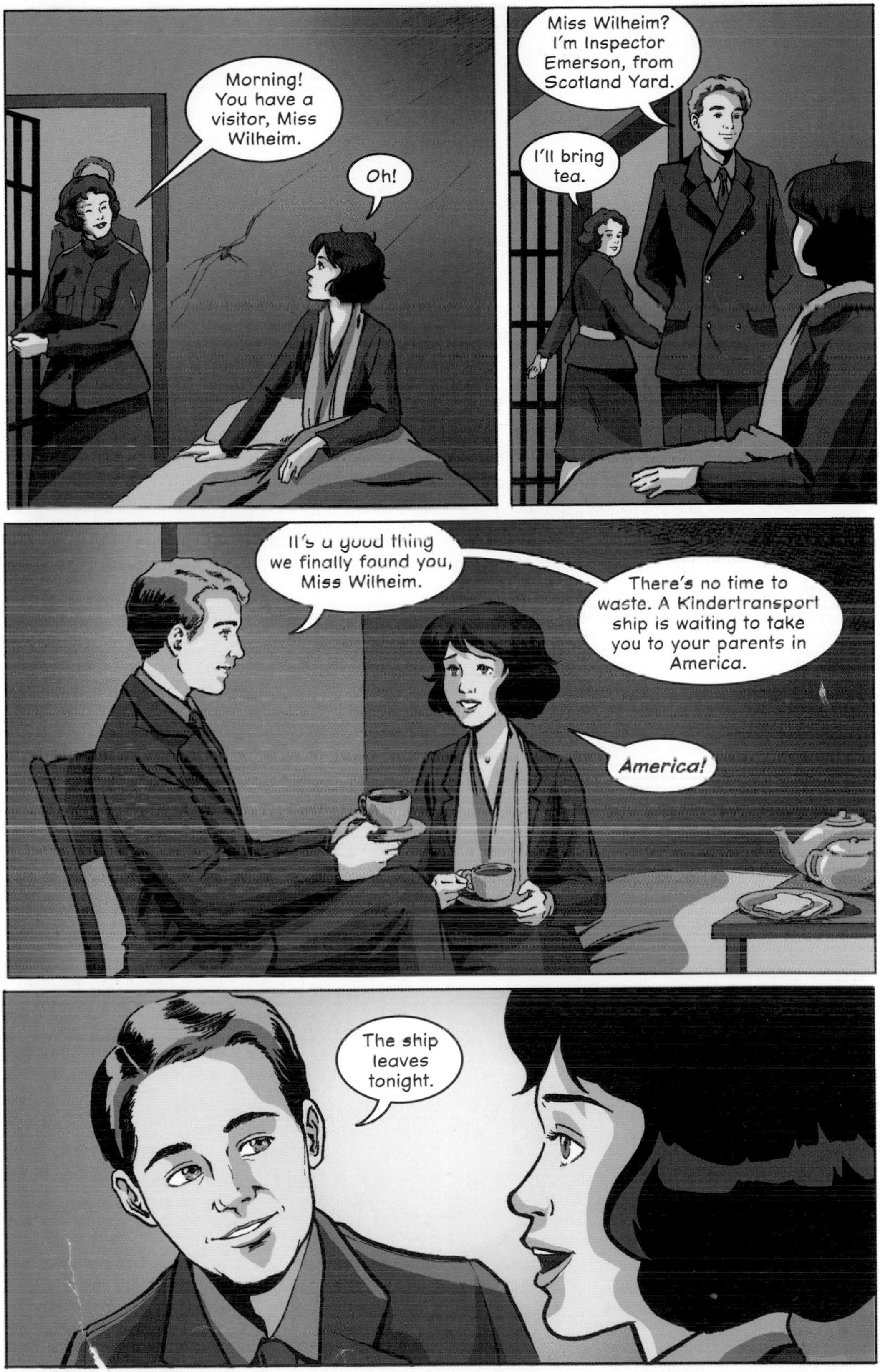
Morning! You have a visitor, Miss Wilheim.
Oh!
Miss Wilheim? I'm Inspector Emerson, from Scotland Yard.
I'll bring tea.
It's a good thing we finally found you, Miss Wilheim.
There's no time to waste. A Kindertransport ship is waiting to take you to your parents in America.
America!
The ship leaves tonight.

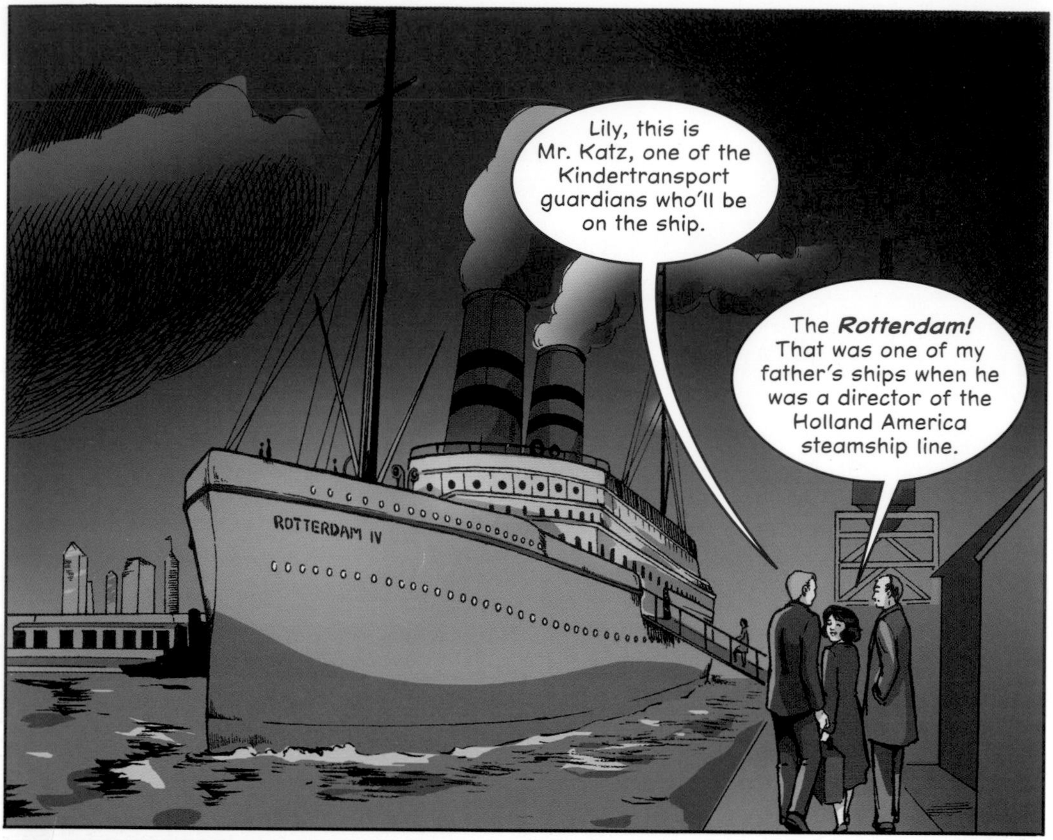
Lily, this is Mr. Katz, one of the Kindertransport guardians who'll be on the ship.
The **Rotterdam!** That was one of my father's ships when he was a director of the Holland America steamship line.
ROTTERDAM IV

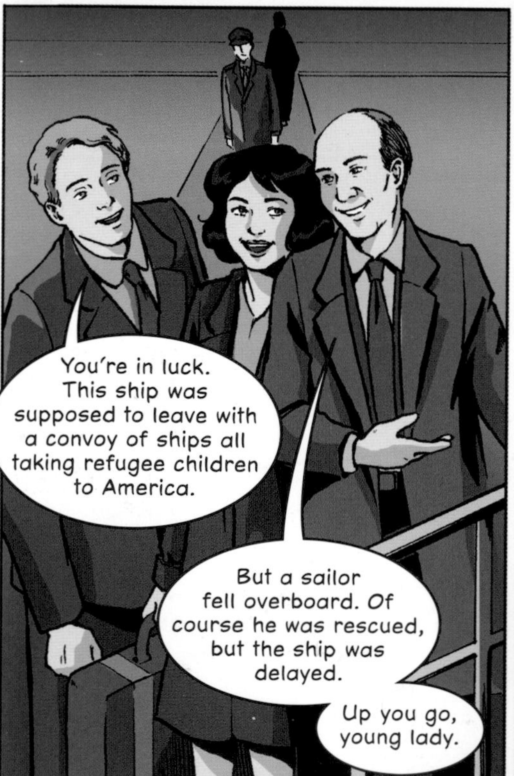
You're in luck. This ship was supposed to leave with a convoy of ships all taking refugee children to America.
But a sailor fell overboard. Of course he was rescued, but the ship was delayed.
Up you go, young lady.

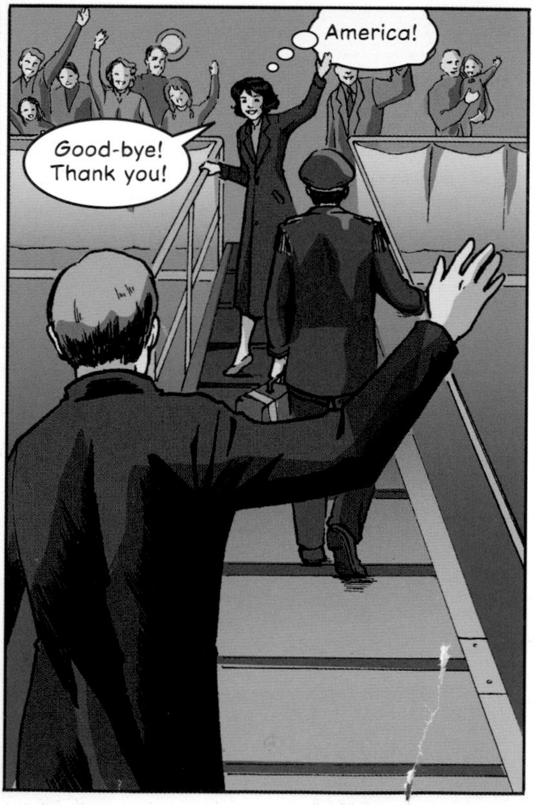
America!
Good-bye! Thank you!

CHAPTER SEVEN: *America!*

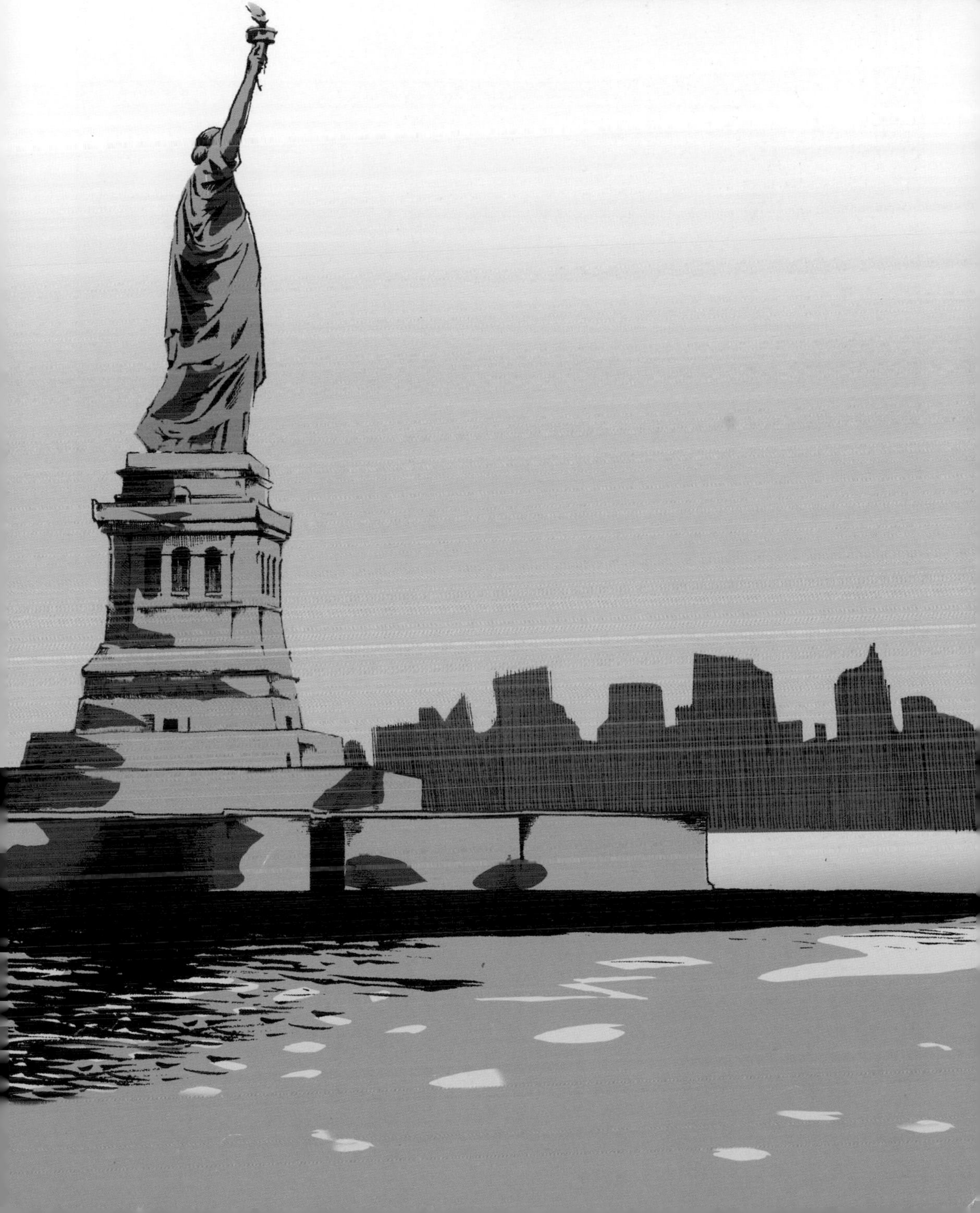

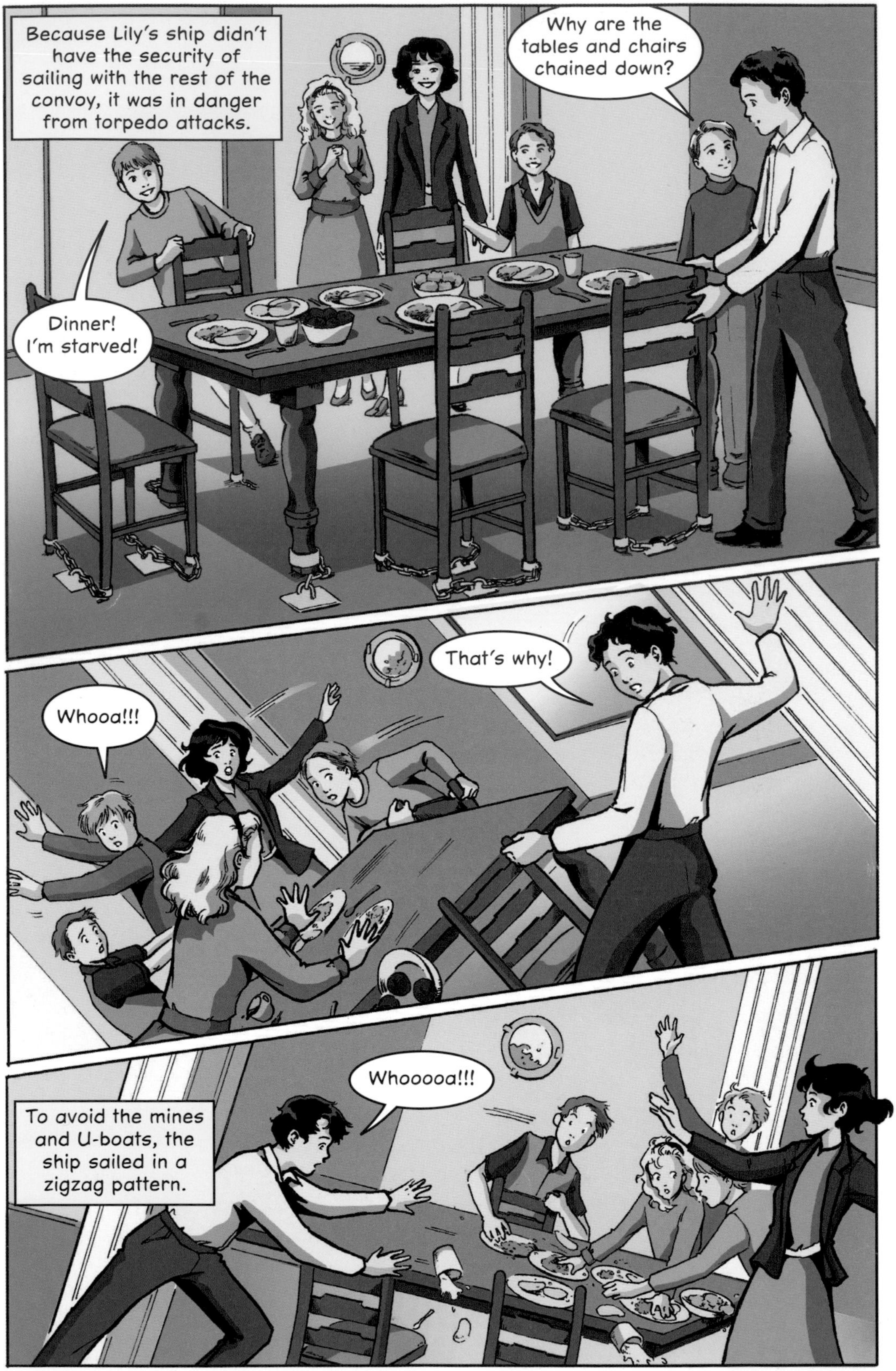
Because Lily's ship didn't have the security of sailing with the rest of the convoy, it was in danger from torpedo attacks.
Why are the tables and chairs chained down?
Dinner! I'm starved!
That's why!
Whooa!!!
To avoid the mines and U-boats, the ship sailed in a zigzag pattern.
Whoooooa!!!

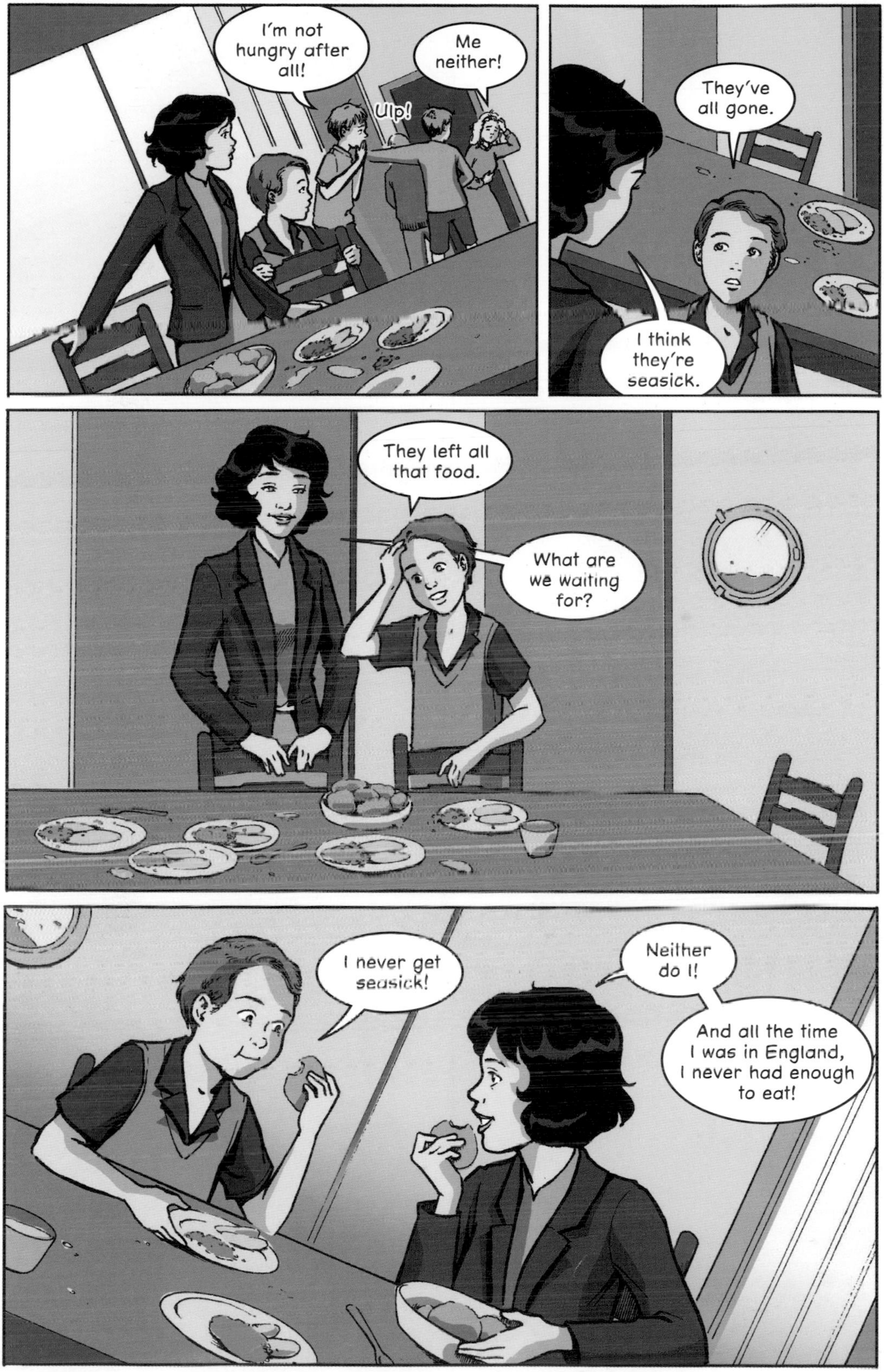
I'm not hungry after all!
Me neither!
Ulp!
They've all gone.
I think they're seasick.
They left all that food.
What are we waiting for?
I never get seasick!
Neither do I!
And all the time I was in England, I never had enough to eat!

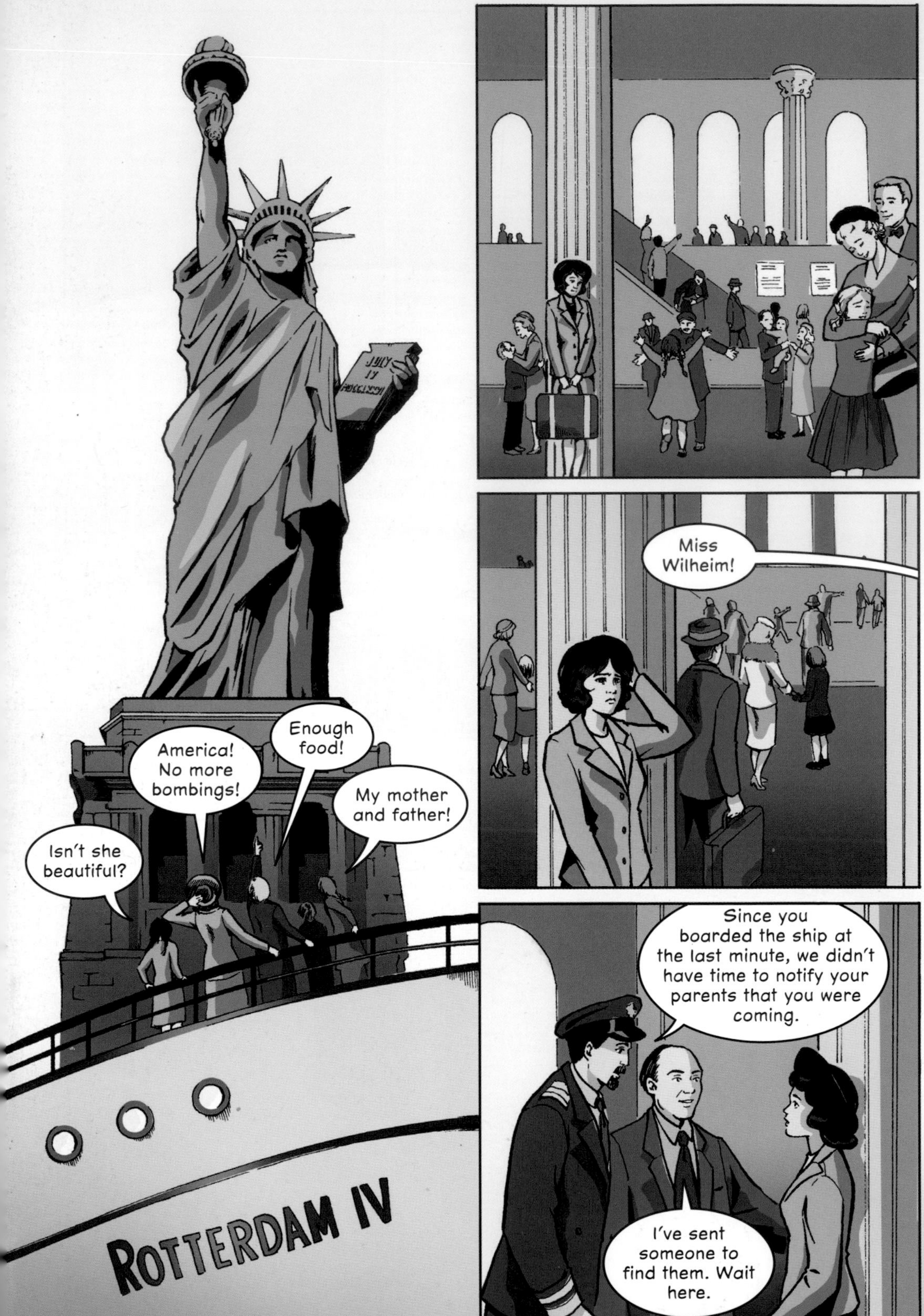
Isn't she beautiful?
America! No more bombings!
Enough food!
My mother and father!
ROTTERDAM IV
Miss Wilheim!
Since you boarded the ship at the last minute, we didn't have time to notify your parents that you were coming.
I've sent someone to find them. Wait here.

CHAPTER EIGHT: *Getting By in New York*

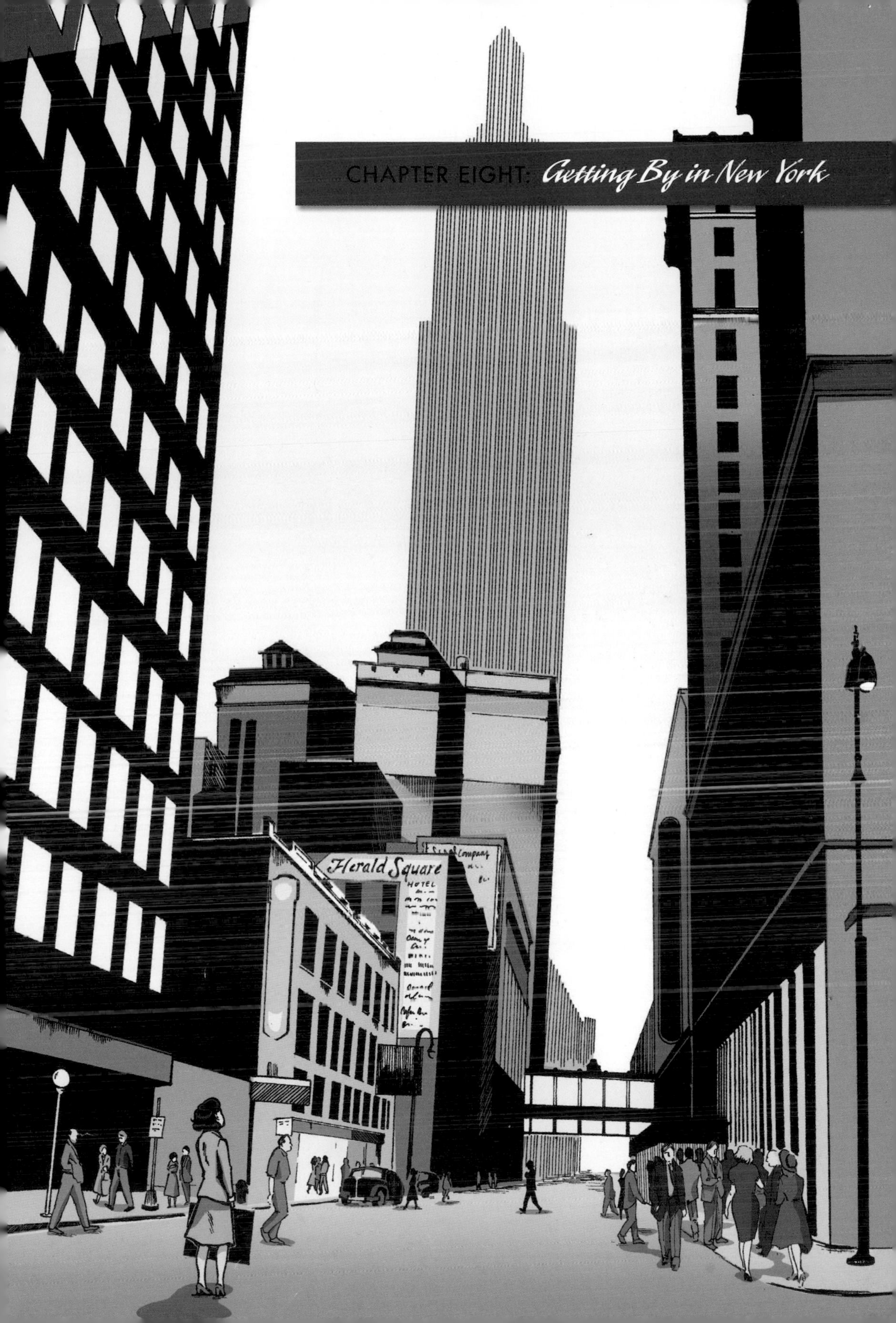
Herald Square
HOTEL
Company

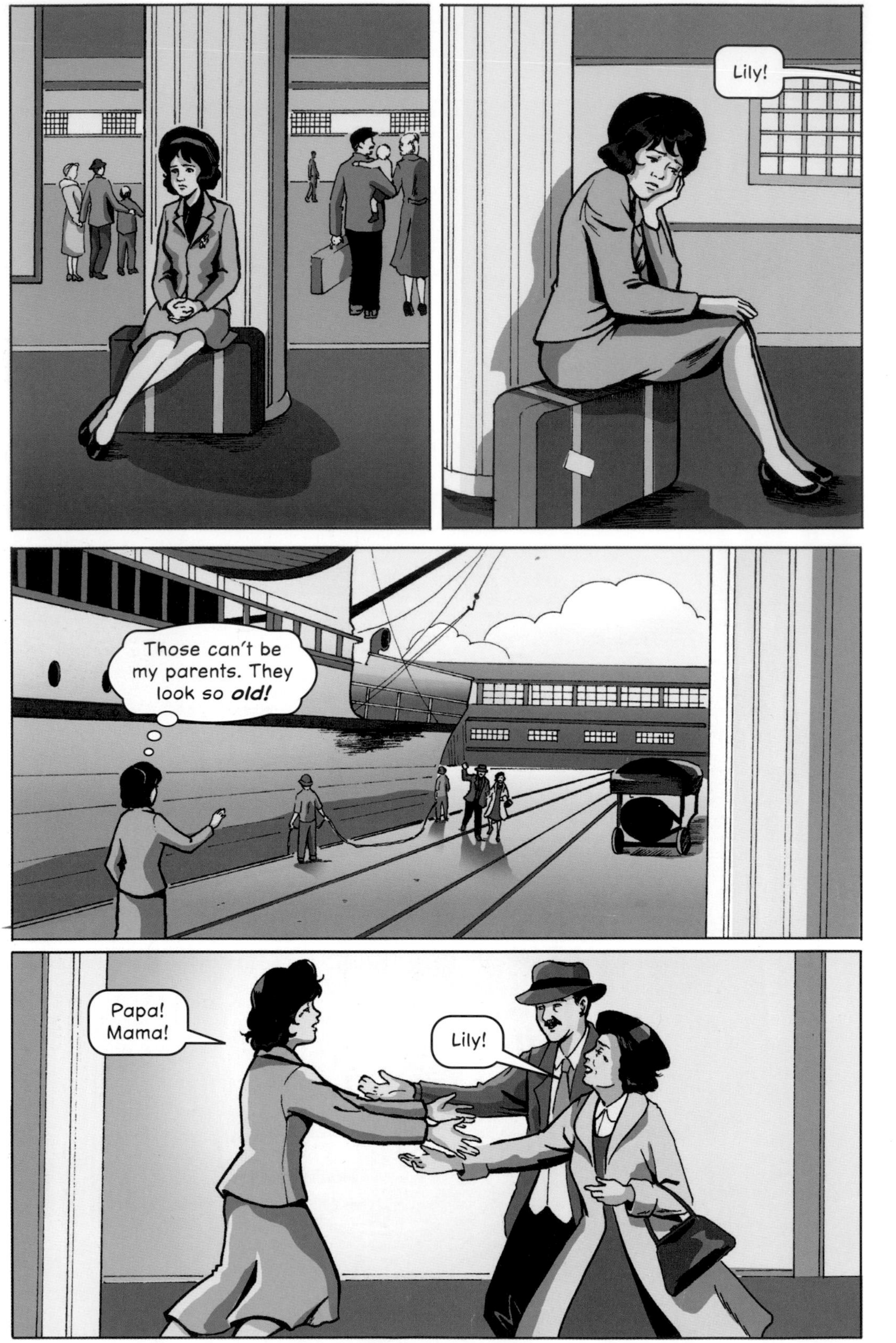
Lily!
Those can't be my parents. They look so *old!*
Papa! Mama!
Lily!

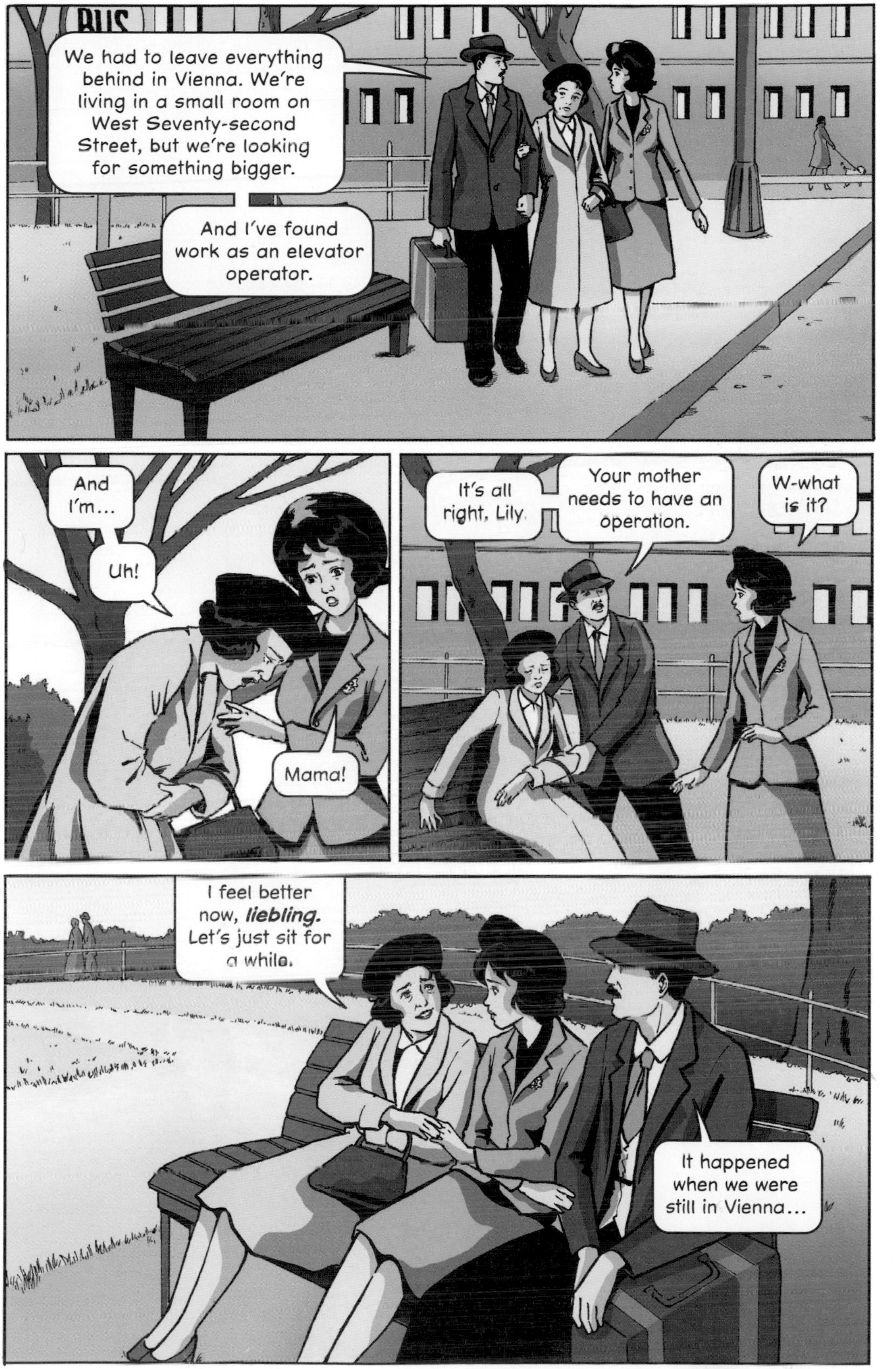
BUS
We had to leave everything behind in Vienna. We're living in a small room on West Seventy-second Street, but we're looking for something bigger.
And I've found work as an elevator operator.
And I'm...
Uh!
Mama!
It's all right, Lily.
Your mother needs to have an operation.
W-what is it?
I feel better now, ***liebling.*** Let's just sit for a while.
It happened when we were still in Vienna...

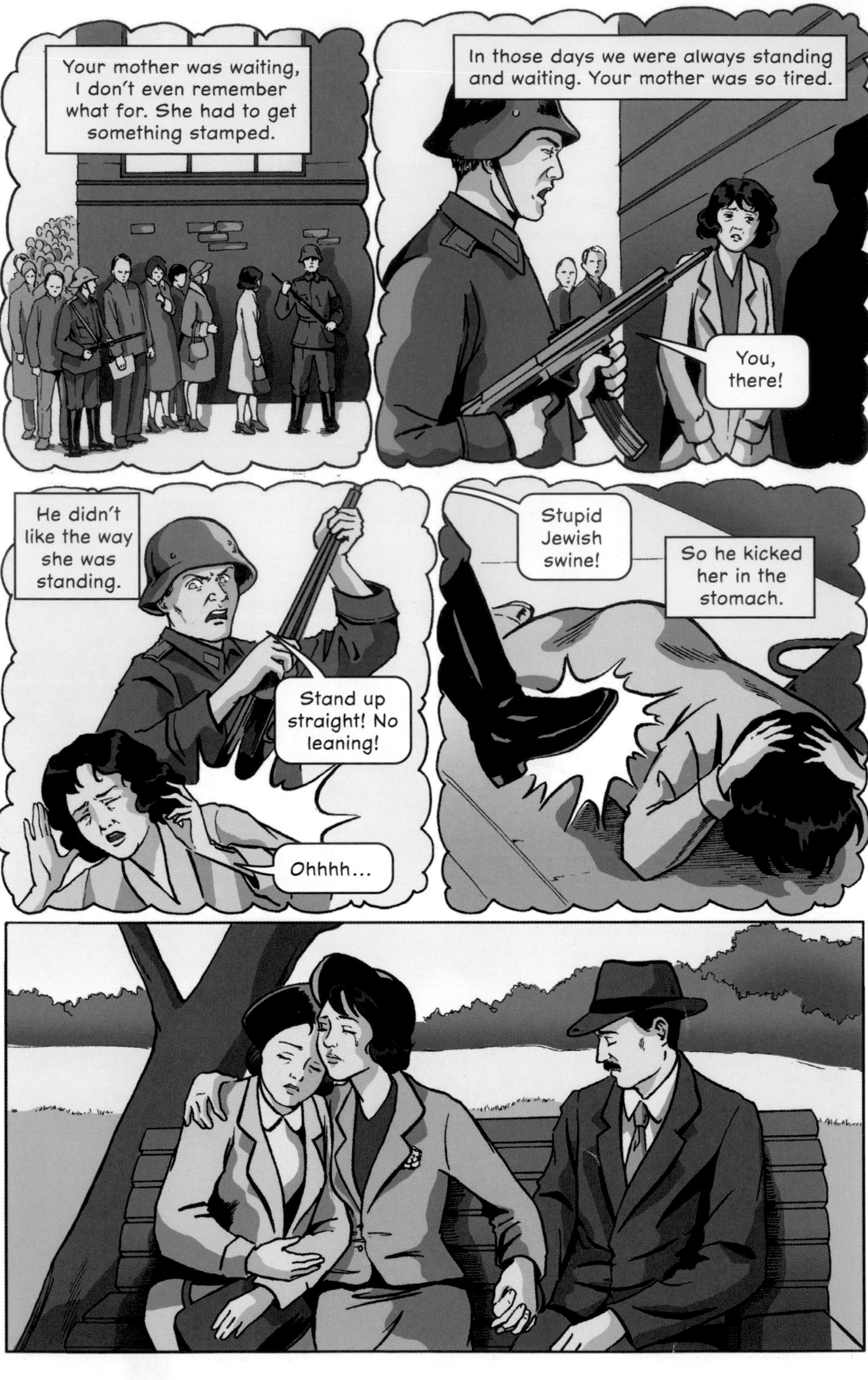
Your mother was waiting, I don't even remember what for. She had to get something stamped.
In those days we were always standing and waiting. Your mother was so tired.
You, there!
He didn't like the way she was standing.
Stand up straight! No leaning!
Ohhhh...
Stupid Jewish swine!
So he kicked her in the stomach.

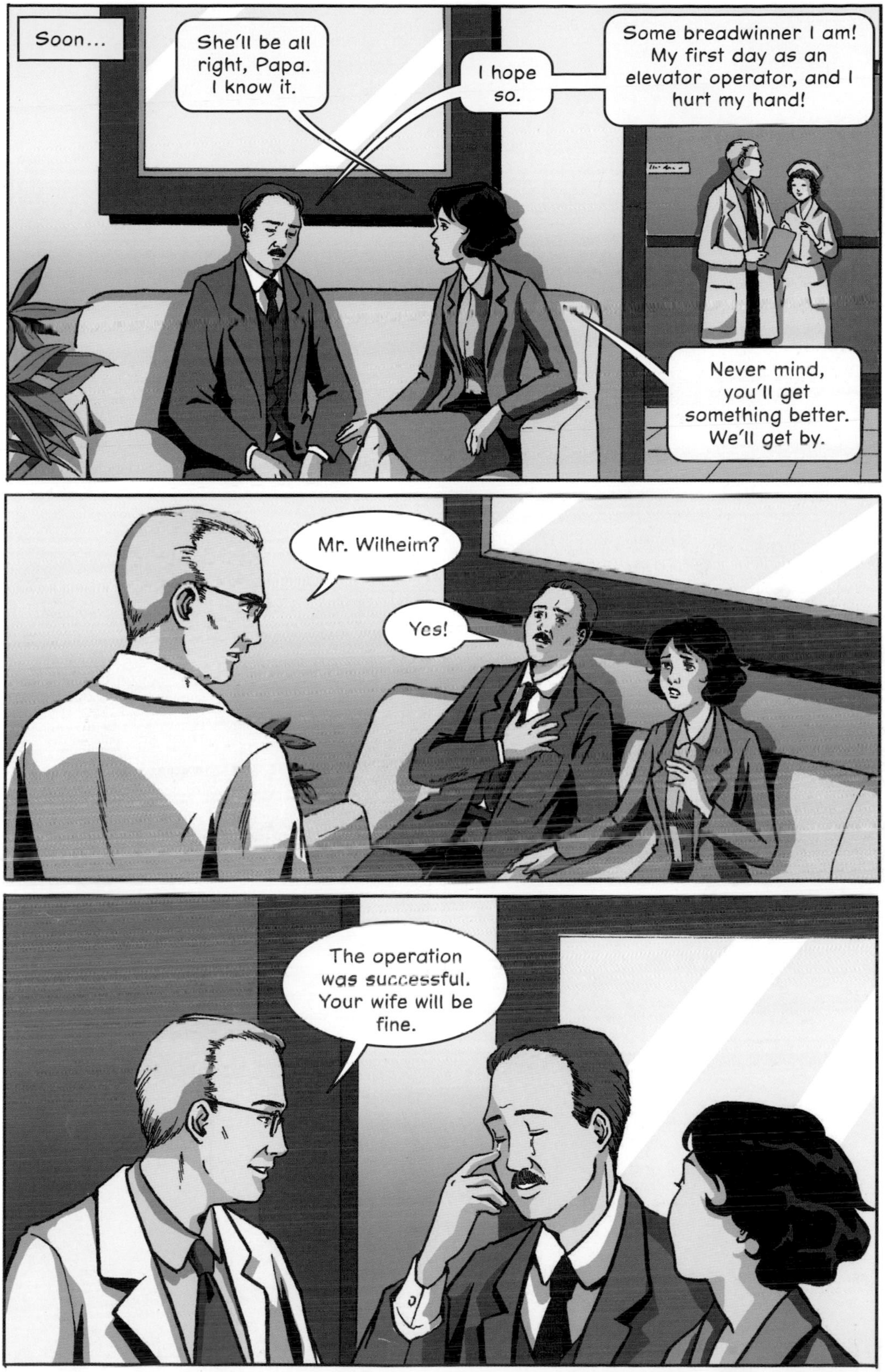
Soon...
She'll be all right, Papa. I know it.
I hope so.
Some breadwinner I am! My first day as an elevator operator, and I hurt my hand!
Never mind, you'll get something better. We'll get by.
Mr. Wilheim?
Yes!
The operation was successful. Your wife will be fine.

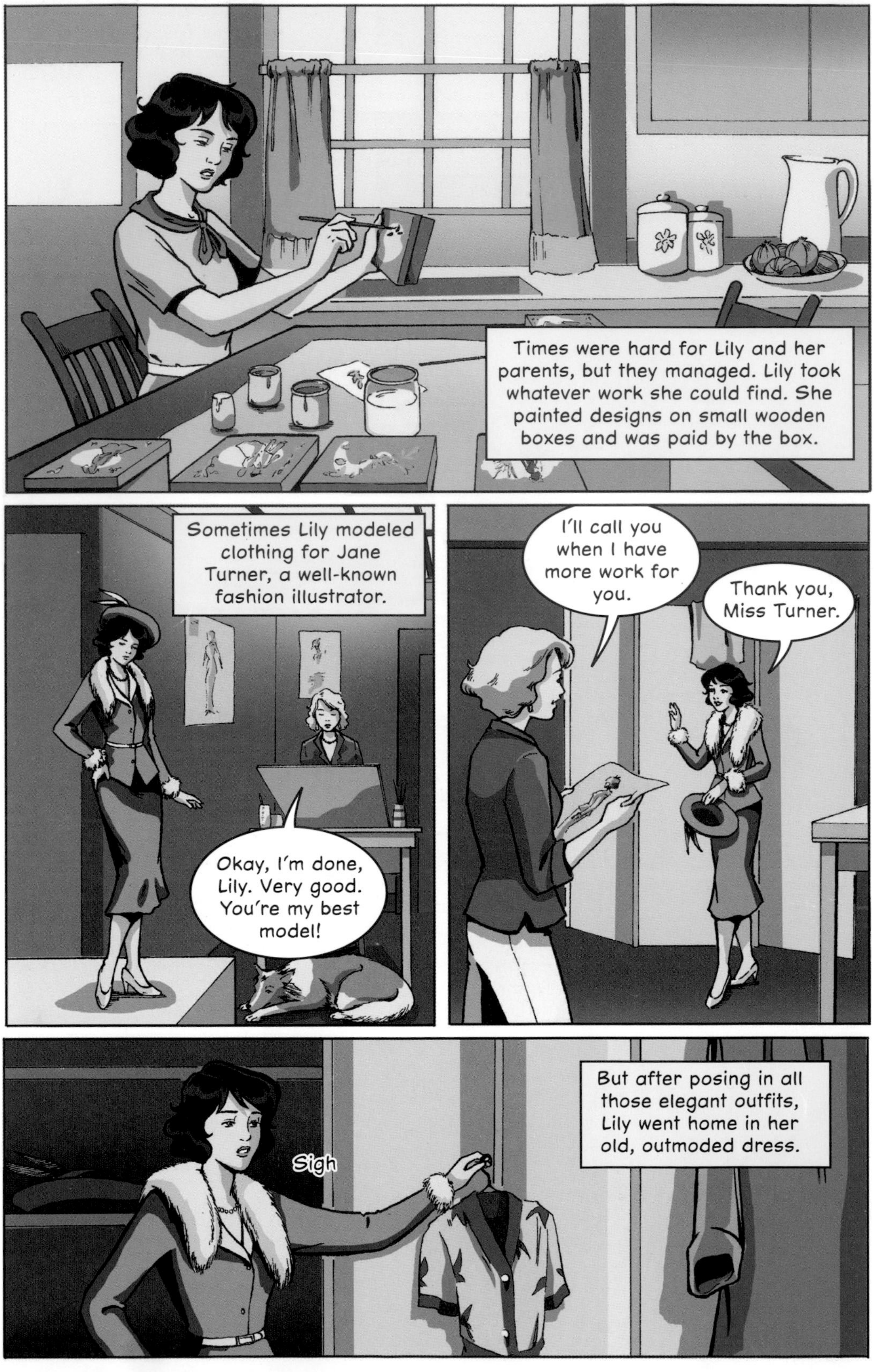
Times were hard for Lily and her parents, but they managed. Lily took whatever work she could find. She painted designs on small wooden boxes and was paid by the box.
Sometimes Lily modeled clothing for Jane Turner, a well-known fashion illustrator.
Okay, I'm done, Lily. Very good. You're my best model!
I'll call you when I have more work for you.
Thank you, Miss Turner.
But after posing in all those elegant outfits, Lily went home in her old, outmoded dress.
Sigh

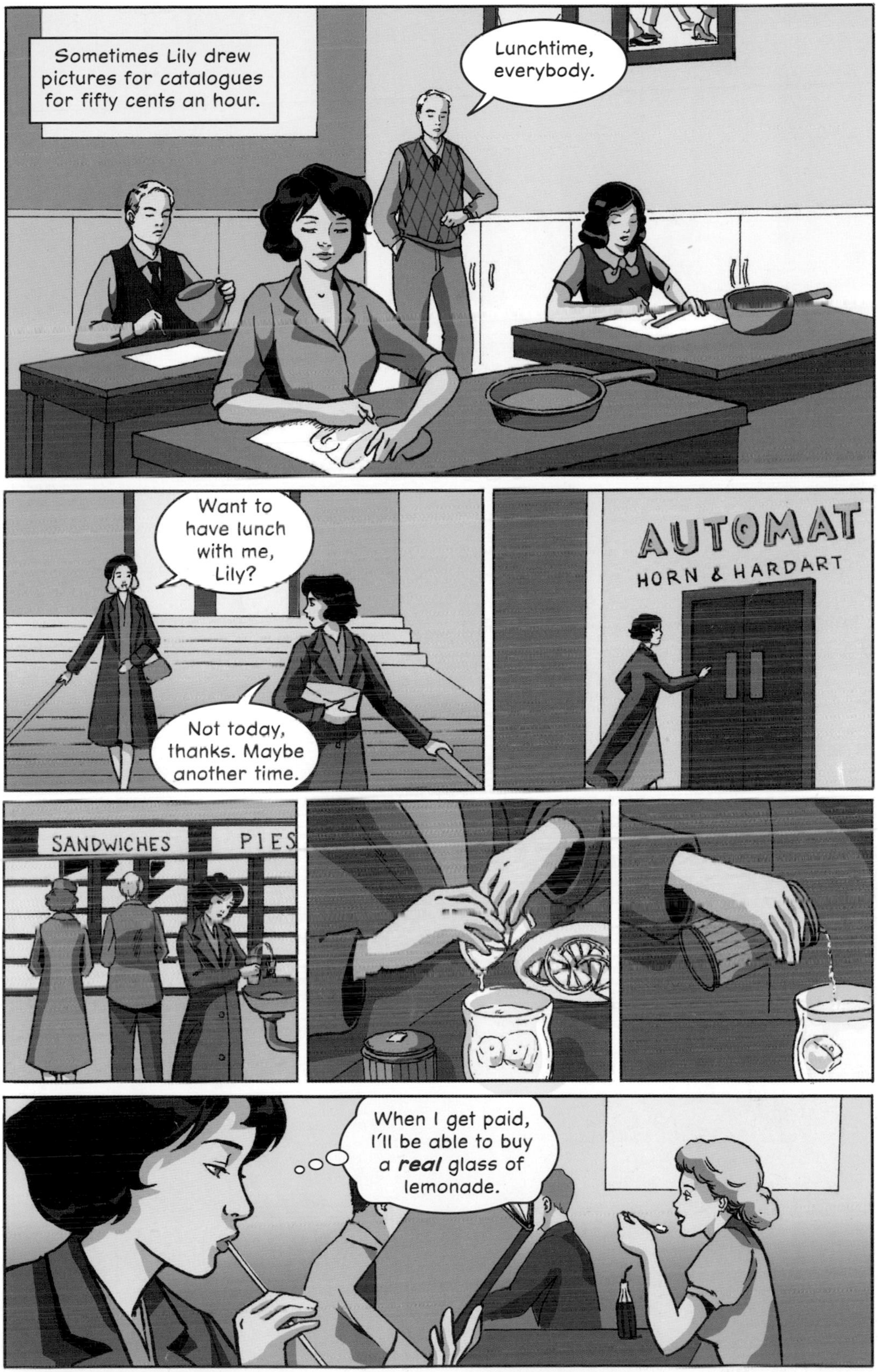
Sometimes Lily drew pictures for catalogues for fifty cents an hour.
Lunchtime, everybody.
Want to have lunch with me, Lily?
Not today, thanks. Maybe another time.
AUTOMAT
HORN & HARDART
SANDWICHES
PIES
When I get paid, I'll be able to buy a *real* glass of lemonade.

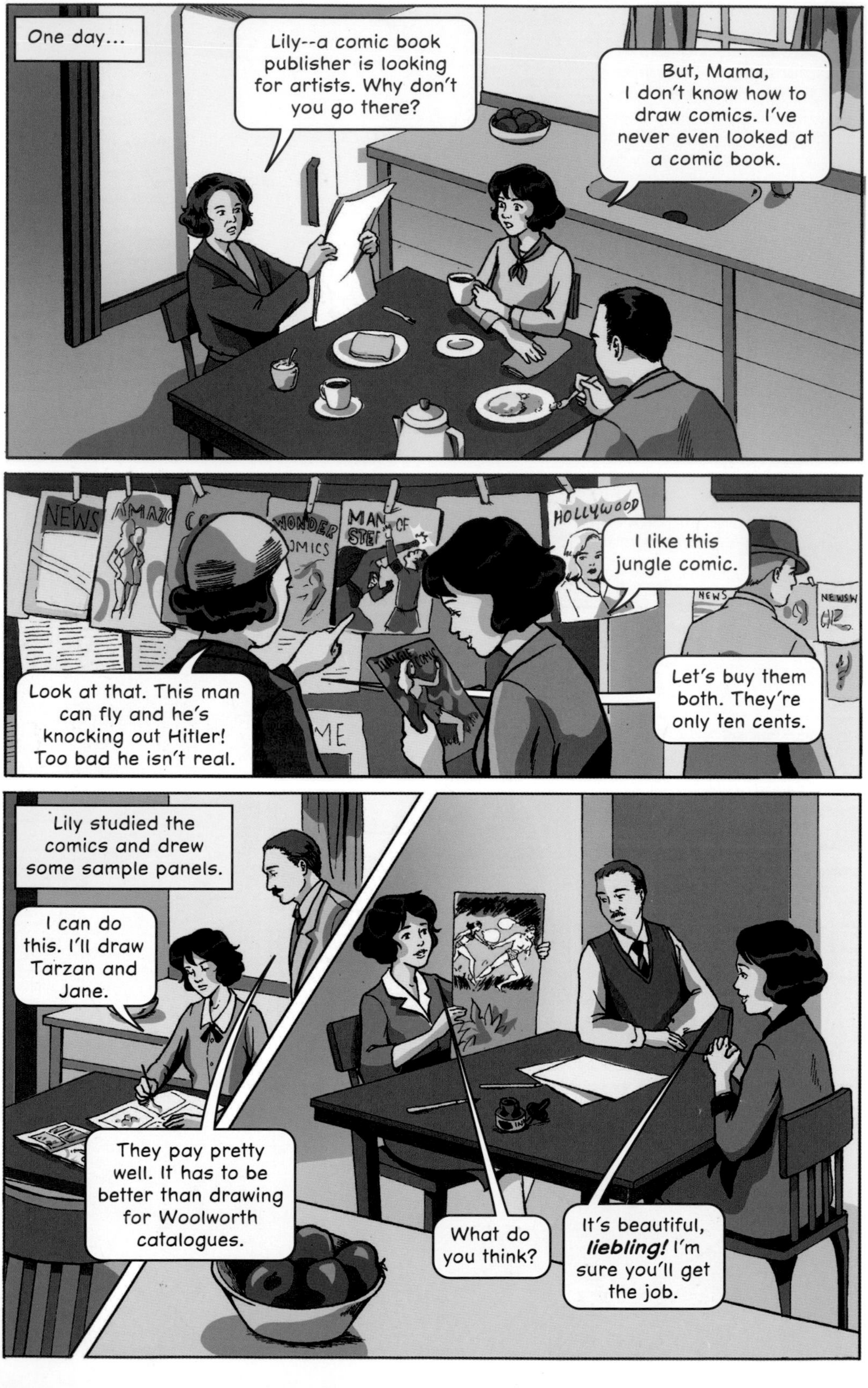
One day...
Lily--a comic book publisher is looking for artists. Why don't you go there?
But, Mama, I don't know how to draw comics. I've never even looked at a comic book.
NEWS
WONDER COMICS
HOLLYWOOD
I like this jungle comic.
Look at that. This man can fly and he's knocking out Hitler! Too bad he isn't real.
JUNGLE COMIC
Let's buy them both. They're only ten cents.
Lily studied the comics and drew some sample panels.
I can do this. I'll draw Tarzan and Jane.
They pay pretty well. It has to be better than drawing for Woolworth catalogues.
What do you think?
It's beautiful, ***liebling!*** I'm sure you'll get the job.

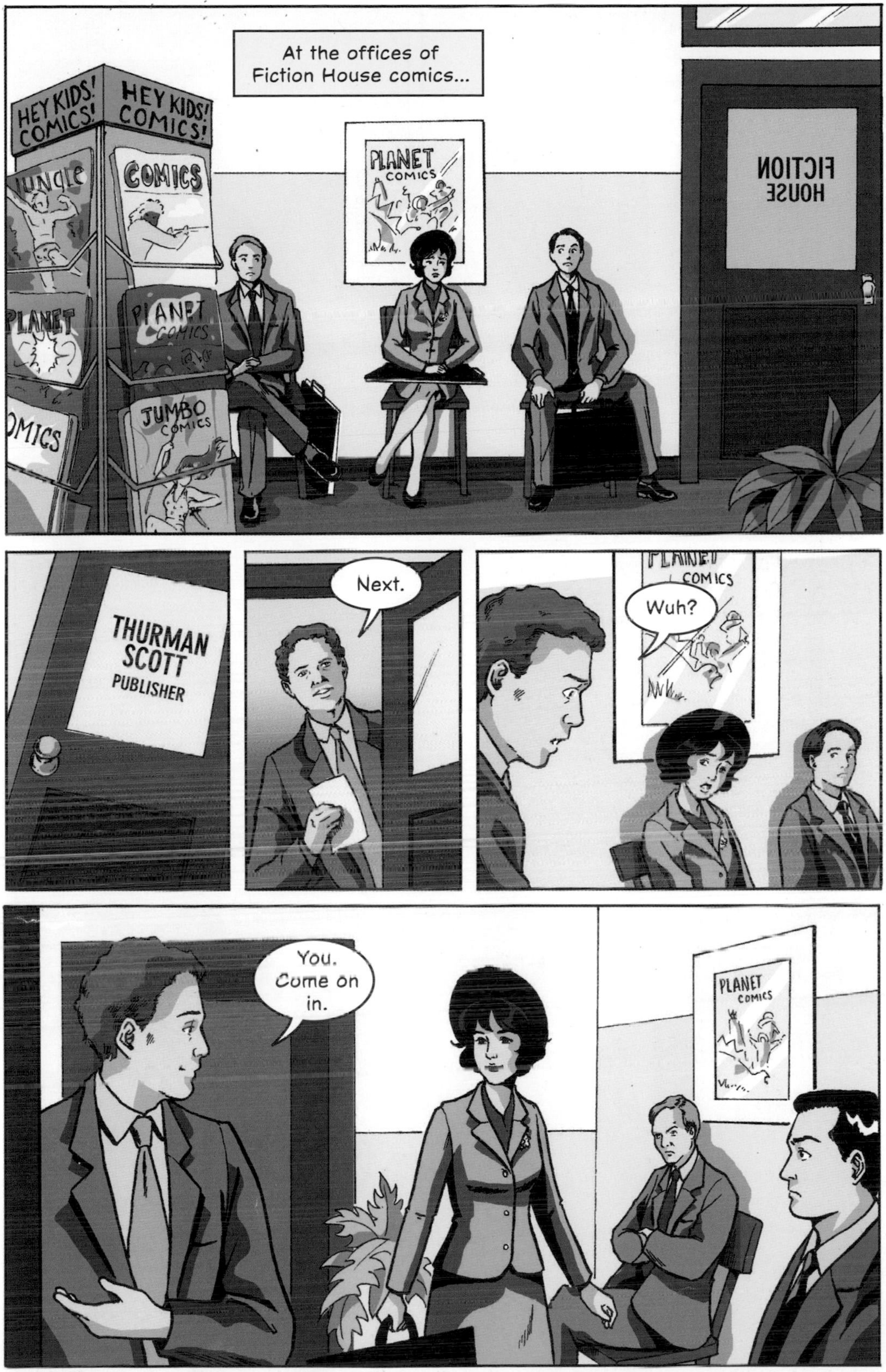
At the offices of Fiction House comics...
HEY KIDS! COMICS!
HEY KIDS! COMICS!
JUNGLE
COMICS
PLANET
PLANET COMICS
JUMBO COMICS
PLANET COMICS
FICTION HOUSE
THURMAN SCOTT PUBLISHER
Next.
PLANET COMICS
Wuh?
You. Come on in.
PLANET COMICS

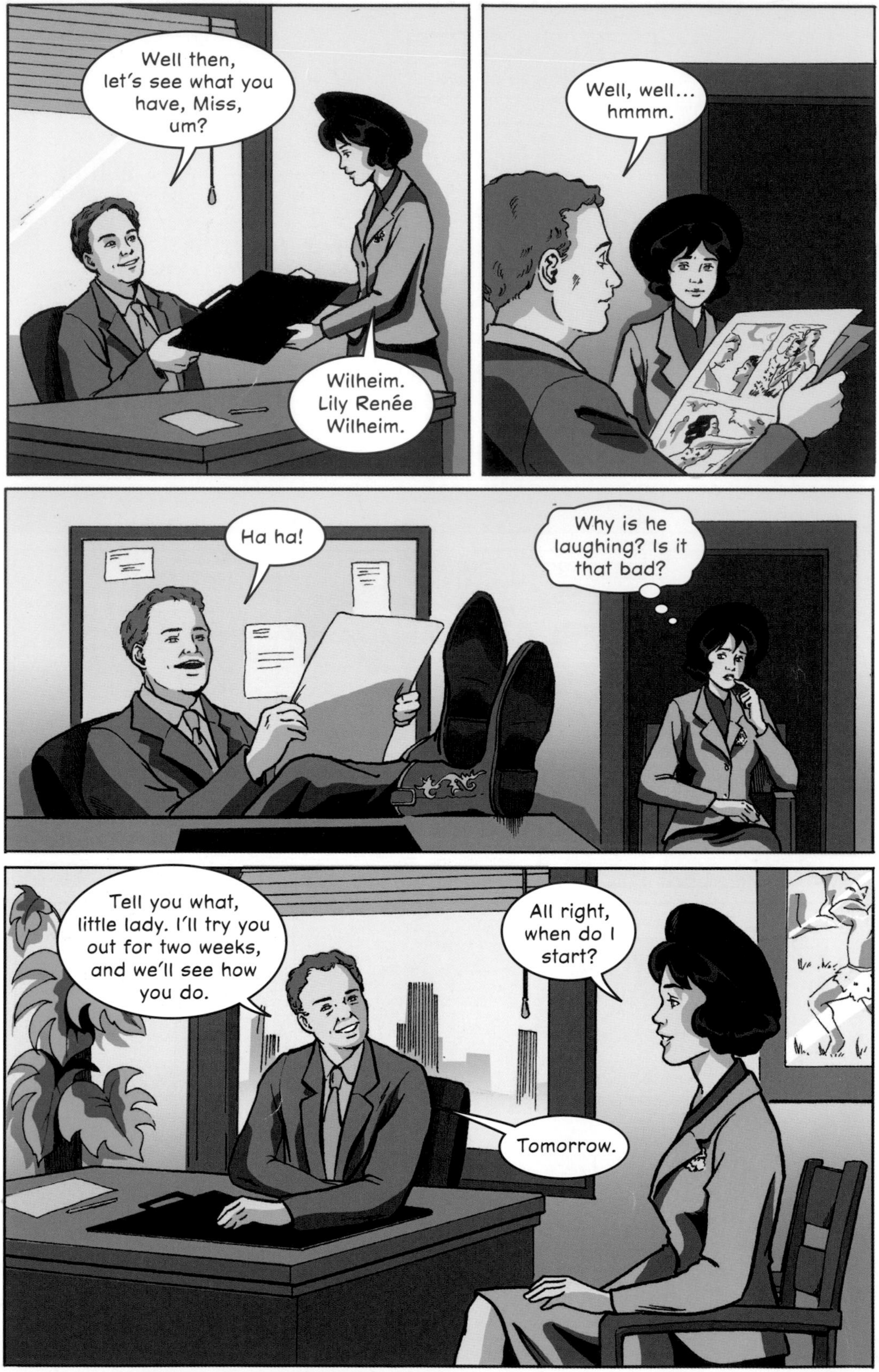
Well then, let's see what you have, Miss, um?
Wilheim. Lily Renée Wilheim.
Well, well... hmmm.
Ha ha!
Why is he laughing? Is it that bad?
Tell you what, little lady. I'll try you out for two weeks, and we'll see how you do.
All right, when do I start?
Tomorrow.

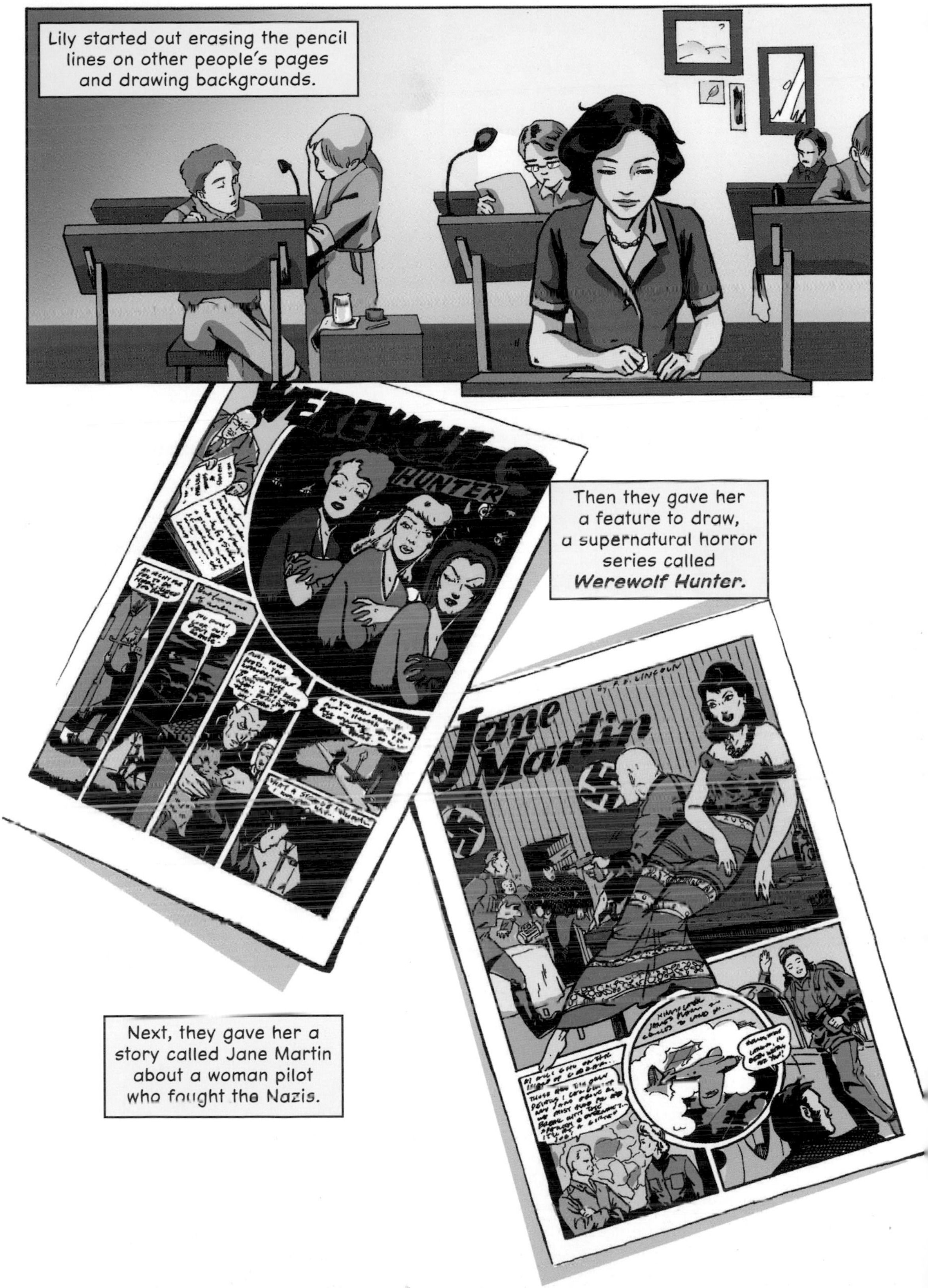

Lily started out erasing the pencil lines on other people's pages and drawing backgrounds.
HUNTER
Then they gave her a feature to draw, a supernatural horror series called ***Werewolf Hunter.***
Jane Martin
Next, they gave her a story called Jane Martin about a woman pilot who fought the Nazis.

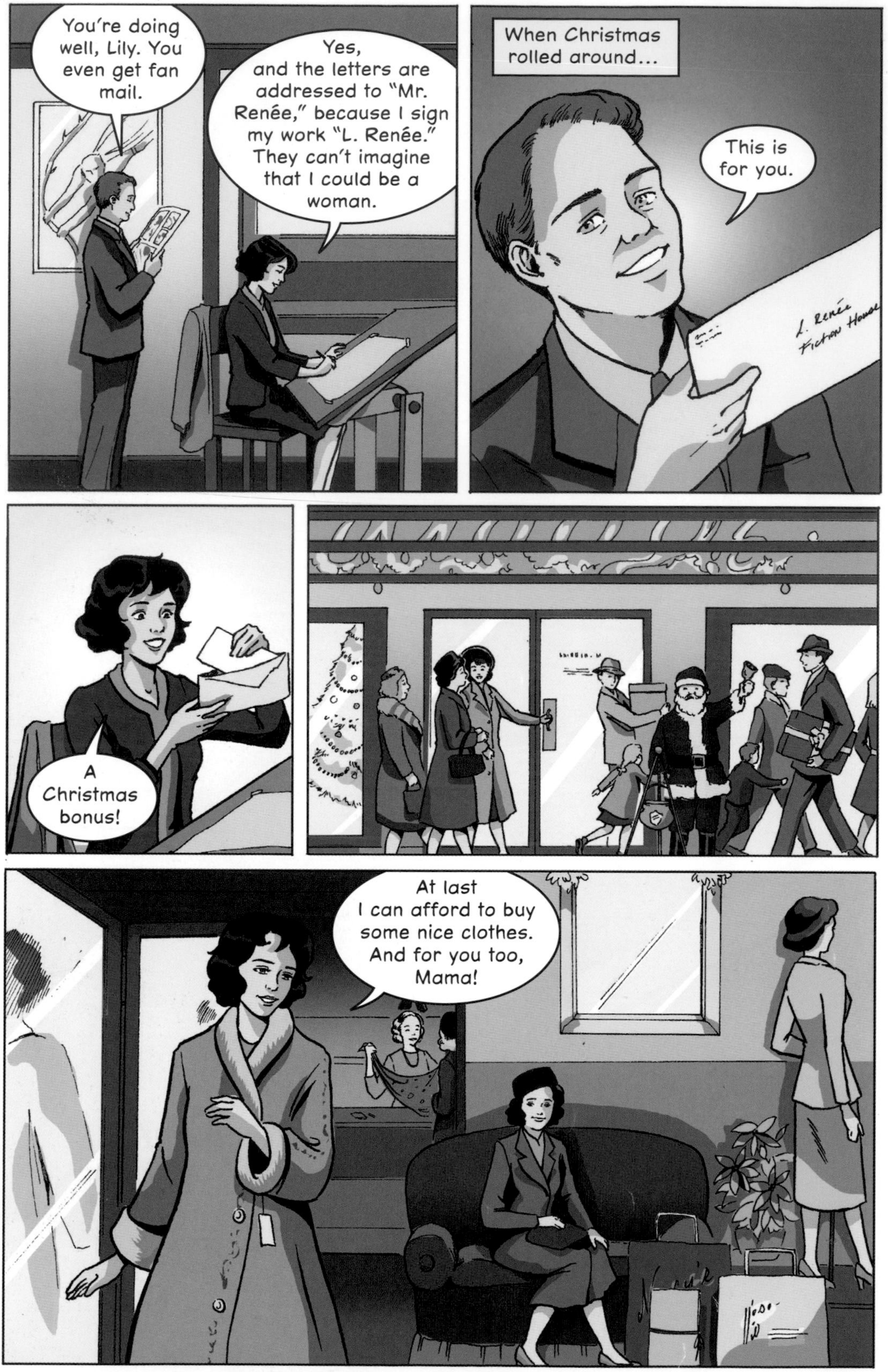

You're doing well, Lily. You even get fan mail.
Yes, and the letters are addressed to "Mr. Renée," because I sign my work "L. Renée." They can't imagine that I could be a woman.
When Christmas rolled around...
This is for you.
L. Renée
Fiction House
A Christmas bonus!
At last I can afford to buy some nice clothes. And for you too, Mama!

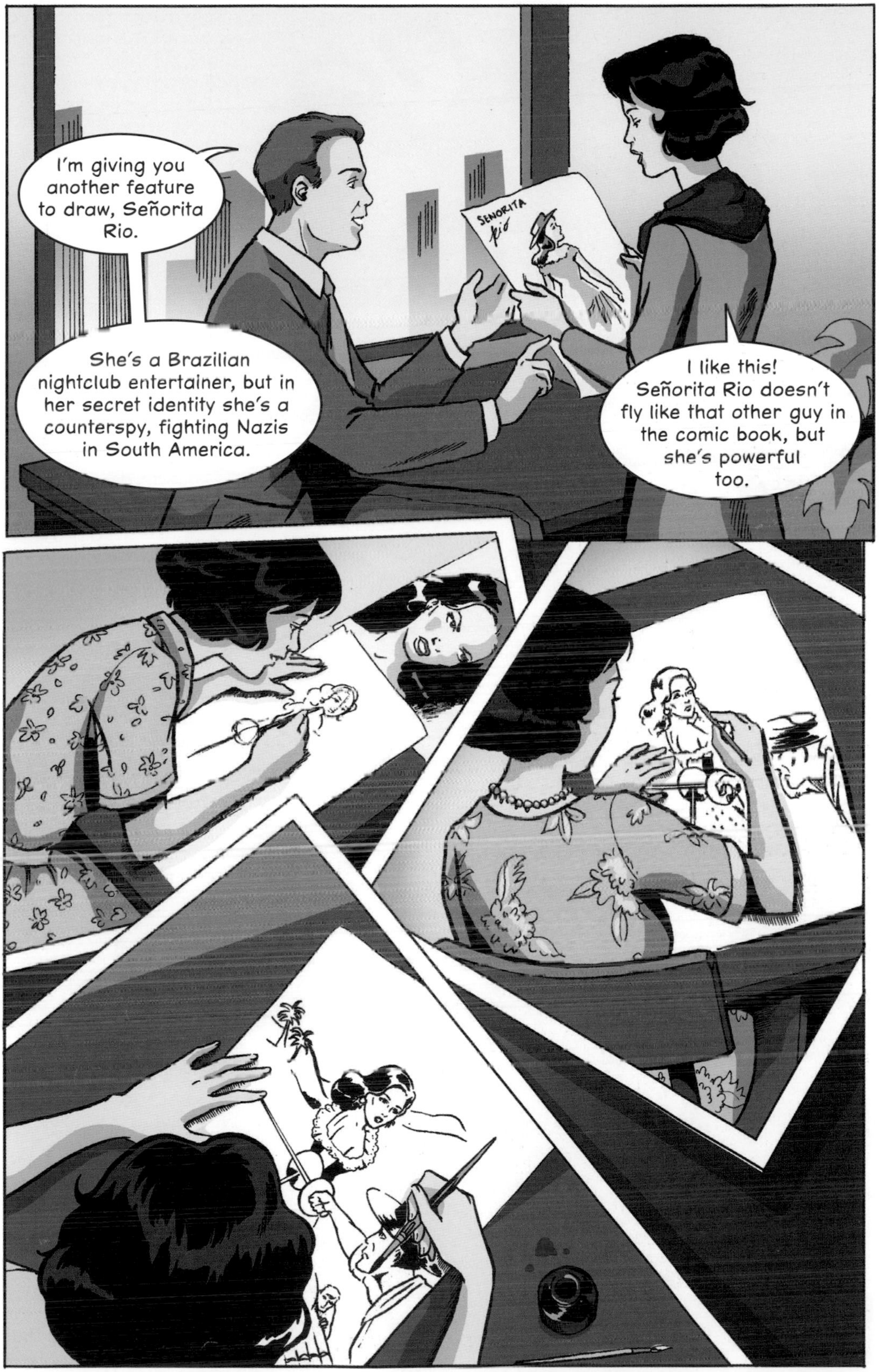
I'm giving you another feature to draw, Señorita Rio.
She's a Brazilian nightclub entertainer, but in her secret identity she's a counterspy, fighting Nazis in South America.
I like this! Señorita Rio doesn't fly like that other guy in the comic book, but she's powerful too.

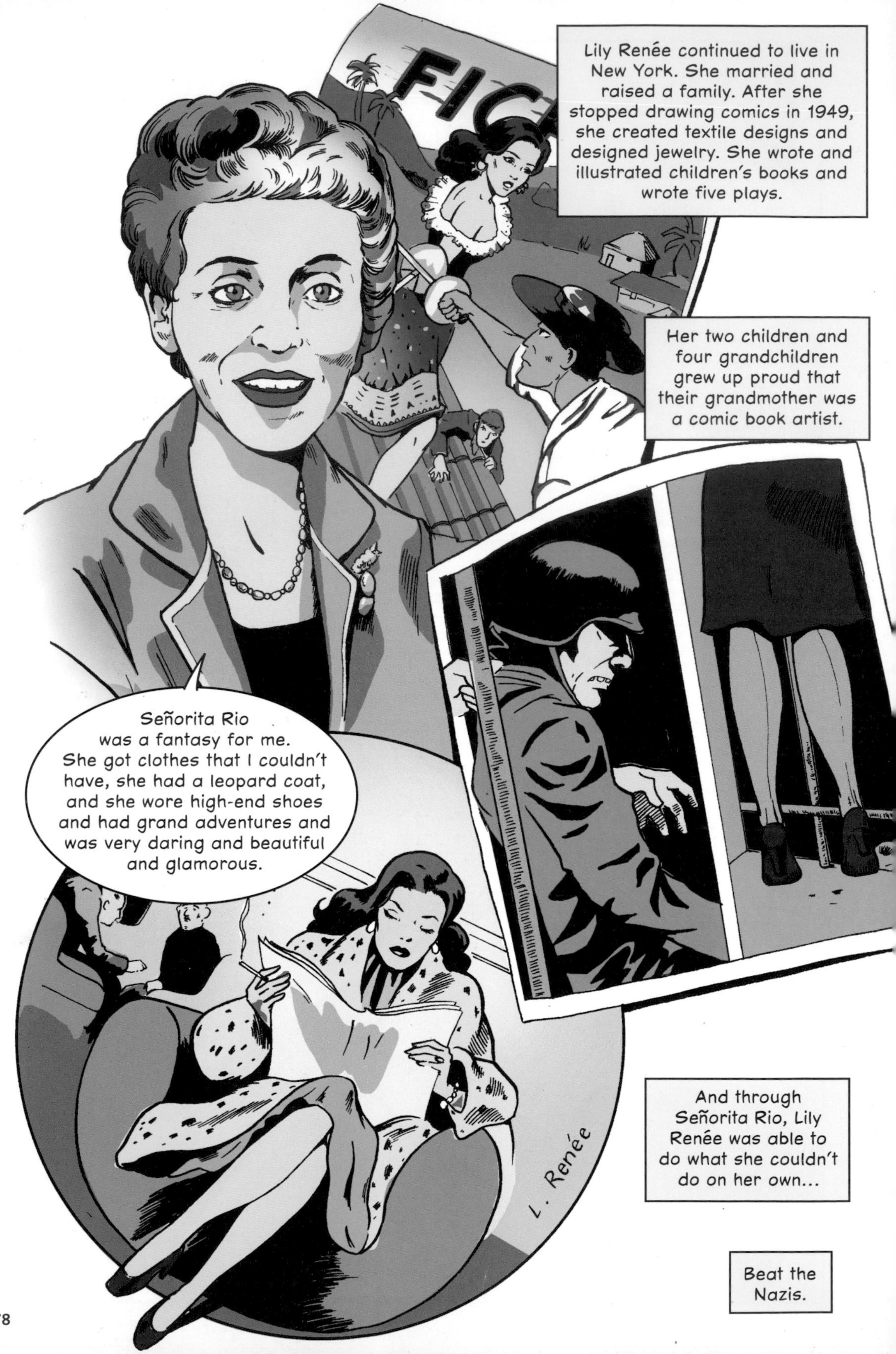

Lily Renée continued to live in New York. She married and raised a family. After she stopped drawing comics in 1949, she created textile designs and designed jewelry. She wrote and illustrated children's books and wrote five plays.
Her two children and four grandchildren grew up proud that their grandmother was a comic book artist.
Señorita Rio was a fantasy for me. She got clothes that I couldn't have, she had a leopard coat, and she wore high-end shoes and had grand adventures and was very daring and beautiful and glamorous.
L. Renée
And through Señorita Rio, Lily Renée was able to do what she couldn't do on her own...
Beat the Nazis.

More about

LILY'S STORY

GLOSSARY, *German to English*

Anschluss: a German term meaning "link up." This word was used to describe unifying Germany and Austria in 1938, to bring all German peoples together into one country.

Blitz: short for *Blitzkrieg*, which translates as "Lightning War." It was so named because the surprise attacks were lightning fast but also because the bombs were like deadly lightning raining down from the sky. Germany started daily air attacks on major cities in England in September 1940. The Blitz finally ended in May 1941.

Kindertransport: Children's Transport. Kindertransport lasted from December 1, 1938, to September 1, 1939, when England went to war against Germany. About 10,000 children escaped from the Nazis this way.

Kristallnacht: Crystal Night, also called the Night of Broken Glass, so named for the shards of broken glass scattered on the sidewalks after the shop windows of Jewish merchants had been smashed on the night of November 9–10, 1938.

liebling: loved one, dearest. This is what Lily's parents called her.

Nazi: a member of the Nationalist Socialist German Workers' Party, the political party that ruled Germany from 1933–1945. The Nazi Party spread hatred and violence against ethnic minorities, the physically and mentally disabled, members of other political parties, and Jews, among others. While they were in power, many people became members of the Nazi Party out of fear.

In the story, the two different types of word balloons show whether people are speaking (or writing or thinking) in German or in English.

The Nazi Concentration Camps vs. *the British Internment Camps*

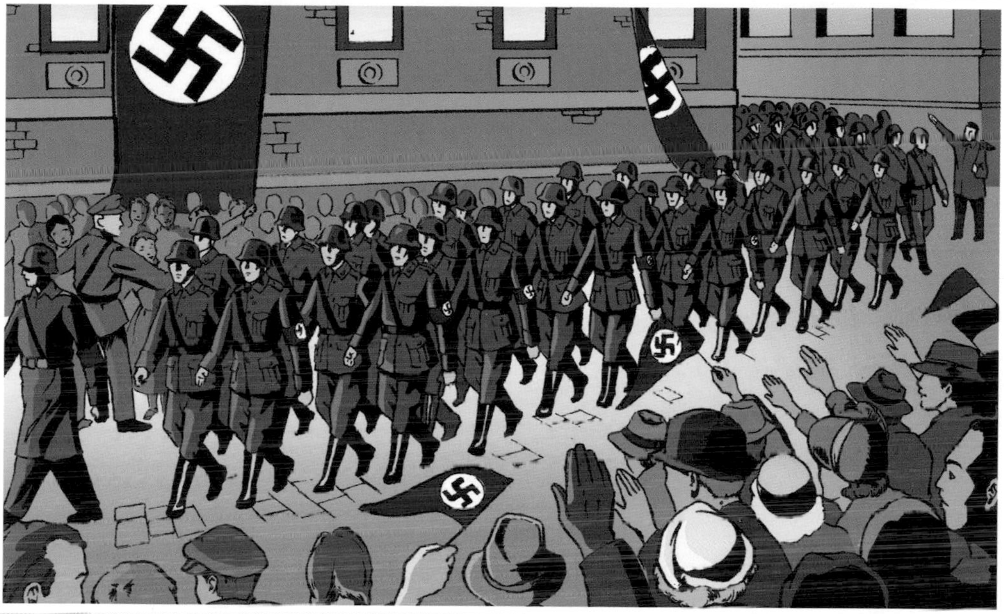

THE CONCENTRATION CAMPS

The first concentration camps were built in Germany in 1933 after the Nazis took control of the country. In the beginning they contained opponents of the new government, political prisoners, and other people that Hitler considered "enemies of the state": Communists, Socialists, Jehovah's Witnesses, homosexuals, and Roma (the nomadic people sometimes referred to as Gypsies). They were called concentration camps because all the prisoners were physically concentrated in one place.

After the Nazis marched into Austria in 1938, they started sending German and Austrian Jews to camps called Dachau, Buchenwald, and Sachsenhausen, all located in Germany. When Hitler invaded Poland in 1939, the Nazis opened labor camps there, where thousands of Polish prisoners died from exhaustion, starvation, and exposure. Soon the Nazis were arresting Jews, Polish people, mentally and physically disabled people, and other "undesirables" from *all* the countries they conquered, and building more camps to confine them. In 1941, the Nazis invaded the Soviet Union and established prisoner of war camps there, for captured Soviet soldiers. Eventually, about 20,000 camps and detention centers were built.

The prisoners were taken to the camps in filthy, cramped trains meant for cattle, with no food or water sometimes for days. Once they arrived at the camps, those who were young and healthy were turned into slave laborers. They were starved and overworked until many died from exhaustion, malnutrition, or exposure. The very young and the very old and all others who couldn't work were immediately sent to their deaths.

No matter what the camps were called, whether they were labor camps or prisoner of war camps, the end result was almost always death for the inmates. But certain camps made no pretense of what they were. Places such as Auschwitz–Birkenau were simply extermination camps. The purpose of the extermination camps was to kill as many prisoners—usually Jews—as they could, as quickly as possible.

For this purpose, the Nazis built gas chambers, rooms filled with poison gas. Auschwitz–Birkenau had four gas chambers, and during the height of the war, up to 6,000 people were murdered in the chambers every day.

Hitler's aim was to destroy all the Jews in the world. By the time the concentration camps were liberated in 1945, he had succeeded in murdering over three million Jews, along with many of his other "undesirables."

It is a miracle that anyone at all survived these hideous places of mass torture, starvation, and death.

THE INTERNMENT CAMPS

In 1939, England went to war with Germany and suddenly all refugees from Nazi-occupied countries were considered possible spies or saboteurs. Refugees from the ages of 16 to 70 were classified as "enemy aliens" and shipped off to internment camps on the Isle of Man and also to camps in Canada and Australia.

These camps were nothing like the Nazi concentration camps, but they weren't happy places, either. They certainly were nothing like summer camps! In many cases, accommodations were very basic and primitive. Husbands and wives were split apart, as men and women were sent to separate camps, although later, England opened a camp for families. On the other hand, the Isle of Man had been a resort island where British families went for their summer vacations. So the people who were sent there (called *internees*) were housed in holiday cottages.

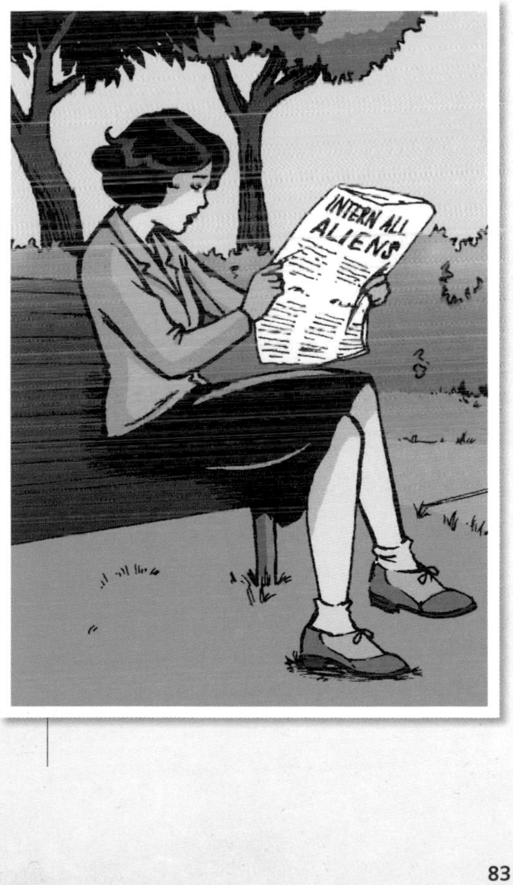
INTERN ALL ALIENS

Because they were not allowed to have newspapers, some of the internees wrote and printed their own camp newspapers. Others formed schools and theaters. Many of the young men joined the British armed forces. They bravely fought the Nazis.

In 1941, when the United States entered the war, the "enemy aliens" were reclassified as "friendly aliens." The camps were closed, but not before two terrible incidents.

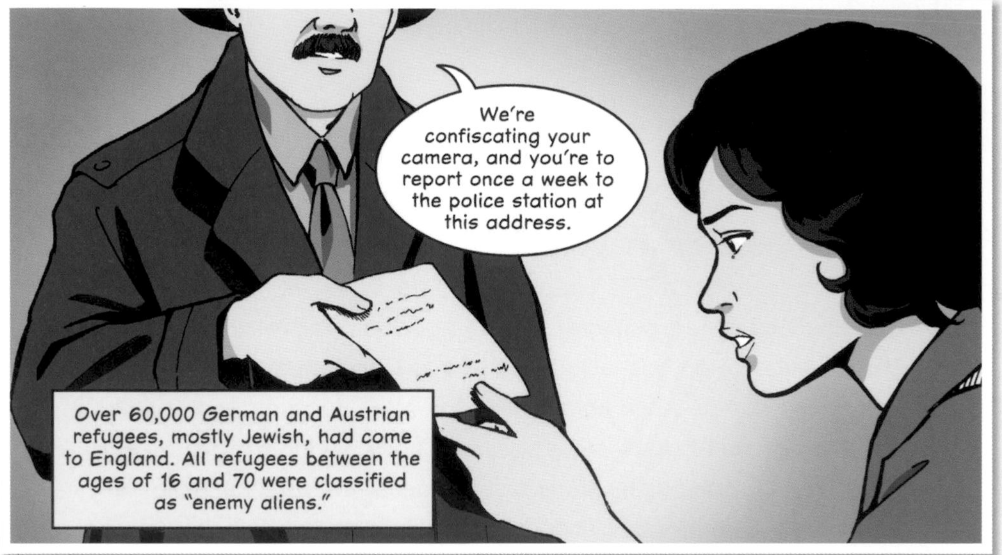
We're confiscating your camera, and you're to report once a week to the police station at this address.
Over 60,000 German and Austrian refugees, mostly Jewish, had come to England. All refugees between the ages of 16 and 70 were classified as "enemy aliens."

In June 1940, the ship *Andorra Star* was transporting refugees from England to an internment camp in Canada when she was torpedoed and sank. All 743 internees, crew, and guards perished.

In July 1940, the ship *Dunera* left Liverpool with 2,542 "enemy aliens," most of whom were Jewish refugees, on board. They were bound for an internment camp in Australia. The *Dunera* was only meant to carry 1,500 people, including crew, so conditions were horribly overcrowded. On top of that, the British guards mistreated the internees, taking away their possessions and beating and insulting them. Moreover, the passengers knew that during the 57-day voyage to Australia, the *Dunera* was under constant risk of being torpedoed by the Nazis like the *Andorra Star* had been.

When the *Dunera* docked in Sydney, Australia, the first person to go on board was a medical army officer named Alan Frost. He took one look at the terrible conditions and filed a report that led to the court-martial (a trial for a soldier in a military court) of the army officer in charge.

AFTERNOON TEA, HIGH TEA, DINNER? *I Give Up!*

Until recently, meals in England had different names and were eaten at different times than meals in Europe or the United States. Dinner, the main meal that most Americans eat in the evening, was usually eaten in England sometime between noon and 1:30 P.M. Then, in the evening, when most Americans were settling down to their heavy meal, the British sat down to high tea.

High tea was a light meal, more like lunch in the United States. But it featured food that might seem rather strange, if not downright unappetizing, to other people's tastes. Traditionally, high tea included something sweet such as scones, cakes, or sweet breads. Along with that would be pickles, cold meats, or poached eggs on toast. And, of course, tea. The tea came from a teapot, never from tea bags in a cup.

During the war, high teas were not as sumptuous as they had been. Fresh meat and eggs were scarce, so British housewives started adding a lot of canned foods to the tea table: canned spaghetti, canned kippers (a small salted or pickled fish), and canned beans on toast. Dessert would likely be canned pears served with canned milk. And, of course, tea from a teapot.

To make things even more confusing, there was another kind of tea, called afternoon tea. This was a centuries-old tradition usually indulged in by wealthy people. It consisted of dainty sandwiches—a favorite was thinly sliced cucumber on white buttered bread with the crusts cut off—along with pastries and scones, served with jams and a thick cream. Tea was poured, usually by servants, from silver teapots into delicate china teacups.

It's easy to see why Lily was confused!

HOW CAN ANYTHING BE WORTH
Less Than a Penny?

If dinner, high tea, and afternoon tea are confusing, British money was even more confusing. There were farthings, ha'pennies, thruppennies, groats, shillings, pounds, guineas, and sovereigns.

And the money had nicknames! A shilling was called a bob, a two-shilling coin was called a florin, and a pound was called a quid. A guinea was worth one pound and one shilling, and a sovereign was a gold coin worth one pound. A groat was worth four pence (pennies), thruppence meant a three-penny coin, and ha'penny was short for "half a penny." There was even a coin smaller than a ha'penny: one-quarter of a penny, called a farthing!

It may seem ridiculous now that anyone would need one-fourth of a penny. But prices were much lower in wartime England. In 1939, a pound of butter cost $7\frac{1}{2}$ pence, and a pound of margarine was $2\frac{1}{2}$ pence. You could buy a pound of apples for $1\frac{1}{2}$ pence and a pound of cookies for 5 pence.

It wasn't until 1971 that this confusing system was simplified into just pounds and pence, but you would still see shillings around for years after that. Ever since 1999, the euro has been used as a single currency in more and more of Europe, making it possible to use the same money as you travel from country to country. But the British have opted to keep using the pound.

Just as the U.S. dollar is worth 100 pennies, the English pound is worth 100 pence. But even today, a pound is still nicknamed a quid!

CHAMBERLAIN *vs.* CHURCHILL

It was Prime Minister Neville Chamberlain, not the more famous Winston Churchill, who declared war against the Nazis in September 1939.

Neville Chamberlain became prime minister in 1937. He had strong experience in government, but many people say he had poor judgment. He was soft and patient in dealing with Germany when Hitler and the Nazi Party came to power. Chamberlain hoped his approach would prevent the outbreak of a major war, but in the end, his weak peace treaties failed to stop World War II.

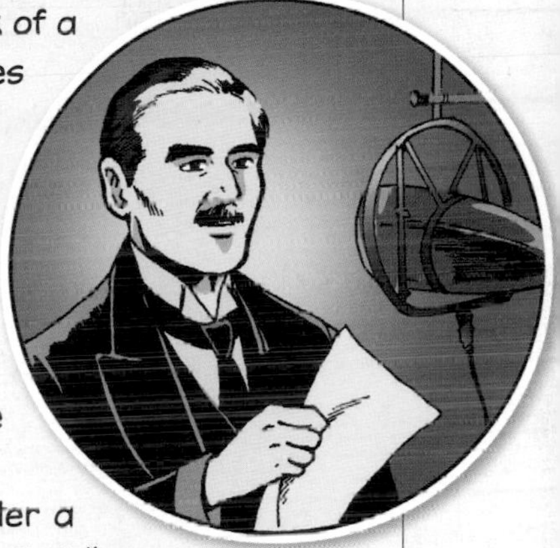

In poor health, Chamberlain resigned in May 1940. This made way for Winston Churchill to become prime minister. Winston Churchill is widely considered to be one of the greatest political leaders of the twentieth century. Many quotes from his speeches are often repeated today.

One of Churchill's most famous quotes, after a devastating loss to the Nazis, was his promise that "we shall fight on the beaches, we shall fight on the landing grounds, we shall fight in the fields and in the streets, we shall fight in the hills. We shall never surrender." Another famous quote was when he praised all the soldiers who fought in the war, saying that never "was so much owed by so many to so few."

Churchill presided over Great Britain for six years, leading the British people to victory in 1945. He is often seen in photographs holding up one hand in a "V for Victory" sign.

History does not paint a kind picture of Prime Minister Chamberlain. His soft policies toward the Nazis, known as appeasement, are still held up today as an example and a warning for current political leaders of what not to do. Churchill himself compared appeasement to being like someone who "feeds a crocodile—hoping it will eat him last."

Then the train stopped in Holland, and everything was different.
Soup for you, from Queen Wilhelmina.
Imagine, people who aren't Jewish, and yet they're nice to us!

Queen WILHELMINA

Queen Wilhelmina was queen of the Netherlands (Holland) from 1890 to 1948. This makes her one of the longest-reigning monarchs in European history. She occupied the throne during both World War I and II, and reigned over her country through many challenges. Known as an intelligent and strong woman, Queen Wilhelmina became a great inspiration to the Dutch (the people of the Netherlands) during their difficult struggle when the Nazis occupied their country from 1940 to 1945.

When she was offered a safe refuge in England during the war by King George VI, she reluctantly accepted. She continued to lead her country from afar. Her radio broadcasts to millions of her fellow citizens were a boost to their morale.

The Dutch people and Queen Wilhelmina regained their freedom from the Nazis in March 1945.

THE *Holland America* LINE

Lily's father, Rudolph Wilheim, managed the Austrian branch of the Holland America Line, a historic and highly respected steamship company. Its first ship, the *Rotterdam*, sailed from Holland to New York in 1873.

The ship that took Lily to New York was the *Rotterdam IV*. It had been built in 1908, and Lily may have been a passenger on its last voyage, because it was sold for scrap in 1940. But in its heyday, the *Rotterdam IV* was first class throughout. It boasted of "56 suites and rooms with brass bedsteads and private baths, and over 100 single rooms, together with a beautiful Palm Court, Verandah Cafe, Elevator, Social Hall, Library, 3 Smoke Rooms, a glass enclosed Promenade Deck, electronically forced ventilation of hot and cold air, etc."

One of the ship's most attractive features was an immense dining saloon that could seat nearly five hundred people. Passengers dined on French cuisine beneath crystal chandeliers while serenaded by a full orchestra. When Lily and the other Kindertransport kids wandered the old ship, its halls must have been filled with faded glory and the ghostly reminders of a long-past age of carefree elegance.

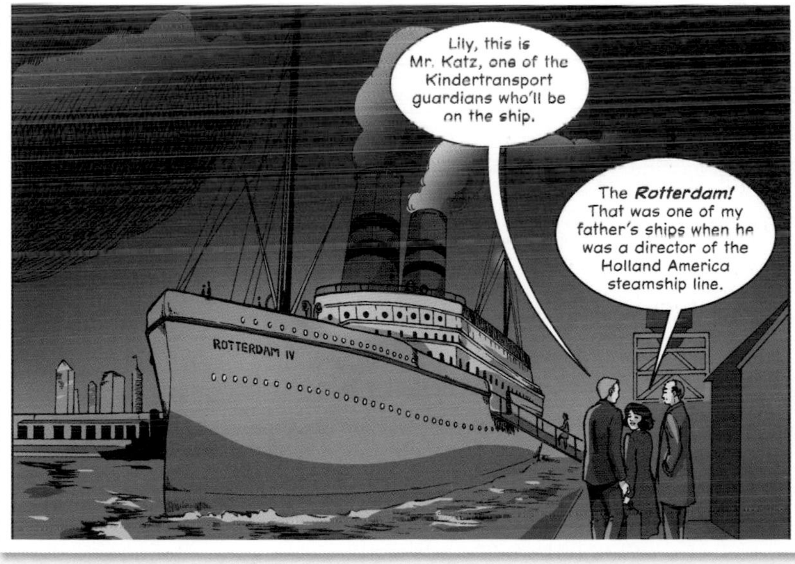

Lily, this is Mr. Katz, one of the Kindertransport guardians who'll be on the ship.
The **Rotterdam!** That was one of my father's ships when he was a director of the Holland America steamship line.
ROTTERDAM IV

Want to have lunch with me, Lily?
Not today, thanks. Maybe another time.
AUTOMAT
HORN & HARDART
SANDWICHES
PIES

HORN & HARDART: *The Automat*

Horn & Hardart, better known as the Automat, was a unique chain of restaurants that was popular from the early 1900s through the late 1960s.

In 1888, Joseph Horn and Frank Hardart opened their first restaurant in Philadelphia. The tiny luncheonette was only 11 feet by 17 feet and had no tables, only a counter with fifteen stools, but the delicious coffee they served made it extremely popular.

It wasn't until 1902 that Horn and Hardart opened their first Automat in Philadelphia, followed ten years later by two Automats in New York City. What made these restaurants so unusual was their way of serving food.

Instead of sitting at a table and being waited on, customers went first to glass booths where women cashiers changed their money into nickels. Then customers took their nickels to a wall of small glass windows behind which plates of food sat on little glass shelves. The shelves had sections for cooked food—mac and cheese, meat loaf, and pot pies were some customer favorites—and there were sections for cakes and pies and desserts. Customers placed their nickels into slots next to the dish they chose and turned a little handle. The glass window popped open, and diners helped themselves to their food. Once they closed the window again, the shelf revolved, and *presto!* there sat another plate of food, ready for the next customer's nickels.

By the 1950s, Horn & Hardart had grown so popular that there were 180 Automats in New York and Philadelphia. In Manhattan alone, there were 40 Automats. By the 1960s, those nickels had become quarters, but the Automat remained a place where people could get tasty, cheap food. The very last Automat closed in 1991.

In the 1940s, you could buy a good, filling lunch at the Automat for 5 nickels—25 cents. Another nickel would buy you a cup of coffee. But poor Lily couldn't even spare that much money and had to rely on "free lemonade"!

Jane Martin
by BOB HICKOK
GUARDING A TOP SECRET JET PLANE IS A HIGH FLYING JOB EVEN FOR JANE MARTIN. BUT SHE FLIES INTO SUB-STRATOSPHERE STORMS WHEN A NATION-WIDE HOOKUP OF FASCISTS LOCK THE CONTROLS FOR A DEADLY, CAT AND MOUSE CONTEST!
YOU CALLED ME, MR. HURRY?
Jane Martin by Fran Hopper

TONI GAYLE
IN THE GAY SETTING OF A FAMOUS WINTER RESORT, GLAMOROUS TONI GAYLE, THE MODEL WITH A YEN FOR DETECTING, FIGHTS A GRIM BATTLE AGAINST A STRANGE KILLER!
J. VALLEAU
THERE'S SUN MOUNTAIN INN, CHILLUNS! NIFTY BACKGROUND FOR WINTER FASHION PIX!
BEAUTIFUL! HOPE I GET A CHANCE TO IMPROVE MY SKIING!
Toni Gayle by Joyce Valleau

IS IT POSSIBLE THERE IS AN OPENING IN THAT WALL? IT LOOKS LIKE SOLID ROCK! I'D LIKE TO --- BUT. NO, I MUST GET DAN OUT OF HERE!
ALL THE NAZIS APPEAR TO BE DEAD AND YET — I HAVE THAT AWFUL FEELING OF BEING WATCHED — THAT SOMEHOW THIS PLACE IS A DELIBERATE SETUP!
THE MARINES ARE STILL WAITING FOR DAN'S SIGNAL— THEY DON'T KNOW HE HAS BEEN WOUNDED! BUT IF I CALL OUT TO THEM, THEY MAY STEP INTO A TRAP!
HAVE TO STOP A MOMENT! MMM — NOW WHAT TO DO? MUST KEEP MOVING, BUT...
...IF NAZIS ARE WATCHING, THEY CAN STILL PICK US OFF— AND IF WE MOVE ON, THE MARINES MIGHT OPEN FIRE!
Miss Fury by Tarpé Mills

The Fighting Femmes OF WARTIME COMIC BOOKS AND THEIR ARTISTS

Up until World War II, for the most part, women were expected to marry, stay home, and raise a family while their husbands went off to work. But the war changed all that. After the United States entered the war in 1941, many young men left their jobs on farms, in offices, and in factories to join the armed forces and fight the enemy overseas. Who was going to take over the jobs they had left behind? Women! The new image of women was of a determined character called Rosie the Riveter. In posters, Rosie the Riveter is shown rolling up her sleeve and saying, "We can do it!"

Women were driving trucks and buses, working in factories and shipyards making ships and planes . . . and, yes, they were drawing comics.

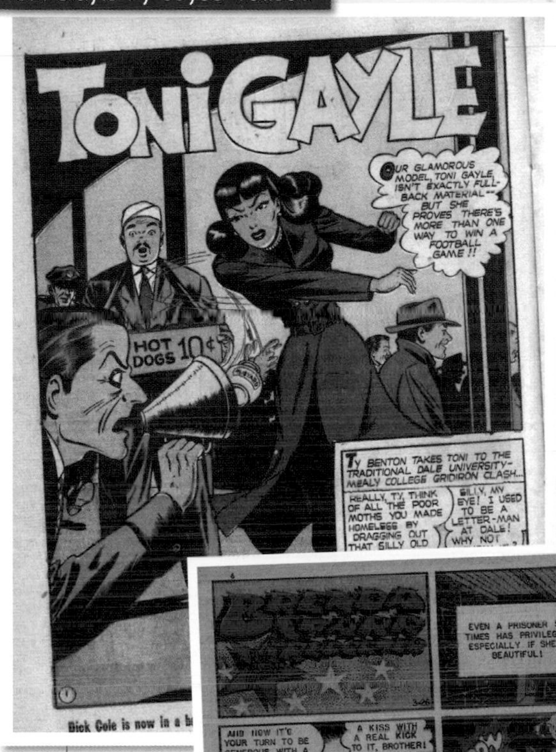
TONI GAYLE
OUR GLAMOROUS MODEL, TONI GAYLE, ISN'T EXACTLY FULL-BACK MATERIAL-- BUT SHE PROVES THERE'S MORE THAN ONE WAY TO WIN A FOOTBALL GAME !!
HOT DOGS 10¢
TY BENTON TAKES TONI TO THE TRADITIONAL DALE UNIVERSITY-MEALY COLLEGE GRIDIRON CLASH...
REALLY, TY, THINK OF ALL THE POOR MOTHS YOU MADE HOMELESS BY DRAGGING OUT THAT SILLY OLD
SILLY, MY EYE! I USED TO BE A LETTER-MAN AT DALE! WHY NOT
Dick Cole is now in a b

Toni Gayle by Joyce Valleau

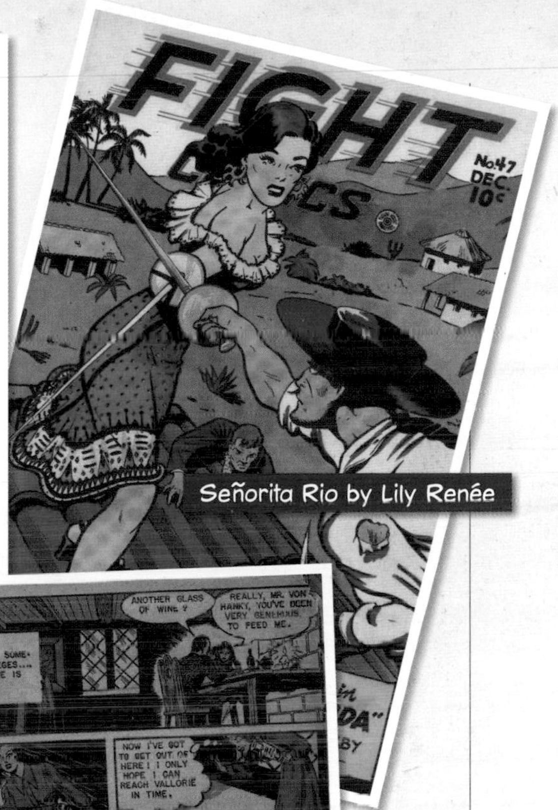
FIGHT
No.47 DEC. 10¢

Señorita Rio by Lily Renée

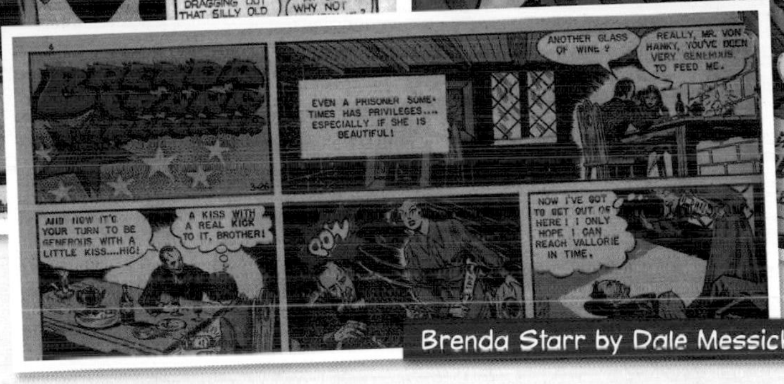
ANOTHER GLASS OF WINE ?
REALLY, MR. VON HANKY, YOU'VE BEEN VERY GENEROUS TO FEED ME.
EVEN A PRISONER SOMETIMES HAS PRIVILEGES.... ESPECIALLY IF SHE IS BEAUTIFUL!
AND NOW IT'S YOUR TURN TO BE GENEROUS WITH A LITTLE KISS....HIC!
A KISS WITH A REAL KICK TO IT, BROTHER!
NOW I'VE GOT TO GET OUT OF HERE! I ONLY HOPE I CAN REACH VALLORIE IN TIME.

Brenda Starr by Dale Messick

The image of women in the pages of comic books changed too. Until the war, women in comic books were usually the girlfriend of the hero. All too often they existed just so that he would have someone to rescue. But during the war, a new kind of woman appeared in comics. Like her real-life sisters, she was strong and determined, but she went one step further. Heroines such as Miss Fury, Black Cat, and the *Girl Commandos* dressed up in costumes like the male superheroes and fought criminals and Nazis. Sometimes they had patriotic names like Miss America. And sometimes they were plainclothes heroines, such as the beautiful spy Señorita Rio, the flying nurse Jane Martin, "girl detective" Toni Gayle, or "girl reporter" Brenda Starr.

And every one of the comics heroines listed above was drawn or created by women!

Lily's PHOTO ALBUM

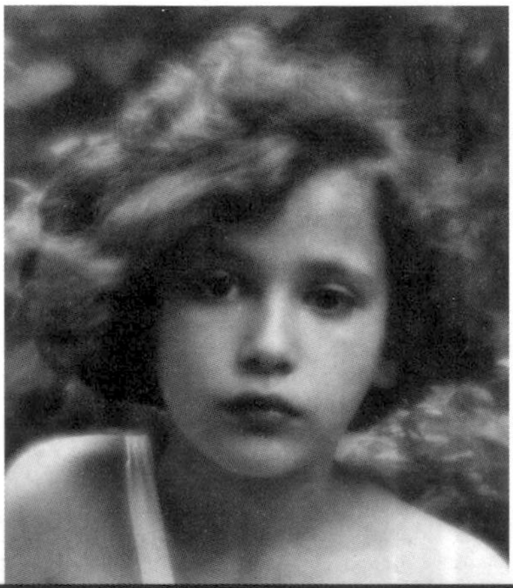

Lily Renée Wilheim at 6 years of age

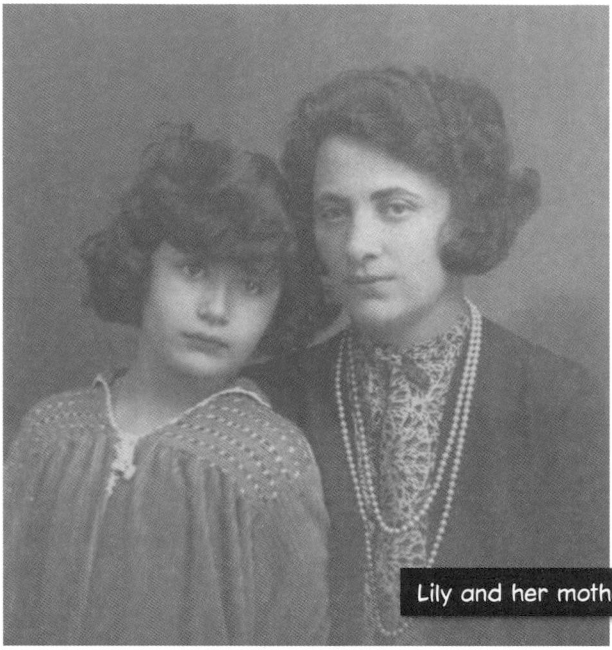

Lily and her mother

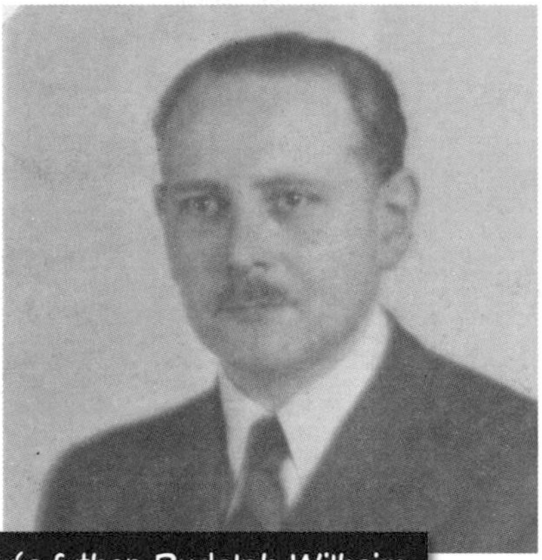

Lily's father, Rudolph Wilheim

13-year-old Lily with her mother and friends

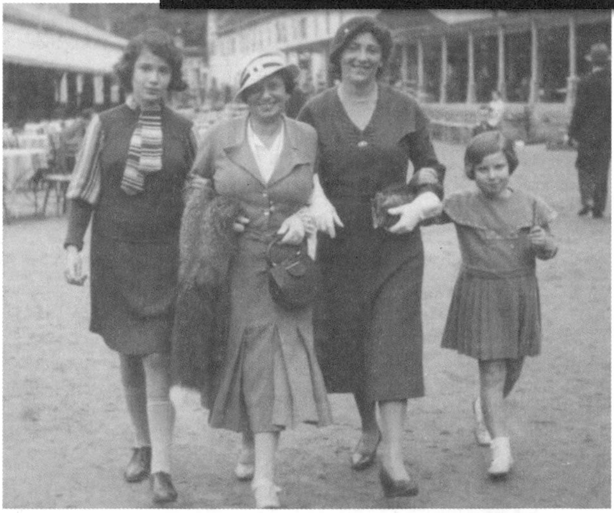

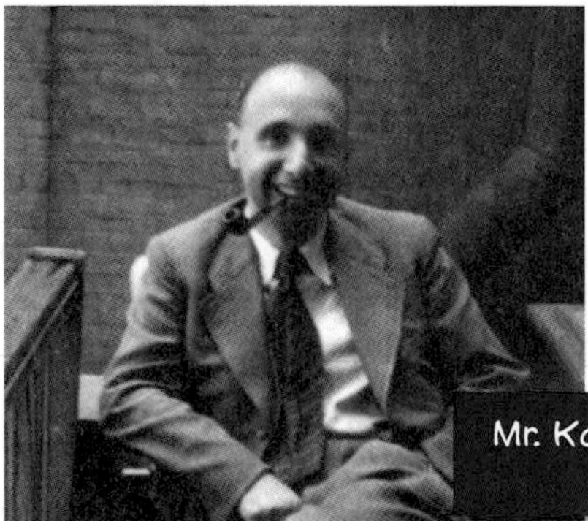

Mr. Katz, who took care of the kids on the *Rotterdam* on their way to America

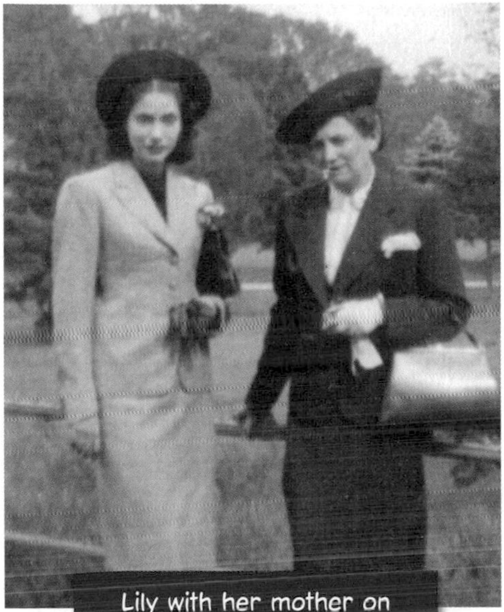

Lily with her mother on
Lily's first day in New York

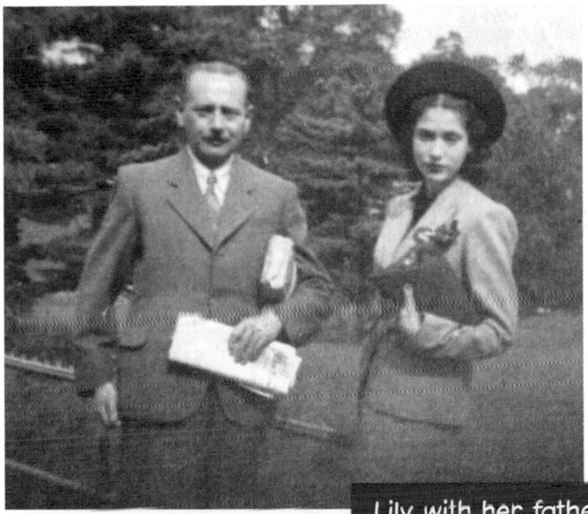

Lily with her father

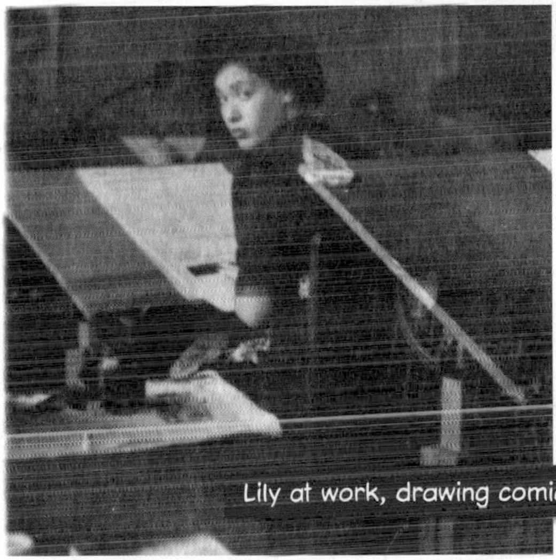

Lily at work, drawing comics

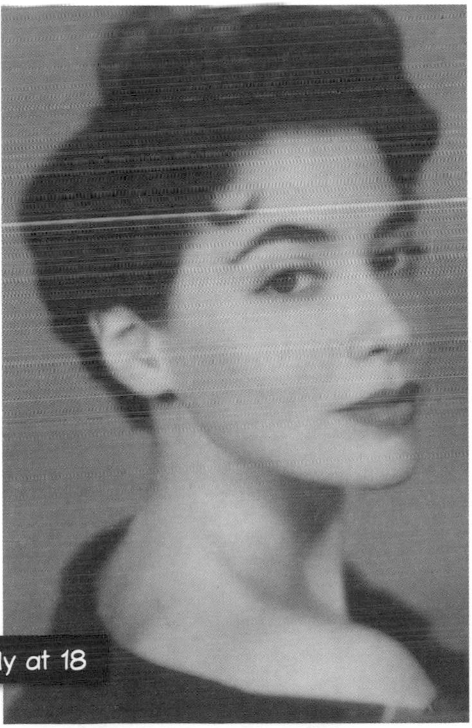

Lily at 18

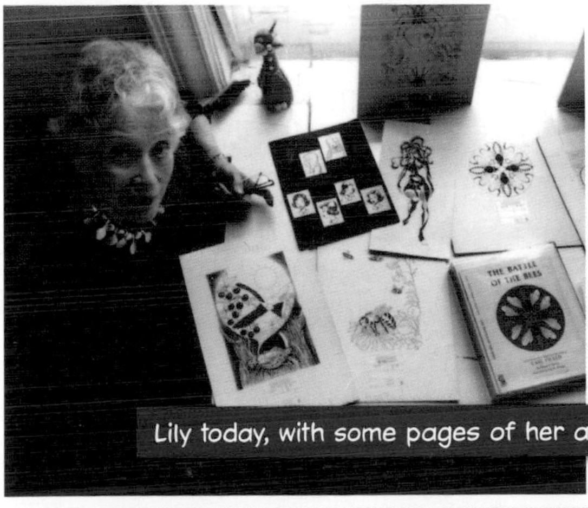

Lily today, with some pages of her art

Trina Robbins is the Eisner and Harvey Award–nominated author of numerous nonfiction and fiction books and comics for children and adults, including several histories of women cartoonists. A pioneer in comics herself, she took part in the underground comix movement of the 1960s and illustrated the Wonder Woman comic book. Most recently, she authored the Chicagoland Detective Agency graphic novel series. She lives in San Francisco with her partner, comics artist Steve Leialoha.

Anne Timmons was born in Portland, Oregon, and received her BFA from Oregon State University. In addition to her collaboration with Trina Robbins on the Lulu Award–winning GoGirl!, her work includes the Eisner-nominated *Dignifying Science* and *Pigling: A Cinderella Story* for the Graphic Myths and Legends series. She has illustrated and painted covers for children's books and provided interior and cover art for regional and national magazines, including *Wired*, *Portland Review*, and *Comic Book Artist*. Her art also appears in the anthology *9-11: Artists Respond* and is now in the Library of Congress.

mo oh likes to draw. She also likes to read, bake, eat (mostly eat), make plants grow (mainly for eating), and sit in the sun. She graduated from the Center for Cartoon Studies with an MFA in cartooning and works on and off as a sketch/concept artist for a small game company. She lives in Massachusetts.